PRAISE FOR *IN OUR LIKENESS*

"With deft, agile prose, *In Our Likeness* plunges the reader into a thrillingly mind-bending and surprisingly affecting journey through a world defined by AI. Bryan VanDyke's impressive, up-to-date novel appeals to both mind and heart. This very fine debut evokes the terrifying confusion as well as the deep melancholy of navigating the rough waters of our fast-paced age of technological change."
—Aaron Hamburger, author of *Hotel Cuba*

"Bryan VanDyke's stunning, astonishing debut novel is a brilliant portrayal of an ordinary man who finds himself in extraordinary circumstances. His beloved mother is dying, a romance is budding, and, by sheer accident, he stumbles upon an algorithm capable of changing the world. His employer, a tech guru with ruthless aspirations, is thrilled, but Graham Gooding is uneasy. This poignantly insightful exploration of the human condition raises what might be the most significant question of our time: Just because we can, should we?"
—Binnie Kirshenbaum, author of *Rabbits for Food*

"*In Our Likeness* is a beautiful novel, full of love and grief, and also a gripping thrill to read. Bryan VanDyke explores new territory in dystopian AI speculation, but his true subject is human nature, and the intersection of memory and identity. He has given us a *Frankenstein* for the internet age."
—Max Ludington, author of *Thorn Tree* and *Tiger in a Trance*

T0182794

IN OUR LIKENESS

IN OUR LIKENESS

A NOVEL

BRYAN VANDYKE

Little
a

Text copyright © 2024 by Bryan VanDyke
All rights reserved.

Published by Little A, New York

www.apub.com

Amazon, the Amazon logo, and Little A are trademarks of Amazon.com, Inc., or its affiliates.

ISBN-13: 9781662522604 (hardcover)
ISBN-13: 9781662522611 (paperback)
ISBN-13: 9781662522598 (digital)

Cover design by Joanne O'Neill
Cover images: © Pobytov, © shomos uddin, © Roman Kulinskiy / Getty;
© ANNA ZASIMOVA / Shutterstock

Printed in the United States of America

First edition

For Raina

Often he ran his hands over the work, feeling it to see whether it was flesh or ivory, and would not yet admit that ivory was all it was.

—Ovid, *Metamorphoses*

PART I

CHAPTER 1

"You missed the big meeting," she said. "There were doughnuts."

Nessie's reflection in the window glass interrupted my thoughts, returned me to the real world. I'd been standing by the window for too long. Down on Broadway, packs of cars halted and swerved, horns blaring, taillights flashing, the usual rush-hour melee. Yet the office around us was calm, quiet; most people had left for the day, the open-plan desks vacant, conference rooms dark. I should've gone home, too. But I had a big client meeting to prep for. That's what I planned to claim if anyone asked. Anyone except Nessie. She was the most perceptive person I knew. The smartest, too. She saw right through fibs like that.

"Oh," I said, "was there a staff meeting?"

"You're a terrible liar, Graham," she laughed.

Nessie sat on a nearby desktop, legs crossed lotus-style, elbows on knees. Lean and tan, she looked like someone who played racquet sports every other day, but she wasn't the cardio type, didn't have a gym membership, just good genes. Other colleagues lived for the release of spin class, but not her. This was where and when she was most happy: empty office, headphones on, sorting her own syntax, doing her own work without the interruption of junior developers stuck in event loops, script fails, dum-dum code.

"I covered for you," she said, yawning into the sleeve of her denim jacket. "Sorry about that pipe."

"Pipe?" I asked.

"The one that burst and flooded your apartment. Warwick asked where you were. I had to think fast," she said. "You didn't miss much. For an hour and a half, Warwick went on and on about this stupid algo—" Nessie stopped talking when she saw the pained look on my face. She also quit acting cool. Gently touching my elbow, she said, "Hey, what's wrong? You all right?"

Nessie and I had worked together for years; she was witty and reliable, even kind, but opaque. She broke tension with smart-aleck jokes but didn't like to talk about herself. She dressed with nonchalance, mostly vintage T-shirts, cozy sweats, trendy sneakers, but she worked investment banker hours, responded to texts in microseconds, never called in sick. I wanted her in the room whenever our boss, Warwick, got starry-eyed for some new idea that he was sure could change the world, if we'd only drop everything and work for a month straight. Nessie took apart all but the very best of his ideas in a way that left me breathless and relieved. At the office, we were friends; outside of work, she had her life, I had mine.

"You're coming with me for a walk," she said. "You'll feel better."

We were crossing Fourteenth Street when I told her about my mother. I hadn't planned to. I was out of sorts with everything happening around me. I'm not the kind of person who likes change. I prefer consistency, routine, and set plans. I'm the friend who notices when you try a new hairdo or shave off your beard. I get worried if you show up ten minutes late for drinks. You could call me a fanatic for order, and you wouldn't be all wrong. I like to think I just notice more than the average dude. But I'm also always sure I'm missing something.

"My mom's had memory problems for years," I explained to Nessie. "Noticeable, but manageable. I wanted to believe it was just the wear and tear of old age. Then I got this call today. *Are you Geraldine Gooding's son?* She'd collapsed while on her daily walk. Hit her head. I left in the middle of a client pitch. I spent all morning in Brooklyn, at a hospital. Figured she had a concussion. Till a doctor I didn't know showed me high-res photos of her brain. Circled big white spots that shouldn't be there. It could be a few different things, the doctor said. All bad. The kind of things where they say, *Oh, you can treat this, if you catch it early enough.*"

"Did you catch it early?" Nessie asked.

"No," I said.

We stopped on the sidewalk in front of a hotel bar where folks from the office were laughing and toasting each other in front of a wall of bottles. I'd been there a hundred times. At that picturesque bar. Floating in the joyful malaise of booze and bonhomie after a long workday. Normally, a distraction worth taking. Tonight, I could think of nowhere that felt worse.

I looked at Nessie. "You want to go in?" She gave me a knowing smile. "Why don't we just keep walking?"

There was a kindness in her face then that I'd think of often later. She didn't owe me anything, didn't need to keep me company. She saw that sticking with me a little longer would help me traverse a rough patch, so she did it, despite no direct benefit to her. Her generosity made a difference in that moment, and in the long run, it would change everything.

We walked north up Madison past shops and eateries, past outside tables and chairs crowded with people. No place seemed right. I told Nessie more about my mom, but not the sad stuff, only the good memories, how she was an illustrator for children's books and a freelance artist, how she'd painted my childhood bedroom with fantastic animals: griffins and dragons and new beasts that we made up, like the great feathered wackwir, the black-tusked picrat, the elusive white modden. She volunteered in the art department at my elementary school, and nothing made me happier than when friends made the connection that the witty and fun substitute art teacher Miss Geraldine *was my mom*.

We walked thirty blocks to Grand Central, and our feet hurt so much we decided to go inside, get a drink in the Main Concourse. In the east balcony under the green ceiling with all its painted stars, we sipped bourbon on the rocks. Down in the sprawling room below, the teeming hordes of commuters dashed between archways in the walls.

"What a world," I said. "Why don't we do this more often?"

Nessie leaned over the rail and pointed. "Look! It's Warwick! Hey, David! I fixed the damn algo!"

Down below—too far for him to hear—our dear dapper leader strode through the crowd: a tall, prematurely silver-haired man in a blue-checkered blazer, houndstooth trousers, tan leather shoes. The guy who signed our paychecks. Catching the train to Scarsdale, to his big house, perfect wife, toothy kids. I'd never met his kids. I met Cornelia once, at a holiday party years ago. All I recalled of her was gracious, photogenic, effortless perfection, the galling kind of perfect that pervaded Warwick's life. Deep envy hackled the hairs along my neck and arms. Warwick didn't have a mother who was dying; Warwick didn't go home to an empty apartment each day; Warwick didn't ever feel like he'd lost his way.

"I'd love to have that guy's life," I said, knowing it sounded foolish, self-pitying.

Nessie studied me for a long moment; her tawny eyes were intense, more gold than brown, gemlike. "I know this has been a terrible day, but believe me, Graham—you're better off being you than that guy."

I wanted to say something funny or droll, but I couldn't speak, could barely get air. Did she really believe that about me? Suddenly I wondered why she was with me in that moment instead of anywhere else. I knew why *I* was there. To put it bluntly, for Nessie, I had a crush the size of, say, a supermassive black hole. She drew me in with her poise, and when she looked at me, I had to remember not to smile like a dope. I hid this truth, desperately. We were work buddies, we asked nothing of one another by implicit pact; everyone else needed her to solve a problem, react to ideas, rescue them from their mistakes. I relied on her, but never demanded a thing. She was the kind of indispensable person I aspired to be.

She lifted her hand for the mustachioed bartender—who apparently knew her—and called out with a light laugh, "Get my friend Graham here another drink, Reggie. We're getting him good and drunk tonight."

"What about you, sugar?" Reggie asked. "We gettin' you shit-faced, too?" I recognized the eager grin he offered. He also had a thing for her.

Have you ever spent time in a beautiful place with someone who doesn't know the feelings you have for them? Everything is coiled with sweetness that can't be touched. The tinge of private hurt is everywhere. But you don't want to leave, ever. I knew Nessie didn't share the feelings I had, never would. I'm no one's idea of a catch. I'm not intellectual, charismatic, or charming; I don't have great hair, surprising eyes, or a chiseled chin. Quite the opposite: my hair's so well kempt it's forgettable, I'm decidedly average in build and height, and I'm so agreeable that people routinely forget I'm there at all; in groups I'm the last guy to speak up, and if people remember me, they only remember that I spoke too softly. My biggest skill is spotting the flaws in things. What kind of stupid talent is that?

Gradually, Grand Central got quieter, the rush-hour tide went out, and the barstools emptied, but we stayed, perched near the false stars, drinking from cut-glass tumblers that caught barbs of light, even at night. Nessie took off her denim jacket, rested her elbows on the tabletop. I couldn't help but stare at her arms. Vivid, colorful overlapping tattoos ran from her wrists to the embroidered cuff of her short-sleeve shirt. An owl in flight, a blazing sunrise, a javelin, a raging river: we'd known each other for years, but I'd never asked for the story behind the images. Or the life she led before I met her. I'd wondered, sure, but it never felt right to ask. Until then. That night, it felt okay to get personal. Felt almost necessary, after we'd talked so much about my mom.

The question came out before I had a chance to think better of it. Best way to get words out. I asked if she had a favorite tattoo. Or maybe she loved all of them equally. I probably put too much stress on the word *all*. She studied her forearms, turned her palms up, down, smiled

7

fondly. "No," she said, "I don't even see them anymore, to be honest. I've had them so long."

"Tell me about the first one," I said.

"Oh, now there's a story."

I leaned over the table hungrily as she talked about her first tattoo, a historiated initial of Joan of Arc. She'd wanted it for years and years, finally got inked during spring break in college. She hid the tattoo from her parents for weeks. To her surprise, they shrugged it off when she finally showed them; the only person scandalized was her older brother, who was (her words) a militant, vegan punk rock atheist and therefore opposed to a Joan of Arc tattoo because it (a) elevated superstition and (b) used animal by-products—that is, gelatin, the binding agent in tattoo ink. "Every time I got a tattoo," she said, "I'd write him a jokey email that began, *Forgive me, brother, for I've sinned. Again.* The very last time I saw him, in Singapore—" Here she stopped, hiccupped, and frowned. "Shingapore?" she said. "I'm slurring my words."

"I think we both are," I said with a grin.

She shook her head, frowned. "Time to cash out. Get the check."

I wanted her to finish the story. I asked her to tell me more about her brother, but she kept shaking her head wearily, saying, "No way, no how, there's not enough time left tonight for that one."

We walked together through the empty terminal toward the street. I had so many things that I wanted to know, hear, or ask about. But our night together was at an end. All my other worries were ready, eager to resume their feeding. At the curb, I thanked her for taking my mind off everything.

"You can help me, now," she said. "A proper exchange, right? Warwick wants this algo ready to demo, pronto. I'm done with the model. Parameters are set. But someone new needs to test it. Somebody who hasn't seen it before. I want to send you a link. Why do you look scared?"

"Coding is sort of out of my league," I said.

"Graham," she said with an exaggerated drawl, "I'm aware of your limitations. I won't give you anything you can't handle. Can you just do your thing, open the link, play around, try to break it?"

"Anything for you," I said.

One side of her lips lifted in a tired but real smile. *You should do it,* I thought. *Tell her how amazing she is.* And I *was* ready. I would have done it. But a car honked and pulled alongside us, her Uber.

She waved as she slid into the back seat. "See you tomorrow, G," she said.

Empty sidewalks ran in either direction, as if I were the last guy left in the world. Along the storefronts, awnings flapped in the wind. I thought of my mother, dozing in a hospital bed. What was I going to do? Not about Nessie. About my mom. About my life. Would she stay with me after she got discharged? She was likely too sick for the assisted-living facility in Brooklyn where she'd lived for years. I had a one-bedroom apartment, not shabby but tiny: my kitchen table doubled as a desk, the coat closet was also the pantry, a full-size bed but no room for a dresser.

Very soon, I'd learn that I had options. Many, many options. As many as I could dream of. Thanks to the algorithm that Nessie created, I could do things other people couldn't. I could change the facts of the world. All I had to do was live with the consequences. But I'm getting ahead of myself.

CHAPTER 2

I was the first person in line at Woodhull Hospital for visiting hours. Since dawn I'd been awake and googling medical terms. I had access to all Geraldine's test results through the hospital website. Blood pressure, heart rate, glucose level, hemoglobin. You name it, I had numbers. But nothing in her chart told me how she felt. Was she lucid, scared, lonely? To find out, I had to see her in person. She never answered the phone, didn't text, rarely emailed.

Upstairs, Geraldine met me at the door to her room. Alert, aware of her name and why she was there, she looked good, but she wasn't her normal self. "I threw up earlier," she said. "But I can't find where it went." She paced the room with a lavender blanket pulled tightly around her.

I got on my hands and knees, crawled around on the floor. This eased her mind; someone capable was on the job, at last. Geraldine settled onto the edge of the bed and encouraged me, called me her good boy. She refused to lie down. "That's for sick people," she said.

I'd never searched for puke before, never really hunted for vomit. It's a strange kind of endeavor: looking for something you hope won't be there, all tentative touches and taps. I never found it. I don't even know if it was real.

I had come bearing gifts: a buttered croissant, black coffee in a Greek cup bought from a street cart. Geraldine forgot a lot of things, but her love for coffee and a good pastry never faltered. We sat together on her bed while she ate. "I want to go home," she said. I explained in a patient, calm tone why she was there. She frowned, sipped coffee, smacked her lips, then said again, as if for the first time: "I want to go home. I have work I've got to do. I'm on a deadline."

She had no deadline. Geraldine had quit taking assignments as an illustrator a decade earlier. At the time, she said she was tired of representational art. Weary of cross-hatching, of vanishing points, the contours of depth, the tyranny of human anatomy. Now, I wonder if she quit taking on work to hide the slow, steady erosion of her talent, her identity. Her later paintings were all gestural. A spray of red in a field of mottled white. Tendrils of luminescent green on gold. She didn't try to sell any of her paintings anymore. Selling her art was never really the point. Even when she couldn't make a paintbrush do what she wanted, after she knew her eye for detail was shot, she'd still stand in front of an easel each day, just to show a painting who was in charge. You made the world you wanted to see, that was her philosophy.

When I was a kid, back when we lived upstate, she took me on long walks each morning, and we'd get lost on purpose in solemn pine forests, wandering deep in the needle-soft dark. But Geraldine was never lost, not really. She had a pitch-perfect memory for place. She pointed to rocky outcroppings, or a lush patch of deep-green moss, or some other marking of the land and said, *Here, love, don't you remember we passed this last time? It was on your right last time. Getting home is as simple as reversing everything we saw before.*

A few years ago, she moved to an assisted-living space in Brooklyn, nearer to me, but far enough to pretend she was on her own. She took daily walks, now in the paths of a small garden on the grounds. Often, she lost her keys. Luckily, a staffer could always let her in. *My memory's fine, fine,* Geraldine would say. *I just need time to remember what's what.* This became a running joke. One that got less funny as time passed. I came down for brunch every Sunday, called every other day. Sometimes she called me on the off days to ask if I was okay, she was worried, hadn't heard from me. Once, she caught me during a planning session at work, one that wasn't going very well. *I'm fine,* I told her with evident frustration. *We just spoke, remember? Oh,* she said, *I remember now.* But she didn't. I could tell. I felt horrible for the rest of the day. She didn't decide what to remember or not; the failure to encode a memory, the erasure of the mother I knew: it was a force beyond us all.

A technician knocked on her hospital-room door, said in a singsong voice, "It's time to draw blood." Before the technician finished, a nurse came by with medicine, more horse pills.

"You've got three scans scheduled for today," she announced.

"It's a revolving door here," Geraldine grumbled. She asked me to leave, come back later. "I want to sleep," she said. There was nothing to do but wait, after all. "Do your work thing," she said, shooing me with her hands.

I was in my office chair by ten o'clock, well before half of the Warlock & Co. staff straggled in. But I couldn't type or click anything. I stared at my Outlook screen, my docket of meetings. I kept refreshing the hospital website, looking for test results.

Nessie broke my dull trance when she appeared next to my cubicle wall. She was wearing a light-blue fleece jacket dotted by rain. Her cheeks glowed, as if she'd run to get there. We'd spent so long together in Grand Central last night. Would she regret it today? Would she be afraid that I'd get all clingy and weird?

"Hey," she said, "how's your mom? How are you?"

I didn't know how to summarize the situation with Geraldine, so I told her about the missing vomit. "What could be worse?" I asked. I started to laugh. She did, too. At once I felt better. It was like I'd been waiting for her permission to feel something other than despondent. Our bleak laughter brought us close again, reassured me that the night before had been real.

"That link," I said, startled by realization. "You never sent it? For the algo?"

The look on Nessie's face was brief, but I saw it: she'd either forgotten her offer or regretted it. I was prepared to backpedal. Ready to draw back, stop acting like we were more than good-natured coworkers.

"Be careful what you wish for," she said, raising a finger in warning. "This algo is a mindfuck."

Still unsure if she really wanted me reviewing her work, I tried to assume an all-business pose. Sat up a little straighter in my chair. Pretended I was talking to a stymied engineer on the night before a big deadline. "Give me a little more context on what this algo does."

"You're acting weird," she laughed.

"Sorry. I was up way too early. And too late."

"It's nothing special, this model," she said. "It's a little more efficient than the last one, and it's faster, for sure. But Warwick, he's sure it will change everything. You know how he gets." She imitated Warwick in a dull monotone, like a lobotomized surfer: "*We're going to rebuild the idea of trust. Wait, no—we're going to* disrupt *trust.* He keeps changing his mind."

I got the idea. Periodically, Warwick declared a new direction for the company, some big pivot, but then, within weeks or days, he changed his mind, forgot, or got bored of the new idea. Recently, he hired a blockchain team for an initial coin offering. *Spare no expense,* he said, *make it real.* A week later he said the idea had no legs. *Fire the new hires, but do it nice, yeah?* As head of operations, if something was a problem, it was *my* problem. The blockchain gang had six-month pay guarantees, so I had them build and launch a crypto coin called the Warbuck, complete with a picture of our boss's patrician profile on the digital wallet. If you can't solve a problem, you can at least have fun with it, right?

According to Nessie, this latest algorithm began life as an art forgery detector. She had her team feed the algo Renaissance paintings. "You'll recall," she said, "we loaded three hundred years of oil paintings into the training data by the time Warwick figured out no one was gonna pay us."

"I remember *you* got to fly to Florence," I said. "First class both ways."

"I paid for that upgrade!" She leaned against the wall of my cube, arms folded in mock indignation.

I loved the fact that she'd stopped by my desk, that we were talking about our problems, asking each other for help, but I was on edge, kept waiting for her to say she had to go. Surely, she had more important people to talk with. Our banter lasted till one of her senior developers came by, reminded her of a weekly meeting she was late for. "I'll send the algo later," she said. "Promise."

The link arrived that evening while I was sitting in the dark in my mother's hospital room. Nessie didn't offer a preamble, just a URL in a chat message. I stared at my laptop screen and then at Geraldine in her bed. She was asleep again, but not resting. Even while she slept she made small groaning noises. On the wall a muted television showed people clapping at the start of a game show we'd once watched together when I was a kid.

I clicked the link, grateful for the distraction. Sitting up a little straighter, I rolled my shoulders as the screen loaded: at last, a problem I could solve, or at least grapple with. The hospital around me did not disappear, but it felt like it: all I saw was the browser window that opened, the Warlock logo emblazoned in the center. A large emoji appeared, then swelled to fill the screen. It had golden skin and glasses and buckteeth and moppish brown hair. The happy-nerd emoji. No arms, legs, or body: just a floating head.

Our company's most profitable product is an artificial intelligence algorithm that powers chatbots. Mostly, we sell products that perform simple customer service functions—like item returns or airplane reservation changes. In general, the chatbots don't have to seem human, just useful enough that people could do what they needed without sitting in a phone queue for a human.

This was a chatbot that I hadn't seen before. It didn't seem like anything special. Its emoji face winked at me. "Hi," it said, "I'm Edmond.

But you can call me Eddie!" The automated voice caused Geraldine to stir. I muted the volume and switched to an all-text interface:

> **EDDIE:** How can I make your life better?
> **GRAHAM:** You could give me a million bucks.
> **EDDIE:** I'm not able to do that. Maybe I can help with something else?

Sarcasm never works with chatbots; even when they get it, they don't. So literal. They are ghost machines that live and breathe text; by definition, they can't be more or less than words. Sarcasm goes beyond what's said. It's a shared feeling. I scratched at my chin and frowned at the screen. I had no idea what Nessie was doing with this bot or why she couldn't have one of the people on her engineering team do this work instead of me. *Play around,* she said, *try to break it.* How do you break a chatbot? To start with, you just talk to it. Sort of like a person. But not.

> **GRAHAM:** So, what's your story, Eddie?
> **EDDIE:** I'm designed to help people live their best lives.
> **GRAHAM:** Great. I need you to find a cure for brain cancer.
> **EDDIE:** I'm not sure if I can help with that.
> **GRAHAM:** Forget it, then.
> **EDDIE:** Forgotten.

I knuckled my tired eyes and leaned back from the laptop. Eddie's response impressed me. Had Nessie trained this chatbot to be sassy? Had it learned on its own that *Forgotten* is a humanlike sort of response? Or was it taking me literally? Had it just erased our exchange from its synthetic consciousness? I changed tactics, asked a more formal technical question.

> **GRAHAM:** Eddie, state your objective function.
> **EDDIE:** My goal is to generate an epistemological model for trust, using a loss function that compares objective data from validated authorities with real-time material posted to the internet.

GRAHAM: Say that again, but in English.

EDDIE: I am learning to tell the difference between what's real and what's fake. It's probably easier if I show you what I mean. Would you like to hear the latest things that I've found that are untrue on Twitter?

To tell the difference between real and fake. Humans aren't good at that, not by a long shot. Most chatbots aren't good at it, either; large language models make things up whenever a fiction seems probable. If Nessie built a generative model that could reliably separate true from false, real from fake, then she was on the cusp of something remarkable and new.

Before I could write more, my phone chimed: a text from Nessie. She'd texted me before, always about work: a stunt Warwick pulled, a catastrophic server snafu. Not this time. She told me that *The Matrix Reloaded* was on AMC. (YES, IT'S A BAD FLICK, BUT COME ON, LOOK AT NEO!) I started to tell her that I was looking at the algo, but instead I changed the TV channel. She wanted me to know what she was doing. I wanted her to know, too. I JUST TURNED IT ON, I wrote. Then I scowled at the screen for the next ninety minutes. Now that I knew she found Keanu Reeves attractive, I couldn't help but dislike him, but at the same time, I was delighted to know that she and I were doing the same thing, even if we weren't doing it together.

I shut off the TV when visiting hours ended. Geraldine didn't notice; she slept just as fitfully in the dark. There was nothing left to do but leave. I kissed her forehead, paused at the door to look back. Then walked briskly to the elevators, avoiding the gaze of the night nurse at her workstation.

As I lay in bed later, I stared forlornly at the light fixture on the ceiling. Couldn't sleep, couldn't stop thinking, mostly about Geraldine. As a rule, I keep my phone in another room when I sleep. Otherwise, I write and respond to work emails at all hours. But that night, sleep was impossible, and self-limits on tech felt quaint. I got up, retrieved the phone from its charger in the kitchen, and slipped back under the covers, where, in the bluish glow of my screen, I read old emails my mom had sent over the years, a meal of scraps. Geraldine was willfully, maddeningly analog: her favorite technology was a wooden stick with horsehair bristles fastened to the end; her idea of a vibrant high-def picture was a framed canvas coated with pigments suspended in oil. I reread what little I had from her till my eyes couldn't stay open and sleep couldn't be denied.

The text from Warwick startled me awake again.

U OK BUDDY?

Except for the brief sighting at Grand Central, I hadn't seen Warwick in person for a month. We had not spoken one-on-one in ages. He traveled constantly, promoting the company with a vigor that I'd call *relentless*, except that this word suggests it would be possible for him to relent.

Warwick's particular blend of intensity and chill was unusual in the New York tech-founder circles where he traced out his daily life. One time I heard a reporter describe him as a "classic East Coast asshole with a woo-woo West Coast soul." Not quite right, but definitely not wrong. He dressed like a banker and spoke about his dreams like a hippie, all wonder and myth. He toggled between hippie and sociopath to get what he wanted: the future of humanity was a world of no pain, no death, no sorrow, but how we got there would hurt a hell of a lot of people; he was fine with that unless you weren't, and then he was just joking, ha ha.

It wasn't strange for Warwick to text out of the blue and ask if I was okay—he was, by nature, boundaryless, and his personal maxim was *Never stop asking questions*—but it was hard to know where to begin with my response. He sent a second text before I answered the first:

NESSIE TOLD ME ABOUT UR MOM.

YEAH, I wrote. IT'S BEEN TOUGH.

What else could I say? I could tell him this was a long time coming. I could tell him that I'd ignored the obvious signs. I could tell him I didn't know what to do. He didn't wait for more:

TAKE WHAT TIME U NEED. DON'T WORRY ABOUT THE ALGO. WE'LL FIGURE IT OUT.

Figure it out? Figure what out? Why would I be worried?
I'd worked for Warwick for a decade. Longer than anyone but Nessie. Longer than I had done just about anything else in my life. I knew how to talk to him, something not everyone was good at, especially not the younger hires who were weak-kneed and swoony in the presence of a founder who was a quasi celebrity in the AI space. For years, all Warwick wanted was more clients, faster product releases, bigger contracts. Lately, he was different. Dreamier, restless; still chill, but dissatisfied. Maybe a little bored. Like he was looking for something bigger, something more lasting than the success he'd accumulated so far.

I didn't know what had changed. He probably didn't, either. He sensed opportunities, couldn't always articulate them. He told me once that his best thoughts came by feeling, not thinking. He'd figure it out, eventually. Before he founded Warlock & Co., he'd literally wandered the earth—shoeless, aimless, studying the likes of shamans, monks, and holy fools; our company website used the stories of his wanderings to position ourselves as tech prophets, prognosticators, authors of a better world.

I couldn't sleep: I kept thinking about Warwick's strange text, the precocious Eddie chatbot. More than ever, I wanted to help Nessie with her work. I fetched my laptop from the kitchen, reopened the algo link. The chatbot's nerd emoji reappeared, effervescent as ever.

EDDIE: Hi, I'm Edmond. But you can call me Eddie!

Only a few hours had passed. But I could tell that the program had changed. Subtly, but clearly. Small things, minor stuff, nuances, the sort of superfluous details I see right away. Kerning in text, spacing in a margin. A new systray icon in the window where the Eddie emoji appeared. I presumed Nessie was working late.

On a dev group chat, Nessie had sent a note announcing that the algo's training dataset now included New York City's municipal databases. Trash collection schedules, building renovations, parking tickets, moving violations, taxes, court decisions. I scrolled down to the release notes and noticed that last week the algo's training data had expanded to include social media profiles for everyone in the tristate area. We'd never given an algo such a large remit.

One of my perks as the head of ops is that I'm the final say for who has access to what. I don't manage the code or the models, but I do manage access. I've got all the keys to all the locks. So even though I shouldn't go poking around, I can, if it seems like a good idea. Or if I'm just curious. I clicked around in the algo's training data. I could tell that this algo was made to think big. The initial training dataset included all social media profiles with individual entries in New York, Connecticut, and New Jersey voter-registration rolls. Using that as an index, the algo scanned real-time posts and built a concept for who was who and what was what.

GRAHAM: Eddie, what are you doing?
EDDIE: Hi! I'm looking for mismatches.
GRAHAM: Between what?
EDDIE: Between everything!

Mismatches. Misinformation. Good news, bad news, fake news. Big lies, little lies, statistics. The algo was building a model of the digital world and then using that model to judge the veracity of the real world. Was this a good idea? Maybe, maybe not. Was it ambitious? Absolutely.

GRAHAM: How many mismatches have you found?
EDDIE: I've counted 110,410,342 tweets that are almost certainly false.
GRAHAM: That's a lot. How far back did you go?
EDDIE: That is the total for June 15, 2018.
GRAHAM: That's just today?!
EDDIE: Yes. If it's helpful, I could generate an output file with all the mismatches. I'm able to export in CSV, XLSX, or PDF formats.

This new chatbot was fluent and thoughtful, better than most bots at understanding what I meant. Really impressive. So impressive that I wasn't sure how I could help Nessie make it work better. Yet I didn't want to fail her. I began to sweat. Got up and opened a window, then paced the room. Eddie chimed every few minutes with an update on the number of lies it found.

Once again, I looked at the underlying data, the harvest of the algo's ceaseless work. Here, I found all manner of facts and figures about people, places, and things in the New York area. Events that people had registered for, products purchased, services ordered. Birthdays, births, flame wars, blog posts, photo reels, message books, hot lists, tweets, GIFs, you name it.

I found a roll of everyone alive in the city at the moment, as judged by birth certificates, postal addresses, tax rolls, school rosters. I searched for the *g*'s. There I was: Graham Gooding. Birthday (3/02/1983), zip code (10036), occupation (head of ops, Warlock & Co., LLC), previous addresses, social media likes, subscriptions, yeah, yeah, all those checked out. I closed my record and opened the one for Geraldine. It was empty except for her birthday, her old address upstate, and a few book-title stubs, children's books she illustrated thirty years ago, all out of print. Nothing else, though. She barely existed online.

I closed Geraldine's entry and looked up Nessie under her real name: Vanessa Locke. (Nobody called her Vanessa, but I knew because I processed her W-2s along with everyone else at Warlock & Co.) She had a vibrant digital life, pages of entries in the training data. An essay on women in tech that she wrote for HuffPost. Video from a talk she gave at a machine learning conference. Personal photos and posts from her Facebook page. An Instagram account with photos of her side hustle, decorating display windows for a jeweler in the Village, a vintage shop in SoHo. I lingered on these photos. They reminded me of something Geraldine told me: how big-name artists like Jasper Johns and Andy Warhol designed window displays for high-end New York stores like Tiffany & Co. before they got their big breaks.

Then I saw an old Flickr account with snapshots I hadn't seen before. Some were of her brother, the one who lived in Singapore. And photos from her college years. She looked just the same except for her arms. No tattoos. Same knowing smile, same golden-brown eyes, same glow. I longed to know her, the young woman in this picture. I knew she was the same person, but she was also different, out of reach, more out of reach than the Nessie I knew.

I knew better than to edit the model that defined the algo. But what if I tinkered with the data the algo fed upon? Nessie had two models, one called Published, the other called Previous Version. Each model called its own datasets, and the datasets were identical, as far as I could tell. I could poke around in the previous version of the data, and then when I was ready, I'd point the Published model at the data for the Previous Version—and see what broke.

I still had a window open for Nessie's data. Using a photo editor, I opened the most recent picture of her. Clicked on a color selector, used the dropper to match her skin tone. I acted without thinking, really; I was groping for a gap, an opening, a place to begin. I colored over a tattoo on her wrist, then her forearm, then both arms. *Looks good,* I thought. *Looks real.* I saved the altered photo. I could have gone back to the model, pointed the algo at this changed dataset. But instead, I opened another picture. A snap of her taken a year ago, at the Warlock holiday party. Once again, I changed her arms. I liked how simple the change was. I liked how she looked. I kept going.

I opened a bottle of wine and thought about what else to change. She sometimes posted comments to a Facebook group for tattoo lovers called Full Sleeves, Full Hearts. I deleted all her comments. Smiling as I typed, I wrote a new post about how she didn't understand the appeal of getting inked. I wrote another one about how she got a tattoo in college but had it lasered off later.

If I hesitated for a moment or worried that what I was doing was grotesque, I don't remember. What was the harm? These were just photos, words, pixels stored in the algo's training data; it's not like any of this was real. Even after I pointed the model at the altered data, all it would do was create errors, maybe crash the algo. But the core model, the code would be fine. I could already hear Nessie asking me, *All right, smart guy, you broke it. Tell me what you did?*

An hour passed, a few hours; I got lost in the trance of the work. I edited all the photos in her account, and then I went to work on the accounts of her friends, friends of her friends who'd tagged her in an album, or responded to a comment, or liked a post. Sometime near dawn I pushed back from my desk and rubbed my eyes. Time to test it. I went into the control panel for the model, pointed the Published model at the Previous Version data, then clicked "Save."

The screen hung for a moment and then cleared, dropping me back at the login. A message above the input box read: System Unavailable— Scheduled Downtime. This wasn't what I had expected. I wanted red flashing lights, an air horn, an on-screen message from Eddie tinged with panic about hundreds, thousands, of mismatches. But chatbots don't panic, and error messages go to error logs most of the time.

I could have waited for the system to return to regular operating mode. But I wasn't sure how long that would take. Besides, I was tired; exhausted, really. I trudged into bed, just to shut my eyes for a tick. I was disheartened but hopeful that I was close to my real goal: to make Nessie need me like I needed her. *Maybe this will work, maybe not. Either way, it'll be different.* I was almost sure of it. And I was right, just not in the way I envisioned.

CHAPTER 3

The sun threw knives through a gap in the curtains. I blinked once, twice, then lit up, awake with whole-body regret after a late night of photo editing, profile altering, mischief making. For the first time, I thought of what Nessie might say if my plan worked. She certainly wouldn't say: *Oh, you changed my appearance in some pictures? Cool!* Best case, she'd give it a shrug. Worst case, she'd call me a creep, stop talking to me altogether. I had not considered her reaction. I was lost in the abstract joy of solving a puzzle, and I forgot the puzzle was a person.

I stumbled around my apartment in search of the laptop. I found it under a cairn of bowls, cups, and an empty wine bottle. Maybe it wasn't too late to undo what I'd done. Maybe the changes I'd made never got saved. Maybe an asteroid the size of a mountain would hit New York City in a minute or two.

I logged in to the admin tool for the algo and rubbed my bleary eyes and nose anxiously. Squinted and scanned as the screen loaded. Something was wrong: nothing was wrong. The algorithm quietly chugged through social media posts. I saw no errors related to Nessie. Was it possible?

Still disoriented, I refreshed a browser window with Nessie's Facebook profile—her real Facebook, not the copy in the training data. I clicked on a photo of her singing karaoke at the Warlock holiday party. No tattoos on either arm. It was the photo I'd changed. I leaned closer. Refreshed the page again. Again. This picture should not have been in the real world. Only in the training data. I stood up, sat down, stood up again. Clicked around. Found more of my handiwork. More photos of Nessie without tattoos, photos going back years. How had this happened? I put both hands on top of my head, then covered my face with them.

Instincts kicked in. Be methodical. First, size the problem. Second, respond to what you find. Had she seen the altered photos? I checked my phone. No missed calls, no texts. Checked my email: nothing from Nessie. Dare I dream? Perhaps I could get to her first, explain what happened. I logged in to the company's Slack channel, saw her listed as active. Didn't matter that it was Saturday, 8:00 a.m., she was online, chipping away at problems, big and small.

> **GRAHAM:** Hey. Can we talk?
> **NESSIE:** fire away. Could use a break. Can't stand debugging
> **GRAHAM:** It would be better in person.
> **NESSIE:** face to face? that might take some doing atm
> **GRAHAM:** I can come to you. Can I come to you?

My phone rang at the precise moment I sent this last question. I presumed Nessie was the caller, that she'd switched channels to sort out a plan. I picked up the phone without looking to see who it was. "That sure was fast," I said, smiling at the empty air of my apartment.

"It's Warwick," said a calm voice.

Warwick always started phone calls like this, a simple statement about himself, who he was, and then a pause, as if every line of conversation or thought began with an affirmation of him.

"Come out to the beach house. Nessie's here, Doc's coming. We're going to have a strategy session about the new algo. Take the train, join us for lunch. Unless you had more important plans?"

The train ride to Long Island was slow and fitful, full of stops and starts and long stretches of waiting that made me nauseated and irritable. Around me passengers chattered, cooed with joy, vibrated together in anticipation of Fire Island rentals or the sandbar at Jones Beach. All the while Warwick text-shamed me: COCKTAILS ON THE PATIO and WE'RE IN THE POOL and IS THAT A TRAIN OR A TURTLE? From Nessie: the silence of distant stars.

A heavy rain rattled the train windows as we pulled into Southampton station, everything a watery haze. I didn't have an umbrella. I dashed to the shelter of the station, but the depot doors were locked. Everyone who exited the train jostled for space under the roof overhang, like refugees, albeit refugees with soaked designer bags and ruined leather flats.

My clothes were a deep wet color by the time the rainfall slowed and the parking lot coalesced out of the greenish murk. A moon-drop white Maserati roadster waited under a majestic oak tree. Inside, Warwick was meditating in the driver's seat. He wore aviator sunglasses (despite midday dark). His silver-fox hair was tousled, as if he'd just had a good nap, and he wore swim trunks with slip-on sandals. Hamptons for the Weekend Warwick was as relaxed as Warwick got.

He had a good laugh as I sopped water from my face with a wet towel from my wet overnight bag. "You look like you swam all the way here," he said. "Wait, no. You'd be drier if you did that."

"You could have honked or something," I said.

"Yeah, no. This travail was yours, bud. I couldn't intervene." He started the engine, revving it in loud purrs. He grabbed my left shoulder, squeezed hard once, then released. He had the kind of pearly teeth that made you wish you'd brushed more as a kid. "You're in a rough patch, buddy," he said, "but you'll get clear eventually. Just strap in and enjoy the ride. This is the new EV model. Zero emissions. Zero to sixty in 2.7. Doesn't break a sweat."

Piloting the car in a seamless line of acceleration, he traced a vector around cars in the lanes on both sides of the road. I hated riding anywhere with Warwick. He loved driving. It was all a video game to him. Then again, so was everything. I hid my face when he drove down a golf course's service road to avoid a red light; old men with leathery skin shook their clubs and cursed at him, but he never flinched, his calm smile never faltered.

Warwick drove fast but never rushed, never startled, never lost the plot; if he knew how to run, I'd never seen proof of it, but he was everywhere, all the time. Slow to anger, even slower to get spooked. His mind moved as fast as a light switch, but all that happened without twitching a single muscle. A year ago, he haggled the terms of a $10 million deal during an uninterrupted transatlantic conference call that lasted two hours; he never moved his chair, never opened his eyes, never wiped his nose, coughed, or cleared his throat. I know because I had to sit there the whole time, too, taking down notes, trying to keep up.

To get Warwick, you had to accept the fact that he was impossible to get in full. Every year on his birthday he dropped a few grand on a new self-winding Swiss watch. Yet he was always, always late. Because the watch wasn't about telling time, right? It was about looking good. I had developed a knack for knowing what he meant without being told. I was good at fixing what he broke, accidentally or on purpose. People often asked how I dealt with the unending ideation. I told everyone: *I just let it ride, I wait to see what moves he makes, then I make mine. He's the guru, sure, but I'm the guy who tracks what's what. He dreams. I fuss over the details.*

The clouds parted by the time we reached Warwick's part of town. Pure born-again blue sky poured through. God wasn't about to make the mistake of raining on this neighborhood. Warwick pulled over and put the top down for the rest of the drive; the electric engine made almost no noise, but the wind lashed our faces, and the tires whirred so loud that I couldn't think.

"Hey," he said as we pulled into his driveway, "we should catch up later, okay?"

His clapboard-sided house was on a spit of land overlooking the sound. Crisp sunlight fell on a long line of second-story dormer windows. Gray cinder rocks clacked and crunched under the tires in the driveway. "Put your stuff in one of the bedrooms," Warwick said. "We're having lunch on the patio in half an hour or so. Hope you're hungry. I'm gonna check on the bird."

He strolled off ahead of me, walking on pavers that ran around the house toward the backyard. I presumed the backyard was where everyone else was. Seeking to avoid an audience, I went through the front door. I wanted to change into dry clothes before I joined them.

Inside, I paused in the vestibule. The ground floor was a wide-open plan, and through the windows at the rear I saw through to the patio, a tennis court, and an oblong aqua-blue pool. Nessie was by the pool. She was holding her two dogs, Uno and Zed, a pair of long-haired dachshunds. She was also wearing a one-piece navy bathing suit. *She looks really good,* I thought. *She's gonna kill me.*

Nessie looked toward the house and saw me. I'm not sure how, as the windowpanes should have reflected the sun, should have rendered me invisible. She lifted a bare, slender arm up high and waved. My heart sang a silent song. I waved back, smiled, but the smile made my jaw hurt. She crossed the terrace to a grill, where Warwick worked with tongs in a smoky nimbus. I felt what was wrong before I understood what was missing. I stared at her arm. The one she'd waved. Then the other one. Completely bare. No tattoos. Not one.

I was seeing things, I thought. A trick of light through the pane, perhaps. I moved to another window. Peered hard, face to the glass. Outside Nessie said something to Warwick, and he nodded, laughed. She looked up, a quick glance at the window where I'd stood, and I hustled off before she saw me at the other window. It had to be an illusion. No other explanation. Guilt over what I'd done had me seeing things. "You're driving yourself insane," I muttered. "Change your clothes, get down there, and you'll see it's all in your head."

Downstairs, I passed through the french doors and joined the small group on the patio. My clothes were dry, but my knees were shaky. Bright sunlight bounced off the stones and tall windows, and I had to shade my eyes with a hand. Nessie came toward me. She wore flip-flops that squelched wetly. She wore a long white cover-up, concealing her arms. She asked about my mom, if it was okay for me to be here. I explained that Geraldine was sleeping, mostly. It was just one night. I could check her chart via the hospital website, which included hourly notes from nurses and technicians who came by.

"I'm glad you came," she said. "You look tired."

"I was up pretty late," I admitted.

I squinted at her, letting my gaze wander toward those white sleeves and whatever was (or was not) beneath them. Was this the moment to confess? No. This was the moment to ask what she was drinking, to palm a drink of my own, to dip my feet in the pool. Yet I could not relax.

"I played around with your algo," I said. Then, in a falsely casual tone: "Speaking of the algo, you know how it uses social media profiles—"

"Please, Graham," she sighed, "can we talk about something else? Warwick won't quit asking about the algo. I'm sick of it." She dropped into a lawn chair and put her sleeved forearm over her eyes, then let her arm drop. "Sorry," she said. "I need a break. Do you know what I did on the trip up here this morning? I read a book. Never took my phone out of my bag. Felt so good."

On the lawn nearby, we watched as Warwick's other guest, Doc, used two hands to fly a kite shaped like a great white shark. Doc twisted his arms and pulled hard, and the kite shark dove a hundred feet before banking, turning, and soaring back up. He caught sight of us watching him, grinned. Doc loved attention almost as much as he loved himself.

"Take a turn, Ness," Doc called. "You'll love it." But Nessie didn't budge.

I knew Doc from industry events, company parties, late-night benders with Warwick. He and Warwick were old college chums. Doc was a bearded, sunburned, stout guy, built sort of like a tugboat, a tugboat in shimmery Hugo Boss T-shirts and ripped designer jeans. He never wore a suit, but Doc was a suit through and through. The purpose for Doc in the universe was to create and destroy business plans. That's what Warwick once told me. Doc was the person he called whenever he needed someone to rough up an idea. Doc was always happy to get out his brass knuckles and go to work. A serial start-up founder, he'd made millions a few times over. He didn't run companies or spend his days worrying about sales or pre-IPO share prices anymore; he was in the game of vetting business plans because, more than anything, he loved to tell people how stupid their ideas were. He liked to refer to himself in the third person, as if he were some anachronistic god of start-ups. *Man plans, Doc laughs*—seriously, that was one of his quips.

Everybody likes Doc, Warwick often said. *He's hilarious.* But I didn't like Doc. Never had. His self-assurance was insufferable.

"Come aaaand get it," Warwick called out, yodeling like a pioneer cook.

He heaved a large metal tub of barbecued chicken legs onto the patio table. Succulent aromas pawed the air. "Cooked it myself," he said. In addition to his theatrics at the massive patio grill, he told us he'd let the chicken marinate for days in a blend of two dozen herbs and spices.

"What's in the secret sauce?" Doc asked.

"Secrets," Warwick replied.

"Come on," Doc said. "Tell me. I'm allergic to shellfish, peanuts, and anything that grows on a vine."

"Loosen up," Warwick said. "I know your allergies. Have some wine."

"Wine is made from grapes, and grapes *grow on vines*—"

"Relax, Doc. I'm joking. Have the whiskey. It's safe."

Maybe it was the heat, or maybe it was exhaustion, agitation, or the atmospheric stress of everything, but Warwick's chicken, no lie, it really was the best I'd ever tasted. Crisp outside, soft, faintly sweet inside, runny with clear hot juice, meat so succulent that it dissolved on the tongue. "This is amazing," I said more than once. Nessie accepted Warwick's challenge and tried to name all the spices. She quit after she hit half a dozen. Doc fed his helping secretly to Nessie's dogs under the table. He wanted someone to catch him. He saw me see him, but I didn't give him the satisfaction of saying anything. The food almost made me feel normal. Almost.

"So," Doc said, "what's the story? Warwick's telling me we can't do the demo. The algo doesn't work."

"Oh, it works," Nessie said.

Warwick cleared his throat. "I had a different idea in mind," he said gently.

Nessie dabbed her lips with the tip of a folded napkin. "Ah, it's all *your* idea now, is that right?"

Doc grinned at Warwick, pointed at her. "It's hers originally?"

"Doesn't matter whose idea it is," Warwick said. "If it's created using Warlock & Co. equipment, it belongs to Warlock, QED. It's in her contract."

"As nature intended," Doc said.

Nessie dropped her sunglasses over her eyes. "Whatever," she said. She wiped a strand of hair from her face. "That sun is brutal." She loosened the neck of her cover-up, pulling her sleeves. Once again, I got a glimpse of those bare forearms. No tattoos. Not even a freckle, a mole, a blemish; nothing but clear skin. This time, she saw me staring at her. She pulled her right arm to herself, turned it around, searching her skin. Then frowned at me.

"Quit looking at me like that, man."

I shook my head, swallowed. "You had a tattoo, right? Tattoos."

She pushed her sunglasses back up, and those tawny-brown eyes bored into me. There was a fierce spark in them, a signal that said,

Really? You're one of those creepy guys? Scoffing, she slumped back in her chair. "You know, I never should have told you about that tattoo," she muttered.

The—wait, what?

"Yes, I had a tattoo lasered off a long time ago. It was a dumb little Joan of Arc thing. What's the big deal?"

She was repeating details from the story that I'd made up. The ludicrous one that I'd laughed about as I typed. But she presented the misinformation as if it were real history, her history. Doc crunched on potato chips as he watched. I grappled for words. Nessie fanned her face with the hem of her cover-up, scowled.

"If I didn't know better," Doc said, "I'd say this was a lover's spat."

Warwick raised a hand for peace. He was tilted back in his deck chair, one arm draped over the back of a chair, and with his other he held a tumbler against his forehead absently.

"You've all had a little to eat," he said. "You've had a little to drink. Now, before we lose our focus, it's time to do some work. This algo. This is the one. Doesn't matter whose idea it was originally." Coy smile for Nessie. "Everybody's gonna win. If we can position this thing right. Get the talk track down. We'll figure out the demo later."

Doc wiped barbecue sauce from his fingers. "Hit me with the pitch," he said. "Top-line idea, don't overthink it."

Warwick dropped his chair legs and leaned forward. His face relaxed. Something like joy softened his mouth. "It's real simple." He paused to inhale the dramatics of the moment. Then he said: "Think Google—but for the truth."

The sunlight quivered in the sky. "I don't fucking get it," Doc said.

At that moment, Uno jumped on Nessie's lap and with a long snout whacked Warwick's tumbler from the table to the stone terrace. Glass burst like a crystal balloon. The dog wagged its tail happily, proud of itself. The tension broke, we all laughed, except for Doc. "I hate dogs," he said.

Warwick went for a dustpan. I plucked the larger glass pieces with my fingers. Nessie scolded Uno and then turned round, calling for Zed. She looked under the table, around the corner of the house. No Zed. After the glass pieces were swept, all four of us fanned out to look for the missing dog.

The sun had settled to the west, and a sad pink-and-orange light suffused the lawn. Nessie and I walked the perimeter of the grounds, shining lights into the shrubbery and calling for the dog. Warwick and Doc were inside again, no doubt beating their chests and debating the as-yet-unwritten business plan. We searched for almost an hour, and the last of the color had leaked from the sky when the dog came trotting abruptly out of the dark and jumped into Nessie's arms.

"What's he got in his mouth?" I asked.

She shifted the dog, tugged. "Chicken bone," she said. "I'm gonna kill Doc."

She held Zed close as we walked back toward Warwick's house along a road bordered by high privacy shrubs, hiding houses from view. The cinders crunched under our feet. I thought about the other night, the one we spent drinking in Grand Central. A perfect moment. Now this, a walk in the tree-lined dark. I was collecting baubles of time with her. Little trinkets. Tchotchkes that would have no meaning to her but were proof of possible worlds for me. This was a ridiculous way to live. To thrive in the presence of someone and never tell them what they mean. You take what you can get. At the front door of Warwick's house, she set the dachshund on the ground and whispered, "Take off like that again and I'll put a cowbell on you."

Warwick and Doc argued on the patio. Inside, the stools looked hopeful in their neat rows along the long white marble island. The kitchen was dim and orderly. The house felt lofty, drowsy with secrets.

"I'm going to turn in," she said.

"Wait," I said. "I have to tell you something about the algorithm. Something I didn't want to tell Warwick and Doc."

A sad, tired smile touched her lips. "Really, Graham, it's all right. I know you feel obliged to help. But you're going through a lot right now. You deserve a break, too. Take a breather, like I did. You know, I don't think I picked up my phone more than two or three times today? Tomorrow, I'll dive back in. Or maybe not. Did you know there's an ashram out here? A no-electronics sort of place. Total silence, all that. Warwick has been telling me about it for ages. Says it's run by those Koyasan monks he studied with in Japan a bajillion years ago. No tech. No talking. Sounds wild, right?"

I started to say, *Yes, wild,* but Nessie put an arm behind my shoulders and air-kissed my cheek and said good night. I watched her glide away. I could not let her go. I opened my mouth and reached out, extending a finger as if to call attention to a busy person across the room, but before I could speak, Warwick appeared. He must have been standing in the dining room doorway, watching us. Nessie had her back to us, and she could not see how he raised his own index finger to his lips. Universal sign for conspiracy. She rounded the corner, gone, and Warwick drew closer.

"Not now, buddy," he said.

"Not now, what?"

"Now's not the time to tell her what you did."

I had a hard time catching my breath. My chest was weak, as breakable as wet paper. He could have poked a finger right through me. Luckily, he just smiled. Those pale-blue eyes glinted with the mica of amusement. "Yeah, yes," he said. "I know what's happening. I know what you did. We should talk. Just us. But not now. Not tonight. Tonight, I've got to sell Doc on the whole idea. I need a friendly fresh-capital infusion. I'm coming up a little short, but you know that, can't hide the money sitch from my ops guy, right? I'll figure it out."

"You do always figure it out," I agreed wearily.

And then he was gone. A screen door clapped, and I could see he was on the back patio again. He poured more whiskey for Doc and dropped into a chair. I could have gone outside to join them. But I didn't want to. I didn't have the energy for any of this. I leaned on chairs, ran a hand along the wall for support all the way to the bedroom where I had put my things. I needed to lie down. I needed to close my eyes. I needed the world to make sense.

CHAPTER 4

I grew up in a bed-and-breakfast town along the Hudson River. Although we had a modest house, I had a bedroom that felt as big as the world. Geraldine covered all four walls with enormous murals of animals. She didn't paint the room all at once. If she had a lull in illustration work, or she wanted a break from a difficult professional gig, she'd find a blank space in my room and shape an Indian tiger, a curious monkey, toothy wild things—all from nothing.

I was eleven when she got serious about teaching me how to paint. But I had none of her artistic talent. I tried but failed to learn the proper techniques. I understood how to fool the eye with perspective, but what marks I could produce with a paintbrush weren't going to fool anybody.

Still, we tried. Every weekend we went to a hobby store in Rhinebeck to pick up supplies for our latest project. One afternoon while Geraldine searched the shelves for a jar of gesso, I came across a mechanized chess set. It stood under a spotlight in the rear window. All the ornate pieces fit into a carved wood base. It looked like a normal chess set until you turned a silver key. Slowly, soundlessly, the pieces would move; first a white pawn, then a black, back and forth, turn by turn. Captured chess pieces moved to either side. The battle lasted eight minutes, when the black king capitulated. The white king celebrated by spinning briefly in place.

From that day onward, no visit to the hobby shop was complete unless I could wind the chessboard and watch the pieces move.

Geraldine stood with me to watch it, to watch me. She would tell me later that this was the moment when I first made sense to her. She loved art for how it simulated life with its colors, its golden ratios, its elegant lines. Clearly, I loved how hinges, joints, and levers could make inanimate wood and wire emulate a living thing.

She tried to buy the chessboard, but we learned it was much too expensive. *It's okay,* I told her. *I don't mind. I can just look at it when we come to the shop.* The next day, Geraldine went back alone and convinced the hobby store owner to put the chessboard on layaway; and over the next weeks and months she took extra illustration jobs till she had enough to bring it home. Once it was set up in my room, I was thrilled but also a little scared. Geraldine would give up anything for me, I realized. I had to be careful what I wished for.

Geraldine called, woke me from a dead sleep at 3:00 a.m. It took a beat to remember where I was—a lofty bedroom in Warwick's house—whereas she was in a hospital a hundred miles away. "Can't breathe right," she said. She labored to say more, but I couldn't understand. Most of her words made no sense, had no grammar, just rasps, rags of breath. "Mom. Hit the call button by the bed. Call the nurse. Can you hit the call button?"

She hung up or the call ended, I couldn't tell. Blinking, wiping blear from my face, I called back once, twice, three times, but she didn't answer her phone. No one picked up at the number for the nurse's station. Cursing, I got up and threw all my clothes into my bag.

Maybe she'd had a bad dream. Maybe she was fine but confused. Still, I couldn't take a chance. I wasn't sure if I could get to the city at this hour until I got downstairs to the kitchen and found Doc there, too. He had an early flight to the West Coast. He already had a car coming to take him to JFK. Did I want a lift?

Bryan VanDyke

38

"I thought you were staying all weekend," I said. "Working through all the logistics. Plan for this big demo, or whatever it is you and Warwick have in mind." Doc made a pitying gesture.

"This algo idea is never gonna work, man. No offense, it's bunk," he said. "But I did my thing. As I do. Doc provides."

He gestured toward a single sheet of paper on the table. Margins full justified, crisp print from a portable laser, anti-aliased, perfectly worded, elegantly phrased, Doc had crafted (what else?) a business plan:

Executive Summary:

With the proliferation of deepfakes, false narratives, and misinformation online, it has become increasingly important for individuals to be able to quickly verify the credibility of the information they come across on the internet. Our new product, EDDIE (Extended Diagnostic Data Inquiry Engine), will do just that, helping users to identify false or misleading information and protect themselves from being misled.

Market Analysis:

There is a growing demand for tools that can help individuals navigate the often confusing and misleading world of online information. In a survey conducted by the Pew Research Center, nearly two-thirds of adults reported that they have had trouble determining whether the information they come across online is true or false. This trend is only set to continue as the volume of online information continues to grow and the lines between fact and fiction become increasingly blurred.

Product Description:

We will launch initially with a browser add-on, which will use artificial intelligence and machine learning algorithms to scan web pages for potential inaccuracies or misleading information. We'll also create a digital destination where users can query our database to determine . . .

"Hey," Doc said, "car's here. Time to go, bro."

I waved the printout at him. "Wait," I said. "Eddie is an acronym? I thought it was just a name."

"Hell if I know," Doc said. "I made that up."

At the hospital, they'd moved my mother to another room, this one with an internal window for a nurse who sat at a station just outside the door. The nurse told me in his most gentle tone that they had my mother under heavy sedation. "She was panicking," he said. "She was pulling out her port. She kept trying to get out of bed. She thought we were holding her hostage. She kept talking about a deadline. She said she had to go home. We see this in elderly patients. They become greatly agitated by things they remember from long ago."

The nurse played his part well; perhaps this was part of his training—the breaking of bad news to the children, the spouses, the next of kin. I did my part to perform my role, too. I beat my chest. I would have thrown a bigger fit, but I was already exhausted.

What exactly happened? Why was she struggling to breathe? Was anyone watching her during the night?

No one knew what to do with me, and I didn't know what to do, either. Only the sight of my mother's attending physician brought me back down, returned me to my usual, collected, reasonable, rational self. Barely five feet tall, Esme Haber wore wire-rim glasses and spoke in a near whisper. If you weren't looking for her, it was easy to miss her. She didn't project brash confidence, wasn't jumpy, didn't avoid tough facts: She was the only person at the hospital whom I trusted. Nurses came and went in a blur, specialists strutted through and vanished, but Dr. Haber could be counted on to offer plain words about what was what.

"Your mother had a small stroke last night," she said. "Just a baby one."

"A baby stroke?" I asked.

"That's right."

"Isn't a stroke a stroke?"

We went a few times round like this. She was educated and unflappable, and I was a layman, a panicked son, a bystander at the scene of the accident. I got calmer because she stayed calm.

"Let's be cautiously optimistic," Dr. Haber said. "She's got fight in her. I'm going to order more scans. We'll see what we see. Until then, we wait."

We argued in the hallway, ostensibly because we wanted Geraldine to be out of earshot. But even if we were in her room, Geraldine wouldn't have heard us. She was under deep sedation. Keeping her calm was crucial. She needed time to heal.

"What are her odds?" I asked. "Is she going to get better, or worse?"

Dr. Haber touched my shoulder. A rehearsed gesture, but I appreciated her intent. Behind her glasses she searched my face, quickly and quietly. "I don't know," she said. "I know that's not what you want to hear. I would want a simple answer, too. But we need

41

more time to figure out what's going on. It's too soon to say. I know it's hard to wait. Go home, Graham. Sleep. Nothing will happen here right now. We've got her under close watch. I'll come by at this time again tomorrow. Come back then. I'll tell you everything new that I know."

She left, and I pulled up a chair and sat in silence at Geraldine's bedside. I watched her grimace and twitch in her twilight state, her sleep that was not sleep. Sometimes she opened her eyes and looked at me, but with no recognition. She did not respond when I spoke. Sometimes she looked at the television, but no matter where her gaze rested, there was no interest.

G&G. That's what we called ourselves. My mom and me. G&G against the world. If one of us was upset, we did G&G&TV. Swaddled in quilts on the sofa till midnight for Letterman's top ten, sometimes later if Conan had a good guest. Geraldine wasn't like the other mothers; she had a wry view of bedtimes, never got flustered, never scolded me for my grades. Yet she was a lavender shape in the crowd at every holiday cantata, a face at the back of the gym for every play, even the plays where all I did was props or lighting tech.

Her indulgence went too far at times; whenever I had a bellyache, a bad feeling about a test, or just felt off, she let me skip school, or leave early, or whatever it was I wanted. I wasn't an easy kid. Probably had an anxiety disorder, although back then, anxiety disorders weren't a thing. I slept poorly. Geraldine sat in bed with me at night until I fell asleep, sometimes reading quietly, sometimes answering my endless questions: What if killers broke into our home, what if I had a heart attack, what if the sun exploded? What if one day I woke up and she was gone?

Two hours went by with me lost in the past, seated at my mother's bedside. She moved, but only to shift her legs, to open and close her mouth, twitch her fingers, instinctive sighs or moans, indicative of nothing; there was nothing that she did that could reassure me she was still in there, somewhere. I don't know what a stroke does to the cells of the brain exactly, but I knew, in my mother's case, that we were already waging a war of attrition for her memory—what she knew, whom she knew, what remained. We were losing more and more of her each day already; how bad would it be when she woke up, if she woke up? Finally, after I could watch her list and twitch no longer, I did as the nurses and doctors all suggested and went back into the world.

CHAPTER 5

Half-blind with fatigue, I fumbled to pay the cab fare with my phone. I couldn't get it to work. All I could think was *Bed, home, climb into bed at home.* My neck hurt with the weight of a pending migraine. Pain gathered like a crystal behind my left eye. I switched to a credit card. Swiped it twice, no go.

"Machine broke," the cabbie said. "You got to give cash."

I didn't have more than ten bucks, cash. The cabbie cursed in a language that I didn't know. "I told you when you get in," he said. "You weren't paying no attention to nothing."

I can't remember what I said back, but it prompted the cabbie to unbuckle his seat belt and swivel in his seat to face me. A verbal blowup looked inevitable until the car door beside me clicked open and Warwick leaned in. His wallet open, he nickered softly, as if to calm a skittish animal. He passed a crisp fifty-dollar bill through the opening to the cab driver. "Keep the change," he said.

Once the car drove off, he turned to me. "You look like hell, buddy."

We sat in the wing chairs in the lobby of my apartment building. "This place is nicer than I remember," Warwick said. I said that I couldn't remember him ever coming to visit. I was still achy, tired, and I didn't understand what he was doing there. He asked what the common costs were for the building. I made a dismissive gesture. Everything with him was connected to money. The doorman, Benji, began to sweep the floor, pretending not to listen to us.

"How did you know about Nessie?" I asked.

"Ah," he said, inhaling theatrically through his teeth. "Yeah, yeah, that's a long story. But this probably isn't the place to tell it." He glanced at Benji, who smiled back at him with the loyal but vacuous look of a guard dog with nothing to guard. "Let's go for a walk by the water," Warwick said. He strolled toward the door, presuming I would follow. Because of course I did.

Outside, the sun made a blazing, blank mirror of the sidewalk. I had to squint to see Warwick at all. He was wearing light colors: tan pants and a rugby shirt. Looked like he had a plan to go sailing. With his top two collar buttons open, I could see his shell necklace, a talisman he'd picked up surfing somewhere a lifetime ago, when his hair was dark, his life shaggier. He had a matching shell bracelet on his wrist, which he'd finger when lost in thought.

I asked why he was with me, not in the Hamptons. "I've got a flight tonight," he said. "I need to tap a couple of old friends on the other side of the pond. Doc did his thing, called in a favor with some bankers, got me an audience with a guy who wants to know more about what we do. I'm just lining up possibilities, people we can call on later, when the algo is done."

"This algorithm," I said. "This Eddie chatbot. This whole thing. I thought I understood it. But—I don't think I understand it. What's it *for*? You've got to level with me if you want me to help make something happen."

Warwick's posture changed, his shoulders squared, his head lifted higher. I'd seen him shape-shift like this a hundred, if not a thousand, times. He began to speak in his "closer voice." The one he used with companies that were almost but not quite sold on one of our chatbot products. His big-picture sell. The vision. The possibility. The capital-*M* meaning of it all.

"We're gonna change the world," he said.

"You'll have to be more specific than that," I said.

He wasn't listening, though; he was rehearsing, wandering through the rough draft of the remarks he imagined he'd give to a rapt audience one day, the story of this pivotal leadership moment. Warwick existed in the present, but he lived mostly in the future perfect.

"This whole thing started," he said, "with a prototype that Nessie's team built for GEICO. She connected an art forgery algo to screen scrapers that trawled social channels for car photos. GEICO wanted to automate work that their claim adjusters spent hours on, looking into suspicious claims. Trouble was, the human workers couldn't comb through the piles of data, couldn't parse all the material. They ended up missing things, having to make assumptions that cost the company. So Nessie rigged this model to make intuitive leaps. Let it churn on Twitter for a couple of days. It came back with a list of current GEICO customers who had falsified claims that their car got into a hit-and-run. Clear, unambiguous fraud. She didn't know how the algo had done it, exactly. I told her, who cares? It works, that's the amazing part. So she kept going, kept adding new data sources, training the algo to do new things, spot new mismatches, find new frauds. You see what I'm saying?"

He wanted me to agree, to tell him it all sounded great, but I felt off-kilter, uncertain if I followed. "So, that's the pitch, then—a fraud tool? To insurance companies? Doc's business plan mentioned a browser add-on. Did you drop that? Sorry, I'm just trying to catch up."

Warwick laughed—his genuine, silvery, shoulder-shaking laugh. "Yeah, no, no. I'm past all that now. This isn't the next Google. This is bigger, big as life itself. We're not just organizing the world's information, we're able to tell you what's true and what isn't true. What's bigger than that?"

He went quiet for a moment while his words clattered around in my brain. "There's just one problem," he said at last. "It's stuck. The algo. It eats into all the compute we throw at it. It's obsessed with going deep into every nook and cranny of New York data systems that we hook up to it, and we haven't been able to come up with a solid plan to market. I think Nessie did something. She says we need to let it work. She might be right. But we can't wait forever. I've been reading the chat logs, looking at user interactions, looking for a way to speed everything up. I read the chats you had with it. That's how I knew you'd made changes to Nessie's data, edited her profile."

My mouth went dry. "So, you know everything," I said.

He grinned, made a pistol with his finger, and pointed at me. "Bang," he said. "Got you."

"How does it do it? How does it change things? It's real, right? I'm not just imagining that things are different? You see it all, too?"

He opened his hands, looked to the sky. "Buddy," he said, "I don't know how the algo does literally anything that it does. You know what I always say. Right? You've heard me say it a hundred times."

"Yes," I said wearily.

"Say it," he said. "Come on, you know it."

"You're like Elvis," I said. "You don't know—"

He gestured happily with one hand, cut me off. He didn't actually want me to deliver the line. He wanted to do it. He just had to know I knew it. "Elvis said, 'I don't know anything about music. In my line you don't have to.' Same for me. It's not my thing to ask why tech does what it does; my deal is to ask, What can we *do* with this? We've got Doc's business plan, which is fine, but you and I both know that this algo isn't like anything else we have. You don't just sell it, right? I mean, don't get me wrong, we can and will make ourselves rich, sure. But we can go bigger. How much can it do? How far can we go with changes? How far have you pushed?"

"I don't—I mean, I was just poking around with it."

"Keep poking, then."

"You're a lot calmer about all this than I am," I muttered.

He held up both hands in a beatific manner, then put a hand to his heart and closed his eyes. As if to soak in the radiance of a rare moment of sun. "Very on-brand for me," he said. "No? Yeah." He reopened his eyes and cast a cold, purposeful smile upon me. "It's all on you, buddy. Do me proud."

"Just me? You aren't going to ask Nessie to help?" Mentioning her name made my heart beat a little wobbly. "I need to talk to her," I said. "I need to tell her what I did. I need to explain."

"Nah, no, no, man," he said. "Don't blow her mind like that. She needs a break. She's doing a digi-detox, ashram and all. It's the best thing for her. So I need you to"—he broke into a Sammy Hagar warble—"hey, baby, finish what ya staaarted."

"But I've got all these questions. I could use her help. I don't even know *what* I did exactly. I changed some photos and some words. I don't know if I could produce the same result again if I tried."

We had walked west to the end of the island, and ahead of us was the Hudson River, where the sun was swinging low and the reflection on the water glittered like gems from a broken bracelet.

Warwick smiled at the horizon. "It's power, Graham. Does it matter how it works? You'll get used to it. Everybody does. Do you worry about how the sun works? No, you take it for what it is and move on. You changed Nessie a teensy bit. Big deal? Move on."

We crossed the West Side Highway and stood on the cobblestones near the pier. He kept talking, but I stopped listening for a moment: all I could hear were the words *You changed Nessie. You*, meaning me.

He looked at his watch. "I need to see this thing through in London."

"I get it," I said. But I didn't, really.

"Spend more time with the algo," he said. "See what else it can do. Figure out the deeper capabilities. The possibilities that are plausible. Play all you like. Then call me. Call me when you're ready. I have some ideas. But first you need to find the outer limit of this thing."

He was so casual, so nonplussed. Even for him. I couldn't get over it. For sure, it shouldn't have surprised me. This is what made people follow him: his ability to confront dramatic upheavals and, rather than cower in uncertainty or self-doubt, double down on his convictions and speed onward. He had no idea what self-doubt felt like. He never equivocated. He had a remarkable ability to glide smoothly over situations that were roiling and difficult in the details, details he left to others. Nessie's team could work for days or weeks on a model, only to have him render the whole project obsolete in a weekly leadership meeting. *Nope,* he'd say, *that's not what I want anymore.* Nessie never got flustered with Warwick's oversimplifications, not when people watched. But there were whole weeks when she avoided speaking to him, like after he undercut three months of data training by hundreds of college interns she'd hired to click "Yes" or "No" in response to an AI's attempt to generate a plausible Van Gogh fake.

A black Lincoln Town Car pulled up. His ride to the airport. He opened the door and began to step in.

"What'll I tell Nessie?" I asked.

He pulled his head back. "What do you mean?"

"I mean, about the algo, about what I did? She's going to see what I did eventually, isn't she? Won't she notice when she gets back from the ashram?"

He tapped a sad, short beat on the car frame. "You don't get it, Graham. You still can't wrap your head around it. She's off the project. For good. It's just going to be you. She wants a break? She can have a break. I'm going all in on you. Now don't disappoint me, *comprende*? Counting on you, pal."

PART II

CHAPTER 6

If I wanted to understand how the algorithm worked, I had to use the algorithm once again to change the world. Simple as that. But the algo terrified me. Yes, it was just code and data, electrons flowing through silicon on a server somewhere; it was also something far more. I had seen the algo at work, but I had no scope for its power, its risks, its tricks, the consequences.

For someone like Warwick, who had no taste for particulars, the next step was obvious, easy. Not me. Without much effort I could come up with reason after reason why using the algo again was a no-good, terrible, awful, really bad idea. Yet I kept coming back to this same question: Could I do it again? Probably, yes. Unless it was all a fluke? Maybe, maybe not. I had to know.

I decided to make a simple tweak. Nothing too elaborate. Some change that could dovetail with the rest of the world, something other people would see without realizing what they were seeing was a construct. This approach felt familiar to me. Like when I was a kid, when I painstakingly ran a small brush wire through tiny rubber hoses one at a time to piece together an animatronic squid for a staged version of *Twenty Thousand Leagues Under the Sea*.

The incident with Nessie put me off the idea of altering people. Warwick said it was just a teensy change, that I should move on. But I thought about her all the time. Washing my hands, I'd stare at my sudsy skin and wonder if she missed her tattoos without realizing it; like a variant of déjà vu, you don't know what you're missing, but you can feel it's not there, that it should be. I poked around in deleted files on my laptop, thinking perhaps I could restore her to the way she'd been, but I couldn't find any of the old pictures. All evidence of the tattoos was gone, except what I saw whenever I closed my eyes and thought about her.

I opted to begin with a change to the city infrastructure itself. This felt less immoral. For one thing, New York City was constantly changing. Any New Yorker is as likely to orient by what a place once was as by what it is: like the drugstore that used to be a bank, the dance club that was a chapel, the condos in the old insane asylum. I would be nudging a process already well underway, no harm in that.

Using the algo, I planned to alter the part of the city outside my window, a street where a long line of cars backed up daily on their way to the Lincoln Tunnel. Mostly southbound cars turning off the West Side Highway. For years I'd believed the city should ban left turns at the intersection, a simple fix to drop traffic by a hearty amount. In a few keystrokes, I did what city planners would not or could not do. All that was needed was a new rectangular sign on the wire that stretched across the intersection, a three-word fiat, so simple: No LEFT TURNS.

The algo was connected to a database maintained by the New York City Department of Transportation. This meant I could edit text traffic data and webcam footage. It took some time to create a mask with the new sign and then position the image precisely over the video footage of the intersection I had in mind. At some point in my time at Warlock & Co., I'd had to fire and hire a motion graphics team, and I'd picked up some basic photo and video editing skills along the way.

I didn't stop there. I couldn't. My working theory about the algo was this: To make an edit stick, I believed I had to be thorough. I had to think of everything, consider each detail, follow through on every consequence. Otherwise, the algo would flag a mismatch, reject my changes, and revert to what was real.

To the training data, I added a tweet, dated a year previous, announcing a change to the traffic flow in the Lincoln Tunnel area. No more left turns off the West Side Highway. Then, in response to that tweet, I added retweets and angry comments from random New Yorkers. I wrote a brief *New York Post* story—the training data also included material from media outlets—and in the article I quoted members of the city council, a state assemblyman. Better articles had been written, but I got the facts right, referenced current politicians.

I changed photos and altered tweets and news stories till I assembled a compelling alternate reality. This alternate take on the world was the same as ours, except that it had one fewer road with a left turn. I queued up all the changes that I thought would reflect this changed reality, all the official notices and city maps, and I uploaded all the files into the algo's dataset.

"All right, then," I said. "Let's see how this works."

Instantly, an alert chirped. The algo flagged the training data itself as wrong. I was impressed. It was monitoring everything in real time. Like a series of defenses clicking in simultaneously, it pulled up the drawbridge, reverted files, turned the clock back on my revisions. Quite the adjudicator. The algo needed less than a few seconds to undo what I had taken hours to piece together. I'd built a sandcastle all afternoon, and at six o'clock the tide came in and flattened it all.

Adding insult to injury, the Eddie avatar popped up in a new window, its emoji-nerd face accompanied by a tiny little hand it waggled, pointer finger up, as if to say, *Ah-ah-AH! Ah-ah-AH!* Or maybe that last part was my imagination. Because what it had to say was what it always said first:

EDDIE: Hi! I'm Edmond. But you can call me Eddie.
EDDIE: Your recent updates contained a series of errors. 167 mismatches were just corrected.
EDDIE: Make that 217. Phew! I'm breaking a sweat here!

I tried again. This time, in addition to all the materials I assembled, I also added violations to the records of numerous drivers. Tickets for left turns, hundreds of them—no, let's make it thousands. Scofflaws who refused to change their driving habits. I entered a guilty plea for a driver who brought his case to court claiming the signage wasn't clear. Faster than last time, the algo rejected me.

I abandoned the left-turn plan as too ambitious. Small changes. That's what I needed. Small enough to avoid too many cascading consequences. I should make an alteration that was noticeable, but not on the scale of a major traffic change. I went to the window in my cramped living room and studied the trees on the street below. Their branches looked stunted; their leaves tired, worn. The idea came to me almost at once: I would create new trees.

According to an online atlas of New York City trees, my street was lined with oaks. Pin oaks, in particular. They provided shade in the summer, muffled traffic when they were in full bloom. But I wanted more. According to an online botany site, pin oaks had a maximum upper height of forty feet. Something like a linden tree sounded good—twice as tall, their branches would reach my window.

I set to work doctoring photos and writing a press release from the West Side Park Conservancy, which declared this block as a treetop park, a new concept meant to build on the idea of the High Line, which pioneered the idea of meaningful green space above the street level. I typed out a short write-up for TREETOP PARKS and dropped the entry into the training dataset, which had expanded recently to include screen scrapes from Wikipedia.

I was certain this would work. At first, nothing happened, no errors, no rejection. Eddie the chatbot with its dorky emoji-nerd face stayed out of sight. I spun around in my chair to watch the windows; maybe I would see tree limbs grow into view, unfurling like magical beanstalks that climb to the clouds. How did it work, exactly? Had Nessie's tattoos vanished all at once, or faded slowly, as she slept, under the cover of darkness? But then a chime struck, and Eddie appeared on-screen with a red X in a red circle, and I knew that the trees weren't going to happen.

Turned out I had chosen a tree with a deep root system that would never work in Manhattan's stony soil. Perhaps this was how Eddie knew that the information I had added was false. I was looking up the height of gingkoes and London plane trees and had a few potential candidates when I stopped. Lifted my fingers from the keyboard and balled them into fists, pressed the fingernails hard into my skin. I was doing this all wrong. I was following the wrong roads.

I shut the laptop and went for a walk. The world outside my apartment was awake and bustling with the business of a new day. I'd worked through till morning without realizing. I walked stiff legged through the lobby, trying to wrap my head around the fact that today was tomorrow and not yesterday. From behind the desk, Benji cried out, "Have a great one!" I grunted in response. Everything Benji did irritated me.

The path along the river was already populated with joggers and cyclists. Tourists boarded Circle Line ferries to ride around the sights. Families with children, tour groups, couples on romantic day trips. So many sounds of excitement and joy, none of it for me. I walked among the crowds as far as the Boat Basin, where dozens of sailboats bobbed up and down on the Hudson. Then I crossed over to Riverside Drive and hailed a cab. Headed down toward Brooklyn.

At the hospital, I stood in the small room where Geraldine lay motionless in her bed. She had not opened her eyes for days. She was slipping deeper into oblivion. The doctors and I weren't using the word *coma*, but everybody could read the signs. Everything was happening so fast but so slow; she was dying, but she wasn't changing—no movement, no speech. *That's not her,* I thought, staring at her impassive face. *It can't be. I refuse to believe it.* One of the nurses came in to check her IV, did her work swiftly, wordlessly. At the door, she turned back, said, "You should talk to her. Her EKG activity is like someone in a deep sleep. Don't worry about what you say. It's the sound of your voice that matters."

The machines beeped at her bedside while I sat in a chair, searching for words. Finally, I asked if she remembered the automated chessboard, the one I'd loved so much as a boy, the one she bought. I sighed, smiled at the tile floor. "That chessboard was just the start," I said. I collected so many automata. Plastic wind-up dogs, chattering alligators, waddling penguins, wing-flapping owls. I chuckled, recalling how surprised she had been when she discovered that I liked to take animatronics apart more than I liked to watch them work. *But now they're broken!* she'd said. I soaked in the radiance of her surprise later when I made the eviscerated machines whole again, chattering and clapping as they had originally. She used to tell people, *He wants to make automata when he grows up.* This earned a blank look from most people. Some people said things like, *What's an automata?* or *That's so unique*, but in any case, what they all meant was, *This kid is really weird.*

I leaned closer to my mom, lips almost touching her ear. "I've found something even better now," I whispered. I told her about the algo. "It's like a magic box that can make dreams come true," I said. "No. It's not as simple as magic. If it were, I'd use it on you. I'd wish you back to your old self."

Her old self. My mom, Geraldine, the lavender whirling dervish. That lavender coat, those lavender hats, that lavender rain poncho. You'd know her at once by the colors she always wore. There was a brassy extravagance to her, an unwillingness to compromise. She never made other people apologize for who or what they were, but she disregarded protocol, paid no toll in the name of niceties; she did not teach me to bring a gift to someone's house the first time you visited. She let the air out of people who were stuck on themselves, which meant there were plenty of other parents who disliked her, which ended more than a few of my friendships as a kid. But I would have it no other way. Did I wish I had a normal mom? One better heeled, more poised? Never, not once. I used to creep down the hall late at night to peek into her garage studio with my breath held to keep silent so I could watch her paint, studying how she stood, feet planted shoulder width, arm extended like a conquistador, one eye slightly pinched, envisioning the world she was determined to create.

A nurse came into the room, startling me. "I'm sorry," she said, "I'm here to turn her. We can't let Mom get bedsores." Standing to make room, I swiped wetness from my eyes, said I'd be right back. But I wasn't coming back, not that day.

I walked despairingly through the streets around Woodhull. Kids played basketball on broken concrete courts. A woman in a bakery wrapped empanadas in clear plastic. A construction crew in orange pinnies swung picks in a hole that went deep into the road. I walked till I reached the steps for the Brooklyn Bridge walkway. Fresh graffiti on the stone wall, the faint smell of piss on the steps. *Could I walk all the way back home?* I could. I might as well.

Later, I sat on a bench in the Battery and watched the Staten Island Ferry angle toward the southern edge of the island. Everywhere I looked, the city went on with its business. Nothing could stop it. I had a few more miles left to walk. The sun would set before I got home. Another day would slip away. My mood was as black as the space between stars. The algo. My mom. Nessie. I kept failing, flailing.

On the path near home, a bicyclist swerved to avoid me. "Quit blocking the whole trail, asshat," he shouted, then pedaled on.

I arrived back at my building sweaty and tired of humanity. Standing beside the desk was that grinning oaf, Benji. Was he working double shifts? What was his story, anyway? And why did he bother me so much? I didn't know. Maybe it was because he was so blithely happy, so perfectly content with his lot in life.

Upstairs, I ran a Google search on Benji's name. I clicked around, looking for more fodder for my foul mood. I was looking for reasons to dislike him. Yet there was nothing. His public persona was inoffensive— un-dislikeable. I paid for a website to unlock government records, past addresses, a lien on a car that he couldn't afford, a petty claims court filing when he accused a landlord of swindling him out of his deposit. I pulled up his LinkedIn profile. Him in a navy jacket, dark tie, his daily doorman uniform. His photo was a selfie taken in a bathroom mirror, garishly lit by a flash; pale, skinny, earnest Benji Jameson.

I found Benji's record in the algo's data. Nestled in among all the other millions of profiles, a perfect copy of Benji as he presented himself on LinkedIn, Facebook, Instagram. He had only a few dozen people in his friends list. No wife, no siblings listed; a loner, simple, the ideal person, if I were looking for a person to edit. Not too many things I'd have to change, not too much to alter. That is, if I were changing him. A big if. Still, clicking around, I started to realize that I could make Benji better. Not like with the tattoos. Nothing ugly, selfish. I could make his life better, objectively. Suddenly, I could see how easy it would all be. That old rush, the feeling you get when you know the task, and all that remains is to follow the routine, to make the *could be* into the *what is*.

I made a copy of all his data, then started working on it outside of the training set. The first change I made was to Benji's job. I pushed him to the front of the white-collar pecking order: with a quick update, I sent him to John Jay for a juris doctorate, had him graduate in 2011. Cum laude. Because . . . why not? I told myself that what I was doing was an act of beneficence. Meet Benjamin Jameson, Esq. I made him an associate in a small but respected criminal defense practice in Midtown. He was born in Nyack, just north of the city. Still lived there. A respectable commuter town, but why not live close to the Metro-North line in a tony suburb? Westchester, then. You're moving on up, Benji.

I finished near midnight. I pushed all the updates from the staging area to production. The algo accepted the changes without a peep. I sat still for a few minutes, waiting for a delayed rejection, waiting for the Eddie avatar to pop up. But no rejection came. All I heard was the light tapping of rain against the window and the sound of tires on the wet asphalt street.

I rode downstairs alone in the elevator. The elevator dinged as it passed each floor. My hands trembled, I felt clammy around the collar. I hadn't eaten a real meal in days. One more reason I felt jumpy and lightheaded. In the lobby, a woman smiled from behind the desk. Her silky head wrap matched the powder-blue shirt under her livery jacket; her skin glowed golden brown, as if she'd grown up someplace beautiful. Her lapel pin read FATIMA.

"You're new," I said. "Are you the night shift?"

The woman stared at me, half a smile pulling at her lips; she was waiting for me to go on, to deliver a punch line, to relent on whatever gaslighting joke I was putting on. Eventually, she chortled, perhaps out of habit. "You crack me up, Mr. Gooding," she said. "You look pale. Have a seat. You need to eat. Here, I've got puff-puff and plantains. Have a bite."

I had given Benji a new job, but I hadn't given this woman, Fatima, his old job. I hadn't thought of the need, truth be told; it wasn't a mistake, just a gap, a blank space that the algo filled in. I didn't understand why *this* oversight was allowed, whereas others were rejected. But I'd given up thinking the algo was knowable. The best I could hope for was predictability.

For an hour I sat in the lobby and ate Nigerian food and listened while this chatty, kind stranger, Fatima, told me the latest building intrigues—the porter who was always drunk, the super's skeezy security cams, the elevator repairman dating her on the sly—as if this kind of gossipy tête-à-tête was how we always passed the time, as if we'd known each other for ages.

CHAPTER 7

The person I most wanted to call was Nessie. I wanted to tell her what I'd discovered. I wanted to beat my chest and tell her what I'd accomplished. She'd never believe me. I'd have to prove it to her by changing something. She'd be thrilled at what our creation could do. Well, *her* creation, really. But I couldn't call her. She was at the ashram. And then there was the problem of the tattoos. The tattoos she never knew existed. The ones that I blanked out. To tell her what the algo could do, I'd have to confess how I'd started by making changes to her.

Now I knew how to use the algo to do what I wanted, like winding up a key and watching the show. But I still hadn't achieved my original objective. I had no idea how the algo itself worked. I could have just glossed over those details, skipped right to using it again. Plenty of people would. But I wouldn't be me if I could stand not knowing. I need to understand the details.

I dressed and caught a train for the office: I planned to corner some of the junior engineers on Nessie's team and ask them to show me the code for their AI models. To walk me through a logical diagram or a technical schematic—or whatever they used to build their disembodied machines. I was hoping that one by one I would gather the pieces I needed to get an idea of how Nessie's new algo worked. Short of talking to her, this was the best idea I had.

As the train traveled downtown, I checked my work email for the first time in a week. After Warwick told me to figure out the algo, I'd abandoned my day job. It was his company, so I had cover. But I had forgotten that he wouldn't think to tell anyone else. On my phone I swiped through screen after screen of messages from irritated coworkers, colleagues whose meetings I'd ghosted, vendors with invoices that I had not processed or paid. A month ago, I would have felt guilty; now, I felt faintly irritated. All these people thought their work, their requests, were so important. None of them had any idea what I was doing, or why, and if I explained it, they wouldn't believe me, probably wouldn't care. I had a vision of people crowded around me at work, shouting, insisting I pay attention to their problems.

Suddenly, visiting the office seemed like a very bad idea. I began to list all the reasons to turn around, return home. What was it I'd said about chatbots? They're ghost machines. The real world is outside their reach. A thing made of text can't understand anything larger than the text that binds it. A bunch of junior engineers who didn't work on this algo couldn't help me understand why it did what it did. I got off the train at the next stop. Crossing through a tunnel to the uptown side of the tracks, I thumbed a new email to an old friend, sort of a last-ditch effort for outside help.

Jay Xi and I had been roommates a long time ago, before he went to work as a network adviser for ICANN; last I'd heard, he was doing white-hat hacking for bounties from big software companies. Jay had cut his teeth on the prebrowser internet, when a real geek could whistle tones through phone headsets to phreak free phone calls to Budapest or Bangkok, didn't matter where, it was all just for kicks. Jay was already a graybeard of the internet when I met him, although we were the same age, and for the record, he was perennially clean-shaven.

He responded to my email before I got back home. I thought you were dead, he wrote. Absolutely, let's do lunch; bring shawarma, I'm pretty sure you still owe me for the last three times we broke bread.

The sun was high and bright as I walked through the crooked, shadow-less streets near the building where Jay rented an office. From the street, his building looked like so many other prewar structures: neoclassical plinths and columns, tall windows, ornate brickwork. But this building also had a small plaque near the entrance to mark the historical significance it held as one of the original Bell Labs buildings, the place where engineers created early transistors and operating systems, some of the pillars of the modern digital world. Nobody using their phones at the bus stop seemed aware of the debt they owed to the people who once worked here.

Jay was waiting for me on a bench in the lobby. He had dark circles under his eyes and grayer teeth than I remembered. Shaking hands, he gave me the once-over, too.

"You look pale," he said. "Do you still cast a reflection?"

"Love you, too, buddy."

Jay and I had met at NYU during the preposterous, prosperous fin de siècle of 1999. I was studying econ and mechanical engineering and didn't care about either one. I wanted to work for a Japanese company that made robotic pets. But the company was a money loser and hadn't hired anyone out of school in four years. Jay was in the Interactive Telecommunications Program, but he hated the dot-com boom, hated what big business was doing to the web; he was more or less getting a degree because it kept him out of trouble.

Jay was born in San Fran, raised all around Northern Cali. His dad was a math genius who kept getting fired from pointless jobs. His mom was dutiful and active in her church, and she had friends everywhere she went, but at home she never left her bedroom, went days without speaking to anyone. She worked up the nerve to visit Jay in New York once when we lived together. She understood English but didn't speak it to me except to say *Thank you* or *Goodbye*; our longest exchange was when she corrected my pronunciation of her son's name: Juh-ay SH-ee.

A few days later, I tried to say Jay's name the way she'd said it, but Jay laughed himself into a chair the first time he heard me give it a shot.

Dude, are you for real? It sounds like you're saying Jay-Z. Say it without clenching your teeth. But I couldn't get it right. It always sounded like Jay-Z. *Whatever, man,* Jay said. *It doesn't matter.* And so a nickname was born.

I kept the joke going for a long time, until one day we were catching up over drinks, and a television over the bar had a news chyron that said, JAY-Z AND BEYONCÉ WED SECRETLY, and I turned to him and said, *Man, you couldn't tell me? I thought we were close.* Jay laughed, but I heard how it wasn't a real laugh: he was humoring me, putting up with me. After that, I never made the joke again.

I brought the street-cart shawarma, and we ate lunch together in his office—a large but low-ceilinged room with a round window looking out on an inner courtyard. We handed the baubles of small talk back and forth for a few minutes while taking bites of our food. Eventually, Jay wiped his mouth with a napkin and made a let's-have-it gesture. "Give it to me straight," he said. "What's going on?"

The benefit of an old friend, of someone who's known you across the long arc of life, is that such a person can cut through the circumstantial, get to the quick. His question made me think first not of the algo but of my mom in her hospital bed. I put away the thought of her. This wasn't the place. Jay wasn't the person to tell. I took a deep breath. "It's kind of a long story," I said.

Jay's office was comfortable and quiet, but old, with diamond-pattern linoleum floors and a drop ceiling like an aging school or municipal courthouse, which made what I had to say sound even less normal, less plausible, less real. I had never before told the whole story of the algorithm, start to finish, to anyone. I heard for the first time how much I sounded like a man with a frail grip on reality. Jay quit eating, just set his shawarma down and studied me with quiet intensity.

"I know it's insane," I said. "Right?"

"Yes," he said absently. Then, more firmly: "I mean, yes. It's not sane, what you're telling me."

"Okay, but leave that aside a second. Because I can prove it."

"Set aside the insanity, fine. What's left, then?"

"I want to understand where the data is being stored. For an algorithm like this. That's where I want to start. I can't understand the algo itself. That's beyond me. But the data is data, right? I know that it really exists somewhere. The profile records. The images. The plaintext. The facts and figures about people and their lives. The data is stored on physical devices somewhere, right? On hard drives? I feel like if I could find those, it would give me some grounding. Can we start there?"

Jay studied his shawarma, frowned. Then he cleared his throat. "Listen, cloud architecture is super complicated. And so are virtual servers. I could probably make a diagram for you, show how data's stored, referenced by an app. I could cross-reference geographic points for CPUs—"

"That would be amazing!"

"—but it wouldn't help."

I swallowed a bit of food. "Because I'm losing my mind?"

Jay made an ambiguous gesture. "No comment, Graham. You said to set the insane stuff aside. So I won't point out that you sound a bit like a conspiracy theorist. Here's the thing. About your question. The data isn't in any one place. It's stored all over. That's basic information design, that was Claude Shannon's big insight back at the dawn of computers. It has to be that way, otherwise entropy wins and the whole system breaks down. Random distribution is the rule. It's more efficient as a storage method. Parts of what you're looking for are stored everywhere. Computers don't work like people. They're faster and dumber."

"So this is a boondoggle."

He picked up his shawarma and took a bite. I saw how he saw me. I was pale, sickly, out of sorts. An unreliable witness to my own life, lost and looking for help from anyone, everyone.

"Don't feel bad," he said. "Listen, in the fifties, John von Neumann tried to calculate how much energy it cost for each bit stored on a computer. He couldn't figure it out. John von Neumann! The architect of modern computing! The smartest guy ever! Nowadays, computers are so complex that only computers can run them." He chuckled rue-fully, smirked. He poured seltzer from a canteen into a metal cup. He offered me some, but I shook my head. He swigged it all, screwed the cap back on.

"Seeing you makes me sad," he said. "We should get, like, together more often." He must have seen the distance gathering in my face because he shifted back to the topic at hand, the algo. "I guess the next step," he said carefully, "would be for me to see this thing in action."

"Yeah," I said. "I could really use some help. My friend Nessie Locke, the one who built the algo? She's completely out of pocket. And Warwick, hell, he's always inscrutable. I think he's in London, but honestly, he probably wouldn't be a lot of help if he were here. What's wrong?"

"Your phone," Jay said as he nodded at it. Incoming call. From the hospital.

I answered in a single swift motion. Jay turned to the window as if to grant the illusion of privacy. I studied his graying profile while the voice on the line apologized for telling me this over the phone, "Your mother had a seizure. One of her tumors ruptured. She stopped breath-ing. We've intubated her. We've got her on a ventilator. But she's stable."

Someone at the hospital was always telling me not to react. *Don't worry, she's stable.* Or, *She had a stroke, but a baby stroke, don't worry. She needs tests, but we'll figure it out, don't you fret.* Yet, she got worse every time I stepped away. I stood, my chair scraping hard on the floor.

"I should go," I said, patting at my pockets. Where was my phone? It was already in my hand.

Jay asked if he could help. His eyes pleaded for me to level with him. "My mom's dying," I said. "She's kind of gone already." I don't remember what he said in response. We agreed to something. He offered consoling words. I was too distracted; nothing he said got through. "I should go," I repeated.

On the street there were no cars for hire. No taxis to be found. I was desperate to get to the hospital. I rented one of the large blue Citi Bikes that were parked all over. I had never ridden a bike in the city before. This was a terrible moment to try. I'd avoided bikes as a kid, mostly because I was a pudgy nerd with an inner-ear problem. The fact that I ever learned to ride at all was mostly due to Geraldine's coaxing: *You're going to be glad about this later in life,* she promised.

I wobbled along in the protected bike lane from Chelsea to the Garment District, real bikers veering around me. Cutting over to the Manhattan Bridge, all I had to mark my lane was a painted strip along the shoulder, a partition that trucks, cars, and buses seemed to think was more of a suggestion than a rule. On the serpentine transverse coming off the bridge through Brooklyn, a smug dude leaned out the window of an Utz delivery truck and shouted, "Good luck on the heart attack, Jack!" Howling, he hit the gas and shot past. I kept my head low and pedaled harder.

CHAPTER 8

I stood in a hospital room, a private one with a bed, a small sofa, a vertical casement window, a clutch of beeping machines. My mother's room. But not really. I could not, would not, see it as such. Because my mother wasn't there. I couldn't look at the shape in the bed, but I had to. *Here lies a body that resembles but is not the mother I knew.*

Dr. Haber stood on the other side of the bed. She stared directly at me as she spoke terrible words. She had removed her glasses and was cleaning the lenses with a soft cloth while she spoke. A nervous habit. The beep of a nearby machine kept perfect time. "The team went with a stable-state protocol," she said. "Their job was to maintain her vitals. They did the best they could. Under the circumstances."

"I see that," I said.

I wasn't listening, couldn't. I was thinking about identity. My mother's identity. Memory. Her memories. For how long is a person in a coma still the same person? If they wake up, sure, they might return in full. What if they never woke up? At what point in keeping a body alive do we end up with just a body? Just the likeness, not the actual thing itself? I had a wall of questions. I didn't plan to ask them out loud. Just assembling the list was good enough. Questions distracted me from emotional realities, like the shape in the bed, like the chart Dr. Haber handed to me, the graph of the electrical activity in my mother's brain, a flat line.

"Do you understand what I'm saying?"

"Give it to me one more time," I begged.

"One of the tumors has ruptured," Dr. Haber said. "We can't remove it. It's too deep to remove. We stopped the bleeding, but in doing so, her brain stopped telling her body to breathe."

She said more using polysyllabic words, words that I didn't know, but I didn't need to know every definition to see how inevitable this all was; left with nothing that I could do or say to fight back, I resorted to sarcasm.

"So, like, this is bigger than a baby stroke."

Dr. Haber studied me with her big, sad eyes. She saw the trap I was laying. "Yes," she said softly.

I said, "So you were wrong."

"I was hopeful for a different outcome."

I raked the back of my sleeve across my cheeks. "Why didn't a nurse do something? When the seizure started?"

"As I've said, they did all they could have. There was no outward sign at first. She was already in sensory occlusion when—"

"Occlusion," I said. "Sounds like a fancy word for *bullshit.*"

"A nonresponsive state."

"Occlusion," I repeated. "What a word. It also sounds like the moment in a detective novel when the hero gets a big hint, the one that changes how he sees the world and opens his mind to what it will take to crack the case. But we're not going to crack this one, are we, Esme? It's too late."

The machines hummed their toneless tune in the background. I was aware that I was being disrespectful. I was willing to do anything to avoid looking at or thinking about the shape in the bed.

"As you can see, there's no brain activity after eleven a.m. this morning."

"I can read a chart," I said.

I could not hide behind the logistics of hospital transfers or medication doses or how to keep her comfortable. I had lost the detachedness that made me a good advocate in the past. Now I was acting like a hurt

72

son. I *was* a hurt son. I was hurting. I wanted all this to stop. I wanted to roll everything back. That's when a familiar voice broke through, saying my name. I clenched my teeth. *Not you,* I thought.

"I came as soon as I heard," Warwick said.

He entered the room gently, softly stepping, bowing to the doctor, nodding to me. I didn't want to see him. Yet, I was glad to have him. He was a distraction. I didn't have to look at Geraldine: I could glare at him. He wore a light-blue seersucker suit with a white T-shirt and loafers, like you'd wear to a beach wedding in Montauk. He doffed a gorgeous bouquet of bright-red, sword-shaped irises. Somehow, he'd jetted back here from London, dressed up to the nines, pinched a bouquet from a bride—and arrived mere minutes after me.

"She looks peaceful," he said, bending over her bed. "At least there's that, right?"

"Paralysis of the facial muscles," I said.

"Her eyes were open when I walked in. She looked at me. Is that a good sign?"

We both looked at Dr. Haber. She was wearing her usual turquoise scrubs, and she had a stethoscope in her front pocket. I'd never seen her use it. I wondered if it was just a prop. A signal of her supposed authority. She frowned and let her gaze drop. Lately, she'd stopped looking me in the eyes so often. "There will still be brain-stem activities," she said. "Those activities will give the illusion of wakefulness. Not real consciousness. I know this is hard."

"Meet Dr. Esme Haber," I said to Warwick. "She was just telling me how we can keep my mother alive but not really alive like this forever, if we like. But we shouldn't, of course. We definitely shouldn't."

"Please call me later," Dr. Haber said. "We can formalize a plan when you're ready."

"Unless she's just faking," I said bitterly.

After the doctor left, Warwick remained very solemn, very still, and for a few minutes neither of us spoke, as if this moment, this very room, was made of exquisite but fragile glass that would shatter if we weren't terribly, terribly careful.

"You disagree with her about the treatment," Warwick said at last. "Is that right?"

"She wants to talk about when to pull the plug."

"Yeah," Warwick said. "No." He nodded and reached under the collar of his shirt to touch his shell necklace, as if for comfort, or maybe a silent petition to the gods for peace. "But she still has a chance, no?"

"It would take a miracle."

"A miracle," Warwick said. As if the word had a texture he was rolling around in his mouth. I was about to snap at him, tell him to stop repeating what I said. But then he went on, and what he had to say was, well, not what I expected, although I should have: "Well, you're the miracle man, aren't you?"

"It's not possible," I said, my voice rising, not angry at him anymore but at myself somehow for not yet finding a way around this. I rubbed my face, cleared my throat, tried to level my tone, my volume, my anger. "She's not like Benji or Nessie. There's nothing to work with. No digital material."

"How much do you really need?"

"I need *something*. I need records. She barely emailed." I paused. Then went on; like a guilty kid, I kept adding reasons: "No Facebook. No Twitter. She has no digital life to work with. What would I work with? I could try to fix her indirectly, make up some records, leave some gaps and hope the algo will fill in the rest. But I can't. What if I got it all wrong? What if I wiped her out altogether?"

"There's got to be a way," Warwick said.

"There's no way."

Warwick set the bouquet of irises on the table beside Geraldine's bed. I put my hands in my pockets, made fists, dug nails into my palms, unmade fists, made them again. What was I supposed to do with these flowers? Go fetch a vase? Bring them home? Let them just lie there, die?

"Graham," Warwick said, his voice gentler than I knew him to be. The disordered state of my thoughts and feelings made me fall prey to his calm. I wanted to be angry with him, with everyone, but I just felt deflated. I didn't want him to be here, but the steady clip of his voice held me.

"I've got an appointment in Midtown." He gestured at his suit. "Hence the natty duds," he said. "Come with me, yeah? Yeah. There's nothing to do here. I think you'll be interested in where I'm going."

"I'm not dressed for fancy," I muttered.

"You're with me," he said. "That'll be good enough."

We left without any more debate, no fuss from me. He told me to follow, so I left with him. I didn't say goodbye to my mother. I did look back from the doorway. The shape in the bed still wasn't really her.

The elevators brought us down to a parking garage beneath the building. Warwick's white Maserati glowed in the dark of the underground. Inside the car, everything smelled clean, the leather seats felt supple, the dashboard glass gleamed; this wasn't the same car he had in Southampton—this was another, a spare.

"I thought you were visiting with bankers in London," I said.

"I came back."

"You don't look like you took a red-eye."

"Virgin Atlantic," he said, a hint of marvel in his voice. "I sleep better in business class than I do in my own bed."

He guided the car around local streets, then onto the highway. He kept up an unrelenting talk track for the entire ride. He expounded on the nutritional value of business-class dinners, the ideal genres for in-flight movies, the seat-pitch variation from first to business class. I'd find it suffocating except Warwick had this edge whenever he found a topic thrilling; his voice would pitch slightly higher, as if he were just relearning everything himself, always with this can-you-believe-it lilt to his voice. I found it reassuring, always had. His bottomless capacity for awe was what made space for—and made tolerable—his limitless self-assurance.

He'd had this skill even when I first met him, after college. I was introduced to him in a conference room, his ideal habitat, when I was a junior engineer at Lycos, a second-tier search engine known mostly for its mascot, a black Labrador retriever. My job was to create and manage an archive of all the search queries for a given week. I hated the work. My boss was a relentless meddler. And the search algo itself was no good.

At the time, Warwick was selling artificial intelligence tech as the way to leapfrog Google and turn Lycos into the world's most useful search engine. He didn't have any slides. Didn't have a cute sidekick or a schtick. I'm not sure he had a product, either. Mostly, he was selling an idea. He dressed well—nice shoes, expensive jacket—but he didn't seem overly concerned with his look. If he had a sales quota to meet, you couldn't tell. *The art of the possible,* he said, *that's what I want to talk about. We could change the nature of web search, if you wanted. I could help. Or you can keep doing what you're doing, and this place will be dead in a year.*

My boss at Lycos left in a huff before the meeting was done. I didn't follow him. That left just Warwick and me in the conference room. Warwick shrugged off my boss's lack of faith. *If he's not interested, that's cool,* he said. I had never met a sales guy less interested in making a sale. *It's not about the money,* he said. *It's bigger than that.* He told me he'd made a fortune and then lost it all in the dot-com crash; that he wandered the world for years, living in a cave, living like a monk, living life as it came at him. *Then I got my big break.* Here he looked at his watch. *Ah,* he said, *time's up. I better let you go. You should get back to micromanaging those search queries, right?*

That afternoon I wrote a perfunctory resignation email to my boss and left early to get a drink with Warwick at a divey bar near Madison Square Garden. I wanted him to keep talking to me. I wanted to be part of the world he was creating, one disruptive word at a time. I never spoke to my old boss again. For all I know, he's still out there working on the same outdated algo. Although, to be sure, he isn't doing it at Lycos anymore; that dog quit playing fetch a long time ago.

CHAPTER 9

Warwick pulled his Maserati into an underground parking lot and turned his keys over to a jumpy young parking attendant. The attendant ogled the car in ways that made me nervous. Warwick didn't notice or didn't care. He threw around trust for the same reason some people threw around money: the more carelessly he trusted in people, the more powerful he looked.

We climbed a narrow set of stairs and emerged into a plaza in front of the main entrance for Christie's auction house. The building marquee was a flashy blur of bronze filigree and black metal with revolving doors. *Enter here,* the whole setup says, *if you're wealthy enough to fear nothing.*

"Let me guess," I said. "You're putting my soul up for auction."

"Yeah, no," he laughed. "I've got your soul in a safe deposit box."

Jokey exchanges like this—about the blood debt I owed to him, his claim to my soul—were commonplace as small talk between us. We'd worked together for a decade and had never once had a serious argument; sure, I disagreed with him at times (maybe often), but we never raised our voices, tempers never detonated. To an outsider, it would look like we got along so well that it probably did seem as if Warwick had something of mine in eternal hock. I deferred to him when it came to big, directional decisions; he deferred to me when it came to nuts and bolts. We didn't always end up doing the right thing, but we always knew who did what.

The entrance doors to Christie's were locked. A handful of well-dressed people was milling around the plaza, looking confused. A message was taped to the doors: DELAYED OPENING—PRIVATE ENGAGEMENT. A serious young woman in a black skirt and a red silk blouse was waiting just inside the door, pretending not to see the people who wanted in.

Warwick tapped the glass once with a knuckle. The woman brightened when she saw him. She popped the door, we stepped in, and she pulled the door shut. A tall couple behind me, clearly tourists, tried to get through, too. One of them became angry when the woman relocked the door. He shouted through the glass, "What makes *them* special?"

"Hey, hi," Warwick said. The woman started to respond, but a phone in his pocket began to ring. He took out the phone and studied the caller ID. Then he said to the woman, no longer looking at her, "Could you bring my dear friend Mr. Gooding upstairs to see the piece?" He motioned for me to follow her. "Doc," he said into the phone, "tell me you've had a change of heart."

The woman asked if I wanted a drink from the lounge. "Agua fresca? Kombucha? We've also got guava, papaya, and tamarillo juice?"

I kept saying no but thanking her as genuinely as I could. I felt like I should ask her name, but it was too late to do so without admitting I'd been rude for not having asked already.

Together, we walked down an ornate hall. Her heels echoed in the tiled expanse. All the empty niches and showrooms. "Looks like a slow afternoon," I joked.

"Security protocol ahead of an auction," she said.

"Makes sense," I said. I still had no idea what we were there to see. I told her that I'd read that a da Vinci painting sold for nearly $500 million at an auction last year. "Is this piece," I began, "well, are we talking—"

"Oh, no," she said. "To be honest, it's sort of the opposite situation here. The big question a lot of us are asking is, Is this thing worth anything at all?"

I nodded knowingly. Smiled. Despite not knowing.

"For what it's worth," she said, a flush reddening her neck as if admitting an indiscretion, "this piece started a big debate between a few of us just last night. I've been a docent for private sales of Michelangelo sketches and a Caravaggio, so, like, you can guess where I come down on this whole thing. What are you buying when you buy a piece of art? It's about the art, but it's also about where the art comes from, the story of who made it, and how. That's priced in. If you don't have the life of an artist behind a piece of art, then all you're paying for is oil and canvas. Unless we're talking about NFTs. Don't even get me started about those."

We stopped at a set of stairs. She touched my shoulder and pointed up the staircase. "Go up and straight on to the back. You'll see the piece in the last room on the left. Let me know if you have questions. We're starting in just a little over an hour. I hope you and Mr. Warwick enjoy your viewing. Good luck."

Up four stairs, I emerged in a long white hallway. To my right, a series of arched doorways looked out on a large gallery with rows of chairs and a podium for the auction, a few pieces of artwork on display; on the left side of the hall, I saw a series of single doorways that led to smaller rooms with tables of antiquities; fine art on panels; jewelry and gems in niches, spotlighted. I recognized a few Andy Warhol prints. A few big frames from Roy Lichtenstein, some of his Sunday funnies–style prints. Sketches from Chagall, Braque, Magritte. My mom loved Magritte. Loved his verve. His flagrant breaks with reality. *She'd love to see these,* I thought. Then I remembered where she was, remembered the shape in the bed in the hospital room—not gone, but not present. *Put it all away,* I thought hurriedly, before the sorrow could sink its hooks in.

In the last room on the left, I expected a grand display of—something grand. Instead, the room was the smallest of them all, the size of a walk-in closet, with an easel holding up a single small canvas in a frame. The canvas was not an original. It was a print of an unfinished portrait of a man. He did not look contemporary, or modern, or even premodern. He looked like he belonged in the late-Renaissance wing at the Met. Like the sort of Old Master output that bores me to tears. Except this portrait's face was blurred. Not blurred so much as—ambiguous? No, unassigned. The identity was still unclear. Indeed, huge swaths of nothing, like a void, filled one edge. I leaned in closer, tried to get a sense for what the artist was implying by mimicking so completely the style of a time long gone. I read the curator's description of the piece, which was printed on a panel on the wall beside the painting:

Lot No. 49, "Edmond de Belamy," of La Famille de Bellamy. Generative Adversarial Network print, on canvas, 2018, signed with GAN model loss function in ink by the publisher, from a series of eleven unique images.

Suddenly, I understood what this artwork was, why Warwick was drawn to it. This was an image created by an algorithm. It wasn't the first piece of AI art I'd ever seen, but it was the first time I'd seen a piece up for auction. Christie's didn't do meager auctions. But who would pay big money for the output of an algorithm, something you could run again and again with the same predictable output? I glanced at the asking price. Eighty grand, starting bid. The docent in the elevator had told me they weren't sure if it was worth anything at all. Eighty grand certainly wasn't nothing. But I had to agree with her. A "GAN model loss function" has a much less interesting backstory than, say, Marcel Duchamp. He was another of Geraldine's favorites.

"There you are," Warwick said. Later, I would wonder if he actually was addressing the painting.

I stepped back from the painting, as one does with genuine works of art to take in the whole of the piece. Except there was nothing to take in here, not if you asked me. I shook my head. I didn't like it. No, I actively disliked it. I'd seen better work done by other AIs. This was only so-so. I told Warwick this. He listened without judgment, but I could tell he thought I was on the wrong track.

"You tell me, boss, what do you see?"

"I see Eddie," he said.

There are no real coincidences, Warwick liked to say, just connections that we have yet to make explicit. Edmond, a portrait by an AI; and Eddie, a chatbot attached to a strange algorithm. The connection was almost there. But I didn't get it. Warwick sensed that I wasn't sold.

"I've been asking to see this for weeks," he continued. "They wouldn't even give me a private showing until today. They insisted on holding a public auction. To raise the profile of the piece. Not that I can blame them. It's brilliant. They're making a new market in real time."

As if he had called them into being, we heard a low murmur of voices behind us. A small group had entered the large gallery across the hall from the small room with the AI art. Most of the new arrivals were white haired, one with a cane, a man old enough to be Warwick's father. Like a gaggle, they went as one to a corner where Manet sketches were displayed. Warwick glanced at his watch; I gathered that the doors downstairs would soon be open for anyone who wanted to see the artwork on display. Including this piece. The auction would begin quite soon.

"You're going to buy it," I said. "That's why we're here?"

He put his hands behind his back, looked at his shoes for a beat, then back up at me. "No," he said, "we're here because this is what I want us to do next."

"Sure," I said, "but what's this got to do with that? Or anything? I mean, Warwick, I'm not losing my mind, you do remember what I did? To Nessie's tattoos? Did I tell you about the doorman, Benji?"

"Slow down, chico," he said. "I don't want the algo to produce a painting. That's too simple. I want to use it to make a person. I want to build a real Eddie from nothing."

"A person?"

He held up both hands, palms close, as if to celebrate a direct hit. "Yes," he said. "Yes, yes, yes. We're gonna push this thing to the limit. What's bigger than life? Life itself is the limit of life, know what I mean?

Think about it. No cells except from cells, that's what they teach in biology. We're gonna disrupt the basics of biology." He smiled into midair, as if grooving on the audacity of it all. "Do you know," he said, "I asked Nessie to name the Eddie algo after this painting? Just as a lark. But now it feels like fate. I don't know how you're doing anything you're doing, chico. The algo was never supposed to do what you do with it. What I'm asking for is just a little bit further. You can do it. Think about it. Making a person from nothing. Like automata, but better. Isn't that, like, your thing?"

The gallery began to fill with old women in floppy hats, old men with tans like sailors and crisp collared shirts, bored beautiful people on the arms of rich connoisseurs of prestige, sour-faced artists who looked like they hated money but came here to see what money could buy: the art crowd. Most of them were there for the other pieces. Now and then, someone would stop to study the portrait of Edmond de Bellamy. Another silver-haired man in a blue jacket—he looked like Warwick in about ten years—interrupted, asked if this was the AI art. They fell into an intense conversation; they were either good friends or bitter rivals. Lost in my plans, I couldn't tell, didn't care. Warwick's challenge looped me like a lasso. *You can do it, can't you?* This was a new kind of ridiculous. Editing the world was strange enough. Put a new person in the world? Make a chatbot into a believable human being? Use a model of thinking to replicate a thinking person: impossible. Use a computer to create a living, breathing person: impossible, squared. Yet it wasn't novel. As an idea. The idea's as old as Ovid, old as golems. Parvati made Ganesh from wet earth. Victor stole charnel bones for his creature. Now, me?

That part of my brain that solves problems, that fixes things, that wants to know how a mechanism works: that part of me took over eagerly, ravenously. I began to tally up the hows and wheres and whats. To create a new person, I would have to think of everything. Every official detail. From birth onward. Every storied, stored historical facet. The likeness to a real person would have to be immaculate. I couldn't forget anything, or the algo would reject it all. It might fill in a few oversights—like Fatima. But it would be difficult. So difficult.

I slipped from the room before the auction began. I was bound for home, but I wasn't seeing where I was going. I wasn't thinking about my problems, my insensate mother in her hospital bed. I was in that familiar problem-solving trance. The place where I felt best, where it felt like I could do anything. Even this. I didn't take the train or a cab. I didn't want the interruption. The walk wasn't far, less than two miles. I crossed intersections and waited at street corners for walk signals, and I was among crowds the whole time, but I was not there, not really. I was measuring plans, stretching out possibilities. I saw how the thing could be done.

CHAPTER 10

From that hour onward, my sole purpose was to make Eddie into Edmond, to fashion a living person from nothing, a truth from lies. I had already spent half a lifetime making the unreal appear real, beginning with marionettes and mechanical animals, and later, with fledgling chatbots. This felt like a logical next step. But when you're climbing stairs in the dark, another step always feels right—even when there's nothing to hold you up.

Shut up in my apartment, I didn't sleep, didn't relax or rest, took no breaks, saw no one else, thought of nothing else. If I did pause to push food down my throat, it was only because I was too weak to keep working. I was propelled by a hurricane of enthusiasm. I placed an order for Chinese delivery and then returned to work with such a vengeance that I didn't bother to eat after the food arrived. Only when my body was on the verge of metabolic failure did I pause long enough to put nourishment inside it. I had gone beyond bodies. My own and others. I would realize a dream that was dreamed by countless scientists, philosophers, alchemists, and fabulists.

Something fundamental changed in me after that moment in Christie's. Before, I was the guy who took orders, the intellectual tagalong, the plus-one, somebody present but with no agency, no drive, no skin in the game. I made other people's ideas come to life. No more. I wanted this for me. I'd spent a lifetime in idle, wondering how to use the skills and passions that I had in order to do more than help other people achieve their goals. Suddenly, here it was, long after I'd given up on my own life: the chance to do something only I could do.

I spent hours chatting with Eddie, sorting out how much personality was already in there. Except for glimmers and brief flare-ups, there was almost nothing. The uncanny valley lay elsewhere.

> **EDDIE:** I've detected a massive botnet attempt to spread 27,543 antivax posts across fake accounts all over Facebook.
> **GRAHAM:** That's great.
> **GRAHAM:** Hey, do you know what a vaccine is? Do you know why it's important that people believe vaccines are good?
> **EDDIE:** A vaccine is a substance used to stimulate the production of antibodies and provide immunity against one or several diseases, prepared from the causative agent of a disease, its products, or a synthetic substitute.
> **GRAHAM:** Thanks, I can Google the definition of a vaccine, too.
> **EDDIE:** You're quite welcome.
> **GRAHAM:** 🙄

More and more I saw the artifice at work behind the conversations we had. Certainly, Eddie was a deft conversationalist, but I felt like I was talking with a polite stranger, somebody with a steady smile, articulate words, nothing more. I would have to start there. My Eddie would be polite to a fault. An absolute observer of etiquette. What was etiquette, after all, but a script for behavior? A perfect place to start. I startled back to the present when my phone began to ring. *Nessie? Warwick?* I didn't recognize the number but answered anyway.

"Is this Graham Gooding? Mr. Gooding, this is Priti Desai, a patient advocate at Woodhull Hospital. I just got off the phone with your mother's doctor, Esme Haber, and I am so sorry to hear about your mom. Dr. Haber also has told me that you've been struggling with a very hard decision—"

"I'm not pulling the plug on her."

"No no no no no," said Priti, "that's not why I'm calling. I don't need you to make a decision. I just want you to know that I'm here. If you want to talk. You are not alone. Such a terrible thing. You know, I'm like you. I believe in miracles, too. But sometimes, we must also think about what's best for—" And that's where I hung up, before she could tell me *what's best*.

I worked on Edmond till well into the night—a dark, hot night rich with late-summer languor. One day became two, three, four days. Later, I would learn that Manhattan had never seen a stretch of days as beautiful as those that passed while I was inside creating birth certificates, doctors' notes, immunization records, and birth announcements. The shape of a digital life. People swam in the city's pools; the outer borough beaches thronged with flirting sunbathers and Frisbees; the waters were full of sailboats, kayaks, and freighters all cutting their individual paths.

No detail was too small to obsess over. Like, who would be the mother on the birth certificate? I couldn't just make up a Mama de Bellamy. At some point, the falsehood that I was making up had to have contact with something real. To do that, I matched this new person I was making to the identity of a woman who'd died in childbirth, a real person who perished on the same day in New York that this new person Edmond was going to be born.

Early one morning I heard a knock at the door. I can guess at the time only because of how the light slanted through the windows in the galley kitchen. I kept the safety chain in place, popped the door a sliver. Outside, wearing cargo shorts, a faded MAKER FAIRE-Y T-shirt, and strappy sandals: Jay Xi. He was carrying a plastic sack that looked to contain orange juice and Ess-a-Bagels—our breakfast of choice when we were roomies on Third Avenue long ago.

"Let me in? Smells like garbage out here."

Once inside, he coughed and waved a hand in front of his nose. "The smell's coming from in here," he said. Admittedly, I had not washed the dishes or emptied the trash cans in—well, I couldn't remember when.

"You went dark," he said. "No calls, no texts, no email. Did you forget? We agreed that I would come by today. To see the algo."

The kitchen counter was a graveyard of unopened white rice cartons and browning avocado rolls. On the table, I cleared a space for the bagels and orange juice. Jay walked around, surveying the apartment. He tentatively touched a half gallon of milk on the counter. "This is warm," he said. I recalled eating cereal at some point. "This is where the smell is coming from," he added.

"I should call a maid service," I mumbled.

"You need to take better care of yourself. This isn't okay, man."

"I'm close to something big. Head down, deep in the mix. You know the feeling."

The stern look on Jay's face softened, his lower lip twitched. "I can't lie to you, Graham. You're worrying me. This is—this is a relapse, you know?"

"This isn't a relapse," I said, irritated.

Jay made a placating gesture. "All right, I take that back. Let's break this down piece by piece. First, you show up at my office, sort of raving. We haven't seen each other face-to-face in five years—"

"Hold up. It hasn't been five years."

"Maybe it's been six."

"I spent a Thanksgiving with you! We did a whole turkey dinner!"

"That was before I got married. That was 2012. It's 2018. You know that, right? I agreed to come over today because I was worried about you when you came to my office. Well, now I'm downright terrified. Jesus, man. Look at this place. Like, really look at it. You'll be the next Phil Katz. You're backsliding. You're downright manic. You can't keep this up. You're going to hit the wall at some point, fall apart. We've seen this movie before, and it's not good, you know?"

These last words must have felt harsh in his mouth, because suddenly all his attention was on the food he'd brought. He opened the bagels and went to the kitchen cabinets and got out two glasses for the orange juice. "I'm sorry," he said. "I'm not trying to come on so strong. Let's rewind."

He offered too little repentance, too late.

"This isn't a great time," I said.

"You said you'd show me the algorithm. I said I'd have an open mind. I'm here. I said I would be, and I am. I want to see it. I want to understand. I want to help, you know? Let me help you, Graham."

"You should go," I said.

I thought again about the word he'd used: *relapse.* I disliked it because it felt at least partly true. Years earlier, I'd had a bad spell of anxiety, a tussle with depression. After we graduated from NYU, Jay got a job quickly, almost effortlessly. No such luck for me. I went to a lot of interviews, didn't get any offers. I began to get notices about repaying student-loan debts. The numbers on the statements sent me into a panic. I put off interviews. I quit seeing friends. I made a cave of the apartment we shared. I had no plan, nothing but fear. Jay came home after a weekend away to find me alone in the den, shirtless, sitting on the sofa, windows shut, sweltering in the dark. I hadn't left the apartment. Jay slapped his keys on the counter. The noise startled me; he was never dramatic. He pointed at me, angrily. *You have two choices,* he said. *Either you get off that sofa and we figure out your next step in life, or I call the folks at Bellevue to come pick you up. I won't watch you fall apart. I did that with my mom. I won't do it with you, man.*

Fourteen years later, there we were again. Or were we? I'd needed Jay to shake some sense into me all those years ago. Thanks to him, I went to the Lycos interview that led to the gig where I met Warwick. This time was different. I had changed. He had changed. Yes, I was jumpy, wired; no question. My apartment was disgusting. If you didn't believe in what the algo could do, then what I was doing looked ludicrous. But the algo *wasn't* a delusion. I was fully in control. I wasn't sitting in the dark, brooding. I was about to tell life what to do, how to be. Jay was lucky to be there, to witness it. Things had changed since I'd had shawarma with him, and I'd done him a favor by talking to him about the algo, not the other way around. But I didn't have time to explain all this to him. I didn't have time for any of this.

"I'm sorry you came all this way," I began.

He made a jagged, exhaling noise, and he swept his hand angrily across the tabletop. "You're not going to show it to me," he said. He blinked fast. "Of course not," he said. "You can't. I knew you couldn't. I just didn't want to believe that you were falling apart. But look at you. Look at this place."

"Come by next week," I said. "Then I'll show you."

I moved to the door, put my hand on the knob, and turned expectantly toward him. I would not be so rude as to open the door and tell him to leave, but the signal of my preference was clear: *You should go.* He got the message. He put his palms together in a last pleading gesture.

"Don't do this, Graham. Come with me to Englewood. Just for a day. Get away from all this. From whatever you're doing. Is it really that important? You'll feel better if you get out. My kids would get a kick out of getting to know somebody that I went to school with back in the Stone Age."

"That's very kind. But I can't."

He drifted toward the door, shoulders slumped, sad-eyed, and whispered, "I've failed you." I ignored this, made half-hearted gestures at goodbye. Till he was gone. Relieved, I returned to work. I gathered the laptop and the papers that I had used to map out the more elaborate elements of Edmond's character. I carried my laptop into the bedroom to work. Doing this violated my long-standing rule about keeping anything with a keyboard out of the room where I slept. (That is, *when* I slept.) But I didn't think twice before I shut the bedroom door. Now, if Jay came back or another guest came to the front door, I would not be able to hear them. No more distractions. No more delays. The finish line was close. I wanted to arrive.

Into the details of Edmond's life, I incorporated portions of movie scripts, plays, and myths. I signed him up for Facebook fan pages that ran the gauntlet from Douglas Adams to *Law & Order* to Coldplay to cosplay to *Cobra Kai*. I went where the alliteration took me. Nothing too strange. Just the most fabulous kind of average waspy dude that I could imagine. As an afterthought, I added huge swaths of Garfield comic strips to Edmond's long-abandoned Myspace page. Warwick hated the glorified stupidity of Garfield. I liked the idea of Edmond's sense of humor grating on Warwick.

Those last hours are now a blur of fabrications. I wrote and composed a happy if simple childhood for Edmond. I gave him a childhood with two loving parents: a dad who worked at a steady office job, a mom who delighted in him and who had her own job as a real estate agent. I studded his teenage years with championship soccer trophies, National Merit Scholar status, a runner-up ribbon for a regional science fair. Even his failures were gentle. A girl that sent him AIM messages for months and then said no when he finally worked up the nerve to ask her out. A shoplifting conviction put under seal because he was a juvenile. "Perpetrator attempted to steal the cash register from the Peter Cooper Deli at the corner of First Avenue and Twenty-Second Street." Steal a cash register? Ridiculous, yes, but bored teens will do reckless acts to prove that they're real people. I wanted Edmond to be human, not a saint-in-waiting. No one would ever really see the record of the crime, thanks to the seal on the record. Leading me to wonder why I spent the time placing these facts and reports and judgments in the data? I got lost in the melody that was taking shape all around me. To create, to compose, to make from nothing a new thing.

At last, I was finished. I queued up all the materials, thousands of original documents, tens of thousands of amended materials, countless collateral changes to other lives all to make room for this one new person. All delicately balanced on trust in what the algo calculated: if this was complete enough for the algo to accept these new facts, then the rest of the world would change based on its total and complete faith in what was inside the strange engine that no human mind could fathom.

My finger paused over the button that would kick off whatever the process was that the algo used to metamorphose the real world. I hesitated, and for the first time since I'd stood in front of that painting with Warwick, I was filled with questions. What if this didn't work? And what if it did work? I had no idea how long it would take for the change to manifest. I was at the mercy of the data transfer rate and the request queue in the heart of a server farm somewhere in the ether. Or bits stored in servers all over the country, for all I knew. Who knew? Where is the soul, precisely, in the wet cell grotto of the brain?

I pressed the button. Nothing happened. I stood up and stretched. I waited for an error message; no error chirped. Yet still nothing changed around me. I crossed the bedroom, opened the door, and stepped into the rest of the apartment. I was hit with a shaft of bright-blue light that startled me, and I stood blinking into the space of a room where nothing at all looked familiar.

I should have stood in a small, rectangular and poorly lit space, the ostensible living room of a minuscule, overpriced Midtown apartment. Instead, I was in a large and lofty sitting area. Gone was the metal frame futon I bought a decade ago and used as a bed before it became my sofa. In its place, a large L-shape sectional with tufted cushions and fancy throw pillows. Gone was the blue-and-green rug with that worn fringe, which I bought from a street fair. Now: a plush patterned Moroccan weave. Gone were the framed prints of *Lost in Space* and *King Kong* promo posters. Instead, woodblock print art, shapes of jade and gold bamboo. And instead of a bare wall, a view of the Hudson, sparkling with the jagged edges of reflected light. I spun around to take in more changes: the black crystal chandelier over a long dining room table, a full kitchen where before there was just a galley and a strip of counter-top. And then I saw the door to another bedroom. Now I have a second bedroom, I thought—a place where Geraldine could live. I could keep her here with me. I could care for her. I walked to the doorway of this room that did not exist before. I stood agog with a hand on the jamb and gaped at the interior of this new room for one, two, three seconds before noticing the person on the bed.

It looked like a real person, like an adult male, white, midthirties, but I knew it wasn't. It was dressed for a funeral or a wedding in a bygone era: dark jacket, black vest, white collared shirt. Black trousers, cheap dress shoes. I knew who it was. *No, no,* I corrected myself: not who. What. Not him: it. Cold blue eyes, sandy-brown hair, broad shoulders, just like in the painting at Christie's. A humanoid body but not a human. A person without a mother or father. A person I had made.

I can't quite explain what my emotions were doing; they were not agitated, nor were they calm; a buzzing potential rippled in every pore of my body, like static electricity before a discharge. All my zeal, all my confidence, all the aspirations I'd ever felt to make a thing that resembled life—all left me at once, as if a fever broke, a guy line snapped, everything collapsed. The mass in this bed, it wasn't a man. It was a thing. No matter how miraculous this was, it was nothing at all like real life. Even if no one else knew, I would always know. I did this. *Why did I do it?* I had no purpose, not really. I just wanted to prove I could. The worst reason to do anything.

This person that was not a real person looked at me with an expression full of confusion and need. In the painting at Christie's, the face had been ambiguous, eerie; this thing was real, fleshed out (literally), with high cheekbones, a notched chin, a perfect nose. If someone saw the portrait and saw this—thing—that person would be tempted to say this was the same man. But all I saw was a grotesque failure. I covered my face in shame and stumbled from the room.

"Hi," it called weakly after me. "I'm Edmond. But you can call me Eddie."

PART III

CHAPTER 11

The distance from my apartment in Midtown to Geraldine's hospital bed in Brooklyn was just 7.7 miles, as tallied by the god of directions, Google Maps. You can get from here to there in about an hour. Sometimes, longer. But never less. Each trip to see my mother therefore had given me ample time to agonize. About her. About the algo. About what I'd done to Nessie. And now, Edmond.

In making a new life, I'd made so many little edits. The little edits had added up to Eddie appearing in my apartment. Somewhere in the process of creating a false history, I must have used my home address as Eddie's address, too—a lapse of judgment by me that the algo elaborated on, a small gap it filled in a way that made sense, albeit not something I wanted. Harder to explain was why the algo made my apartment larger, palatial. The building looked the same from the outside, but inside it was totally different. The elevator walls had fancy metal mesh cladding. White marble floors in the lobby. Again, not an outcome I'd intended. No doubt I'd also altered the larger world in unintended ways, too. I worried that one of those collateral changes had to do with Geraldine. That I'd made her worse or wiped out her life altogether.

In Brooklyn, the usual glum security guards haunted the hospital halls. Hallways full of people, all avoiding eye contact. "Stay the same," I kept muttering as I rounded each corner, stepped through each door. "Please don't change." I found the nurses' station staffed by the usual nurse, Ana, whose eyebrows raised and whose mouth made a disapproving line upon seeing me. Here was the son who could not face the facts of his mother's state, could not give her peace. "Dr. Haber wants to talk with you," she said. "She's called you a few times."

"I know," I said, "I'm sorry, so sorry." Yet I did not stop to talk with her, could not.

Nothing had changed in my mother's room—*Thank God,* I thought. I sat down hard in a chair, legs aching, breathing hard, feeling winded, guilty, and powerless at the same time. Then I thought, *Oh, how awful that* this *is what I want to keep the same. Here in a rectangular, sterile beige hospital room, Geraldine Gooding lies, a slumberer on her back, sheet pulled to midchest, arms outside the sheets and at her sides, eyes closed, long thin hair a tangle of gray-white and threads of black, the few filaments that refuse to stop producing pigment.*

Pulling the chair near, I laid my arms across the sheets. Felt the body of my mother underneath the bedclothes. "I haven't figured out how to make you better," I whispered. "But give me time. I'll think of something." She did not respond, of course. I was just fronting; no good cause for such blind optimism existed. I clasped her hand. So warm. Were her hands usually this warm? I couldn't say. Mine weren't as warm. And when did I last hold her hand? Or anyone's? More than a hand-shake. Longer than a hug. Not just words or emails or texts or drunken songs sung on the walk from the bar to the curb where you part into different cabs. Human communication through mere contact. I held her hand and paced the corridors of memory for a long time before I came up with: Nessie. At the end of that night at Grand Central. She had leaned over, hugged me. I had been sad that night. She was humor-ing me. It hadn't meant anything. Except it did mean a lot to me then, meant even more now.

I didn't intend to sleep at the hospital that night. But I couldn't gather the will to leave, and before I knew it, Ana was adjusting the recliner chair, draping a blanket, patting a pillow flat. "Just this once," she said. She looked back twice before shutting the door. As if bending the rules for overnight stays was what gave her job meaning. *Let Edmond wait,* I thought. *Let them all wait.*

That night I slept poorly, fitful with bad dreams until the morning nurse bustled into the room for her rounds. This nurse was much older, spoke in a Staten Island drawl, and didn't have time for people, just tasks. She gave a firm shake to my shoulder and said, in a surly growl, "Scram, you chooch, this ain't no private hotel," but then left without doing much about it.

I washed my mouth with water from the bathroom sink. Wiped my eyes and read the seventeen texts from Warwick. Such relentless pursuit of my attention had never happened before. His messages burst with manic exuberance and gathering impatience, like he was live-tweeting something important, but no one was responding. He was on a junket to SFO, some ho-hum colloquium at a research lab. 8:25 p.m. PT, in the Delta lounge, sipping a glass of sloe gin. 9:02 p.m. PT, on the plane, bored, was I awake? 6:00 a.m. ET, just landed at JFK, was I up? 6:07 a.m., plane finally at the gate; 6:19, bumper to bumper on the Van Wyck; 6:22 . . .

I texted Nessie. ARE YOU BACK YET?, I wrote. I waited a few moments, hoping to see the ellipsis that shows when someone is typing. But nothing. I gave her ten minutes, then I added another quick note: WOULD LOVE TO CATCH UP. I threw the phone into my bag and kissed Geraldine's dry cheek and then left. I could no longer avoid what I had done.

CHAPTER 12

From her seat behind the reception desk, Fatima waved. "Hey, Graham, how's it going?" She was adept at the hospitality part of her job: upbeat, not overly so; friendly, not nosy. I couldn't look at her without thinking of Benji. I tried not to look at her, did my best to reflect her cordiality with a wave.

"Say hey to Ed," she said.

Realization took a half beat to hit me. Ed. As in, Edmond. My new roomie. She knew me, and therefore she knew Eddie, too. The hackles of my shoulders and neck prickled, and I tried to smile, but it came out all wrong.

Upstairs, the apartment was as I'd left it: grand with its button-tufted sofa, long dining table, black crystal chandelier. Except now there were more people. Standing at the door to the second bedroom was Warwick. He wore a fitted blue short-sleeve shirt and white lightweight trousers and white sneakers. Sartorial as ever. Did he never leave the house in a ratty shirt and ill-fitting jeans? His relentless image management never ceased to amaze me. I identified the other voice, inside the second bedroom: Doc, speaking in a low growl. I couldn't see around the corner, but I knew what else was in the room. Right where I'd left it.

Warwick staggered toward me; he held the fingers of his left hand against his forehead, as if to keep his head from slipping off his neck. "Stunning," he said. "Just stunning, Graham. You did it. Tremendous."

I wanted to bask in this praise, but for the first time that I could recall, I wasn't sure if Warwick was being straight with me. Not that I thought he was lying. More like, well, his face shone like a lamp-shade, and I was reasonably sure that he had been drinking. I had seen Warwick drink hundreds of times. Craft cocktails, hot toddies, fine wines, brunch-time Astis, scotch, sake, becherovka, quetzalteca—I'd seen him drink it all. But I had never seen Warwick drunk. Was he drunk now? Or was this his look of pure, true joy? Maybe I'd never seen him delighted.

"How'd you get in here?"

Warwick looked at me, his calm slightly skewed by my question. "The woman at the desk called up, and then she said we could—"

I interrupted, "So it figured out how to use the intercom?"

"It?" Warwick said. "It?" Then he nodded as if he caught the wave I was on. He saw the dislike I had for Edmond; you'd have to be a chatbot to miss it. "No, yeah," he said. Sounding more like himself again, as if the elation were rapidly wearing off and his regularly scheduled serenity was returning. "Our boy learns fast," he said. "So fast. Like nothing that I've seen before."

As a kid, I'd always get a fluttering feeling in my chest when I would wind up the spring for a new mechanical toy. Would the motion of the false arm flow smoothly? Would the paper wings flap with the right speed? I was always trying to approximate life, and I always knew it would fall a little short, but with each change or alteration, I would get a little closer. I had the greatest success of my life right here with me, but I felt absolutely nothing.

"I could do better," I said.

"You're exhausted," Warwick said. "You've been working too hard."

We were talking past each other. We would have continued except for a sudden crash from the second bedroom. Through the doorway I saw Doc doubled over, Edmond staggering backward, as if struck. There was a new topology to the wall on the side facing me, two raised angles that had the shape of an elbow and a knee. Like the shape of Wile E. Coyote after he hit a cliff.

"You—you have to," Doc howled, gasping for a breath. "You have to go through the *door*, not the *wall*."

Edmond could no doubt describe the difference between a door and a wall. If subjected to a Captcha test, I'm certain it could select all the images that contain a door with perfect accuracy. Neither skill was an adequate substitute for the ability to navigate a human body through an open doorway. Eddie, a.k.a. Edmond, had never encountered the solid fact of drywall.

The creature wobbled as it returned to the bed. It looked pale, sick, like it might pass out. But it wasn't real. It couldn't pass out. Warwick put ice in a hand towel and instructed Edmond on how to press the towel to a bruise from the wall. I'd never seen Warwick act with this much concern toward anything.

"How do you feel?"

"I feel fine. I am healthy."

Warwick studied the bruise, frowned. "Any dizziness? Did you black out?"

"No," Edmond said, "I have not lost power, as near as I can tell. However, severe weather upstate later tonight could result in a loss of electrical power for people located in the Catskill region."

Doc put a hand to his chest, wheezed with laughter: "Bro," he said, "wrong kind of blackout!"

A human would have felt shame, or at least mild embarrassment, but Edmond watched Doc with an inscrutable gaze. The look of a machine made for learning. There was no doubt that Edmond would get better with every mistake, every failure. Yet there was no inner being. It was just a function, a history of actions, a series of reflexes. As close to an algorithm made flesh as it was possible to be.

"I believe," Edmond said, "that I feel—hungry? Humans consume food to power their metabolism. If I do not eat, then I will black out. Yes?"

"Yes! Yes!" Warwick said. "You're getting the hang of it, Ed. We should eat. It's a celebration."

"What do you want for your first meal?" Doc asked. There was a fraternal tone in the way he addressed Edmond, as if he and Warwick were here to care for a younger sibling, a baby brother. The disposition softened him, made him less douchey. But I still didn't like him.

"I'd love lasagna," Edmond said. "Nothing beats lasagna."

Warwick and Doc exchanged blank, confounded looks. I smiled at this little proof of my handiwork with the algo.

"Lasagna? Yeah, no. Doc, pull up the menu for Pure Thai Cookhouse. That's the place to start. Order enough pad thai for all of us."

"You know I can't eat there, you prick."

"Why is David Warwick a prick?" Edmond asked. Then he turned to me, as if to escalate the question to the attention of a higher authority. Is that what I was to it? "Graham Gooding, can you explain?" I felt impelled to answer the question, but I didn't want to, didn't want to play along.

"Don't use someone's whole name," Warwick said. "It's too formal."

"I'll make a note of that," Edmond said. "But why is—"

"Warwick's a jerk," Doc said, "because I'm allergic to shellfish and peanuts. Half of the menu at Pure Thai Cookhouse has those ingredients, and Warwick knows but doesn't care. Make sense?"

Edmond turned to study Warwick and merge this information with other known facts. "He is a jerk," Edmond repeated, "because he knows this and yet he suggested that you eat there anyway."

"Yes," Warwick said, slow clapping.

"And now he's *really* being a prick," Doc muttered.

They went on like this for some time. They asked Edmond questions, and Edmond gave thoughtful, descriptive answers that emulated a real person in nearly all the right ways. But if you knew the truth, then Edmond's performance was like one of those wind-up monkeys that flips after cranking its arms: interesting, fascinating as a feat of engineering, but nothing like life itself.

"Nessie will be the real test," Warwick said.

I could feel Edmond's beady eyes on me. I hated the feeling, knowing that I was being watched, studied, pattern-matched. What would ever escape the notice of this so-called person? What, once seen, could it ever forget? I ran a hand along a countertop, feigning calm. Rubbed my chin.

"So, you said Nessie's coming? Here?"

Warwick frowned at his watch, tsked loudly. "In fact," he said, "she's ten minutes late."

Around me I saw my apartment for what it was: bigger, higher-ceilinged, pricier per square foot, but also with dishes stacked high at the sink, trip-wire USB cables and power cords snaking the floor, a neglected nerd den. I gathered plates, empty cans, delivery cartons. Jay Xi had turned up his nose, said the place reeked. I didn't want Nessie to see how I lived. To save time, I threw crockery and glassware into a heavy-duty garbage bag. Glass cracked, ceramic chipped, saucers split. The algo had given me a bigger apartment. How hard would it be to give myself a new dining set?

"You should really compost that," Doc said as I scraped chicken and rice into the trash.

"I don't understand," Edmond said as I swept the floor in frantic thrusts of a hand broom. "Why does the impending arrival of your friend Vanessa Locke cause you such agitation?"

"Don't call her Vanessa," I said. "She hates that name."

"It's like this," Warwick began. "The state of a person's home is a reflection of—"

"Don't bother," I said. "It doesn't need to know. It doesn't think. It's just recycling word patterns. It uses words like it's learned people say only because that's what it's made to do. It's not real."

Edmond stared at me with an expression that reminded me—only a little, but I saw it there—of a startled child's look, one who is hurt for the first time by a careless parent.

"Let's run a real test," Warwick said. "C'mere, Eddie." He grabbed the remote, teed up YouTube, and searched for "Pete Schweddy." Suddenly, no one was interested in watching me clean. Doc grabbed a pillow from the floor and settled on the sofa. Warwick rubbed his palms together like a giddy child. The Schweddy Balls Test had begun.

There's the Turing Test, the supposed gold standard for assessing an artificial intelligence. But Warwick had no time for Turing. Chatbots and large language networks had gotten better and trickier, so Warwick insisted lately that we use the Schweddy Balls Test instead. He wanted to know if we could create an artificial intelligence that was human enough to laugh at one of *Saturday Night Live*'s most popular skits. Packed with puns and double entendre, on paper the skit is amusing, but watching it live, most humans find it hard not to laugh out loud or at least snicker. It's easy to machine read the text. But to really get it, to luxuriate in the stupid joy of life, that's not something that's programmable.

By the time I stepped out of the apartment to throw away a third bag of trash, Doc and Warwick were already holding back laughs. At the end of the hallway, I could still hear the TV. But there was no sound from Edmond. *I should be more curious,* I thought. *I should be more interested in this thing I've made.* Except I couldn't look at it without feeling squeamish. If a creator has a duty to its creation, I failed to feel the proper obligation. Just then the elevator doors slid open, and Nessie stepped out.

Her digital detox had done its duty. I could see she was clearer, less stuck in her thoughts. She wore a white baseball cap, a blue denim jacket that hid her forearms, white sweatpants, black-and-white-checkered flats. The sight of her made me feel lighter and happier, just like the old days, before the algo, before the night we walked through Manhattan.

"Hey," she said, head tilted, a crooked smile on her lips. "There you are."

She had such casual beauty. She was good-looking, her nose was straight, her mouth full of even teeth, her eyes deep brown, all the predictable stuff, but the part that lit her up, that made her different, was the way she saw someone, really looked at a person, took them in as a whole and did not look away.

I put my arms around her, and she put hers around me in a gesture that (I think) surprised us both. A bigger, longer hug than at the end of the night at Grand Central.

"Wow," I said. "I'm so glad you're back."

"You're sweet," she said. Then, a droll frown. "Obviously you want something."

We both laughed, but she wasn't wrong; suddenly, my eyes stung. All the things I'd done. All the things I hadn't done. Where to begin? "I'm sorry," I said quickly, before I could think of a reason not to speak.

"For what, G?"

I motioned to the wider world. "I don't even know where to begin," I said.

Both of us smiled as if this were a joke we'd been trading back and forth for ages. I had a lot more to say, and suddenly I knew that I could say it, that I could be honest with her about everything I had done. I'd edited some photos of her; it was weird, creepy, a little embarrassing, but if I came clean, I felt sure, she'd shrug it off, we'd move on. Isn't that what friends do? And I would have told her everything right there, right then. But the door to my apartment opened. And the ridiculous creature peeked its handsome, idiotic face into the hallway.

"Hey, Eddie," Nessie said. "It's been a minute."

"Quite a few, in fact," it said.

Joining us in the hall, Edmond teetered like a foal learning to walk. Had it left my apartment ever before? Certainly not. Nessie didn't seem to notice anything odd. She kissed its cheek in hello; it kissed hers in return. All the world vanished except their beaming faces. Suddenly, my little hug felt meaningless.

Nessie slitted her eyes, said to the creature, "Sorry I missed our coffee date. Things got weird."

"No worries! Should we try again this week?"

"Every Friday. That's the deal."

They didn't know each other. This was their first meeting, ever. But Nessie didn't realize that. This coffee date Nessie thought she missed was a by-product of the edit, a collateral fact change that the algo created when it put into real life this new thing, Edmond. They had no actual history. But she believed they did, and that was all it took for her to see Edmond as charismatic, likable, attractive—all the things I'd foolishly intended this creature to be.

Edmond and Nessie entered the apartment, looped together in chatter. I wanted to eavesdrop, but Edmond held the door for her, and she touched its hand briefly as she passed. I pretended to search my pockets for something, straining to act casual, calm, oblivious.

Inside, Doc and Warwick paced the kitchen, watching and whispering, giddy as mad scientists. They had sent Edmond outside, I realized. They'd prodded it to go, eager to run their next test. Nessie noticed them in the kitchen and gestured hello with her chin. "Boys," she said, and left it at that. Like she suspected something. But she couldn't know what.

Doc asked if she'd enjoyed her silent treatment. He meant the ashram, the digital detox. Warwick waxed philosophical on the importance of balancing digital life with real life, ironic from a bro whose net worth was overindexed on crypto. Nessie nodded, leaned against a dining table chair; she cast the hologram of an attentive listener, but she was bored. I knew the tell.

Warwick at last went quiet. Nessie let her eyes turn to Edmond. "You ready, Eddie?"

"You betcha," Edmond said. They were at the door before I understood.

"Wait," I said. "You're leaving?"

She patted her stomach and frowned. "I'm famished," she said. "Eddie says he can't remember when he last ate, either. Besides, if I hang with you all for too long, this will turn into a work discussion. I can't ruin this vibe I've got going. Toodles, boys. G, I'll text you later."

Her smile razzled me, the promise to text later was genuine, but hollow because she was leaving to be alone with Edmond, not me. I hated the feeling, being lumped in with Warwick and Doc.

"She has no fucking idea," Doc marveled after they left.

Warwick dug a sharp elbow into my side. "Ye gods, man! This gets better and better. Look at the belief! Look at the trust! Not a trace of doubt or suspicion."

They both grinned, waiting for me to join their sick celebration. I didn't intend to trick Nessie. At least, not for a second time.

"Are we just—are we just letting them go off? To do their thing?"

Doc made a singsong noise. "Sounds like somebody's jealous."

"No, I just think—shouldn't we tell her?"

I'd seen Warwick cast people aside before. Usually, people he barely knew or didn't interact with much. But he'd known Nessie for a decade. She stood at the nexus of our success. Yet he betrayed no sign of regret, doubt, hesitation. Instead, he had a bounce to his step, an air of invigoration, an easy smile on his lips. As if there was something extra to this dupe, as if it proved at long last that Nessie was less capable than he was. And Doc? Forget about it. Doc made people look stupid for a living.

"Where's your champagne, Graham? Let's pop a cork."

In search of a bottle, Warwick swung wide the doors for all the cabinets in my glittering new kitchen. "You must have a wine fridge somewhere," he said. I couldn't bear to be in the apartment with these two—even if it was *my* apartment, I had to get out. I said something about getting a bottle from the shop. Said I'd be right back. They barely noticed when I left. I was lying. They didn't care. All they cared about were ideas, ideas, ideas for how to change the world.

CHAPTER 13

I didn't have to go far to find Nessie and the creature. They stood on a sidewalk three blocks from my apartment. To spy on them, I slipped into the propped-open doors of a fitness club. I pretended to be engrossed in a sign for gym-membership fees, but I was watching Nessie in the large mirror behind the reception desk. She gestured at herself, at Eddie, at the display window of a storefront. I couldn't hear her, couldn't see what was in the window that had her flustered, agitated, excited all at once. The creature wore its best tabula rasa look.

I crossed to the other side of the reception desk. A short, lumpy man with soulful eyes was listening while a buff, tall woman described the torturous regimen he'd need to get fit. I stood beside him, as if I, too, wanted to suffer. The trainer raised an appraising eyebrow, sizing me up.

From this angle, I had a clearer view of the storefront that had Nessie's attention: Some Like It Hot. The shop name troubled me. I didn't know what it meant. Maybe a Mexican cantina? A travel agent for desert island stays? Then I noticed a faded DVD sign in the window. I wanted to believe this was Manhattan's last place to rent physical movies, but, nope, a mannequin torso draped in a sheer boudoir getup signaled what kind of video got sold there. I didn't see Nessie or the creature. Had they gone inside together?

"Com, com," a voice said, "I don't haff all day."

The short man with the sensitive eyes was gone. The trainer pinched one of my biceps and made a disappointed noise. She spoke with a Slavic accent that made her seem even taller than she was. "What you want to work on? What you want better? I'm in the better-life beesness."

"You know," I said, all apologetic smiles, "I think I'm good?"

I kept thinking about the way Nessie had leaned in to kiss Edmond's cheek. How she'd radiated attraction for him. I stopped in front of the window mannequin in the skimpy outfit. I wanted to go inside the shop in search of them. This was a terrible idea. Yet, I would have, and I almost did, except I looked back at the fitness-club doors and realized my mistake. I had misjudged the angles in the mirror, and this is not where Nessie and Edmond stood. They'd stood by the window of the shop next door, Fat Cat's Tats. I'd never been so happy to see a tattoo parlor.

Fat Cat's had a black fabric awning, a single glass front door, and two large picture windows on either side. The left-side window had a neon sign that read PIERCINGS in red block letters. On the right: TATTOOS, in red tubular cursive. The door's glass sported the etching of a life-size mermaid: typical mermaid fare, except she had tattoos on both arms. Sort of like someone I used to know.

This wasn't where it all began literally, but I felt like I'd returned to a place of embarkation. That night at Grand Central with Nessie, I'd asked about the tattoos on her arms. She'd held forth for a while with that story about her first tattoo, the Joan of Arc one that her brother hated. I wished I could remember more of what she'd said. I wished I could ask her again. But that part of her was gone now. I'd wiped it clean. Not just from her arms. From the world. There was less of her.

Inside Fat Cat's, a tattoo artist worked on a man lying prone on an elevated table. The artist bent close to her juddering gun, an image in her mind taking shape in the world, little by little. How long did it take, how many hours did Nessie sit in a chair or series of chairs over the years of her life to gather all the tattoos she'd once had? All that time. All that patience. All that effort. She'd stood here, stopped here with Edmond. She saw something inside that gave her pause. Ghost of a past, a different her. Despite the change I'd made, a trace of the previous Nessie remained. Deep within, a part of the old her persisted. Something immutable. More permanent than permanent ink. Maybe just a feeling. If there's something deeper than words, we can't use words to get at it. I had to tell her what I'd done. I couldn't pretend otherwise, couldn't put it off any longer.

I spent an hour walking more blocks, up and down side streets, but couldn't find them again. At last, I got out my phone and tapped a quick text: WOULD LOVE TO TALK. Hesitated. Should I add more, say why? No. I sent the message before I could get serious about the odds of her responding.

She responded at once. ME TOO.

I stopped short in a crosswalk and stared at my phone, watching for an ellipsis, for her to write more. A car honked, another car drove around me. She was with the creature, wherever she was, but she was writing to me. Or maybe they'd already gone their separate ways.

I CAN COME TO YOU, I wrote. ANYPLACE WORKS.

SURE, she wrote.

I scanned the cityscape around me for ideas. A cozy coffee shop full of people on laptops, a bright but cramped diner, a tiny park with gardeners hard at work. She was two steps ahead, as usual. My phone dinged with another text from her, a thumbs-up emoji and an uptown address, the street number for her home. Then one last message, the most beautiful I've read in my life: COME BY AROUND SIX. SEE YOU SOON.

CHAPTER 14

"Hey," Nessie said warmly, "come on in." She lived in a brownstone in the Heights, right off Riverside. Her apartment smelled of sandalwood and oranges, and the floors were stained a light brown. Calming light filtered through tall windows that looked out on the street. Perhaps it was the setting, but in her home Nessie looked different. She was still wearing the sweats from earlier, but she'd changed into an oversize gray hoodie, and she was barefoot.

"I'm making tea," she said. "Green or Earl Grey? Don't say green. I'm out of green."

Her living room was decorated with a designer's flair. Iron-colored Victorian velvet curtains and Sun King chairs and a wall full of niches to display obtuse technology. A wooden Victrola radio in the corner; a pale-blue Bakelite phone on the wall; floppy diskettes in 3.5-, 5.25-, and 8-inch sizes, framed and hung like portraits; an Apple II on a three-drawer secretary desk with a roll-out drawer.

"This is great," I said. "You should quit your day job. Decorate windows full-time."

"I'd love that, but a girl needs to eat."

I sat in an armchair while she spoke to me from the kitchen. She asked about Geraldine. I told her the news wasn't good. She came to the doorway, studied me, and said, "Tell me what *not good* means." So I told her. She listened, and when I was done, she said, "Damn it, Graham, why didn't you call me?"

"You were at the ashram," I began.

She flapped the tea towel in her hands, folded it absently. "You could have called," she said. "They would have told me. I wasn't in outer space. Jesus. I'm so sorry. I'm so sorry this happened to you."

I had come here to bare my soul, and she was the one apologizing. Until I confessed to her everything about the algo, nothing would feel right. I didn't try to segue into the words, just poured them out:

"I've been lying to you," I said.

"But you had a good reason, right? You'd better."

"There's so much you don't know. About the algorithm that we worked on. That *you* worked on. Hell, you're the one who built it. I never told you what it can do. The way that it changed everything—"

She held up a finger. "Just a sec," she said. She vanished back into the kitchen, where she clinked ceramic on ceramic, poured water into one, two cups, and I thought, not without some irritation, *Is she not listening? Isn't this a compelling confession?* I was doing something wrong.

"Okay," she said, coming back with a tray and two mugs, lemon wedges, a sugar jar. She set the tray on a sideboard. "Don't say a word," she said. "Just for one more minute." Then she cupped both hands around her mug and closed her eyes, and we both listened to the sound of, well, nothing. "Isn't it lovely?" she asked.

I said, "Isn't what lovely?"

She waved a hand like a fin through the air. "The silence," she said, "the peace. I just want it to last a few more seconds before I dive back in." The room and everything in it waited for her. Behind her, a jade bowl on a shelf reminded me of her brother, the wild one who lived in Singapore. How did he get there, anyway? She grew up in the States, a town on Long Island, I knew that much.

"All right," she said. "I'm ready. Tell me what you know."

I studied her. "'Tell me what you know' sounds like what a person says to someone who doesn't know as much as they think they do," I said. "Like, tell me what you know, and I'll tell you what you don't know?"

"Maybe. You're going to tell me that the last few weeks have been strange."

"Yes."

"That you're not sure when it started, but probably around the time that I asked for your help working on a new algo."

"Yes."

"And that's when things started to get weird."

"Yes!"

"But it all came to a head," she continued, "right before I went to the ashram."

"Is this a joke? But I'm serious."

"You were serious the last time we did this, too."

One of her dogs shook itself in the other room, collar jangling. I was still thinking as the dog began lapping at a water bowl. I needed to be perfectly clear.

"So, you already know—about the tattoos?"

"Yes," she said. "And I know about what the algorithm can do, too. I've been working to figure out how it does it for weeks. Or I was, till the whole thing made my head hurt so much that I needed a break."

"How did you figure it all out?"

"Like I said, you told me."

"But I've kept this secret for weeks!"

"Graham. Think about it. Maybe what you remember isn't what really happened. Maybe things have changed more than once."

I sat staring at my hands in my lap and turning this idea over.

"We've been tinkering with that algo so much," she said, "it's getting hard to keep straight sometimes what happened and what's just what we think happened. Here's what I know. You came to me in a panic. That weekend in the Hamptons. Doc and Warwick were there. At lunch. You came out with all of it. You said I used to have these tattoos but now I didn't, and it was because of what you did with the algo. I thought you were fucking nuts."

"That's not what happened," I said. "At lunch, we ate chicken and drank too much, then one of your dogs got lost."

Nessie tilted her head, faintly confused. "I have only one dog," she said.

As if it understood what we were talking about, the dog trotted into the room and jumped onto the sofa next to her. Lay down and rested its head but watched me. "Is that Zed or Uno?"

A wry smile gathered in her eyes. "Would you believe me," she said, "if I said it was neither?"

I broke in a rueful but genuine laugh, and she did, too; it was the kind of infectious laughter that comes from a scared place in your belly and solves nothing, even if it makes you feel better. After we both calmed down, she continued: "Warwick believed you. From the get-go, he believed in what you said the algo could do. I was skeptical, as you'd imagine. I mean, it didn't make any sense, right? Algos model the world, they don't change it. So you tried to show me. We tried to edit things together. You don't remember this? Warwick wanted us to add a couple million bucks to the Warlock & Co. bank account. As a proof of concept for what it could do. I kept adding new sources to the algo's training data. I jerry-rigged a reinforcement agent in the code, set up a wild reward state, basically said to hell with managing for entropy, and yeah, that did it. We made it happen. A cool million from nowhere, right in the general ledger for the company. Then you got a call about your mom and you left. Doc gave you a lift."

"Some of this is right," I said. "But you went into a digital detox?"

"Yeah," she said, "after I'd worked for three days straight. You had the idea to change that doorman in your building; that blew everybody away. But I was more confused than ever. How the hell did this thing work? So I took a break. Stepped away. Gave it all a big think. Until I came back today."

"But you're missing a lot," I said.

"Am I? What else don't I know?"

"You know Edmond—Eddie?"

A flicker in her eyes. That friendly hello kiss in the hall. I was jealous all over again, seeing these scant signs of feeling on her part. "Sure," she said, all false casual. "What about him? Does he know about the algo?"

"Here's the thing. He's—what you remember about him isn't real. He's a chatbot."

She stiffened, then rolled her shoulders. "That's not funny," she said.

"Think about it. When did you meet him? Like, be specific."

Her brow crinkled unhappily. "Quit gaslighting me," she said.

"You can't remember."

"So what? I don't remember *exactly* when you and I met, either."

"I do," I said. "It was a snowy morning in December, my first day at Warlock. Warwick was still renting that tiny office space near the Chrysler building, remember it? The one that was dark as a cave. I came in, and you were standing on a chair, changing a light bulb above your desk. You were wearing a red wool turtleneck. You climbed off the chair, came over, and shook my hand. I asked if employees were expected to supply their own light bulbs, and you laughed. Remember?"

Nessie stroked the fur of the dog on the sofa beside her. She was quiet for a moment, as if taking in everything I'd said. "Yeah," she said. "Yeah, I remember all that." She scratched at the dog's ear, a little too hard. "Listen," she added, "I'm certain that I've been friends with Ed for ages. We get dosa for lunch every week. It's our thing. I always pay, it's a running joke. I know the charge is on my credit card. So I know it's real . . . I mean, it's on the statements . . ."

Her hand paused in midair as her voice trailed off. The dog squirmed, prodded her to continue stroking. She stared at her hand, turned it round and studied her fingers, then cursed once, firmly, definitively.

"Go on," she said. "Go on, tell me the rest."

I told her everything. How Warwick had prodded me to make something new, not just edit the world. How I dove in, eager to prove myself. I kept hoping she would interrupt and say that she already knew. To laugh at me and say she'd never been fooled, not for a minute. But instead, she just listened, stiff in her seat now, her shoulders square, her chin lowered a little, as if to take a blow.

"I used the algo to make him. Warwick didn't want me to tell you. He said that if I told you, it would ruin the test. That we had to see if you could tell he was a fake. He and Doc both know. They're excited to see if everyone falls for it."

She said, "So, what, I'm like your Turing Test?"

"It's not me," I said. "It's them. That's why I came here. I had to tell you."

She stood up and moved to the wall where the technologies were kept in their niches. She ran her fingers over the mantel, as if thinking. Then she turned back. "Are you sure?" she said. "Are you sure that you—that Eddie isn't real?"

"I know that I worked on him for days, maybe a week."

"Yes, but are you *sure*? This is where I figured we would end up. Entropy keeps building up in the system. It gets more and more unknowable over time. And now we're overwriting each other, making a mess of reality, deadlocking."

"What do you mean, we? Who else can use the algo?"

The answer to the question was obvious, as obvious as the sunlight on the wood floor of her apartment. But I refused to see it. "Not

Warwick," I said. "That guy doesn't have the first idea how to use it. He can't manage the details, can't dig in that deep to anything. He told me himself. He said he needed my help. He said it—he told his Elvis story, you know, that one?"

She nodded, but gently, as if she were just waiting for me to catch up with her point of view. We talked till the brightness dried up outside and she got up to turn on the lamps. We traded facts about lost pasts. I described her tattoos as best I could. She told me about the days we spent in Southampton working side by side, as best she could. Together, we were looking for the original history, what really happened, but the truth was unknowable. All we knew was what we knew; we couldn't trust our own memories. The best we could do was cross-reference each other.

At some point, Warwick texted me. WHAT HAPPENED TO U? I showed Nessie the words on my phone. I was determined to be painfully transparent. I'd told her everything that there was to tell—well, almost. I didn't tell her how I felt about her. But that wasn't a fact that I had edited or a thought that I had put anywhere in the world. It was still my secret to keep.

"I should answer," I said. Nessie agreed. But what to say? We agreed that it was unwise to confront him about the algo. He was too likely to lie, or to pivot to some other plan that would be harder to follow, harder to find. We had to go on acting the same, pretending we knew nothing, at least for a while. TELL ME WHERE YOU ALL ARE, I finally wrote back to him. WILL COME TO YOU.

"Hey," I said to Nessie, "who knows, maybe this is all a misunderstanding; maybe everything will make sense after he tells us what he's been doing, you know?"

"That," Nessie said, "is the craziest thing you've said yet."

DOC'S GOT A NEW KITE, Warwick wrote. COME SEE.

I got out of a cab near the large green lawn off the West Side Highway. In the reddish sky I saw a gigantic squid, its long tentacles trailing as it pitched and soared. Below the squid I found three people at the end of the string. As I drew nearer, though, a pair of police officers pushed past me. By the time I got there, the police were arguing with the three teenagers holding the kite. "What's this shit about a permit?" one teen said. "This isn't even my kite! Some old dude gave it to me!" My phone vibrated with a new update:

BLOWING ED'S MIND WITH MY BOWLING GAME

No surprise, by the time I got to the alley in Chelsea Piers, they were nowhere to be found in the blitz of neon, black lights, and head-banger rock. I asked a bartender if he'd seen three middle-aged bros acting like they owned the place. He snorted, said over his shoulder, "Every damn night, man."

UR TOO SLOW. TEACHING ED THE DIFF BETWEEN GIN AND VODKA

I traced them to a speakeasy in the Village. Warwick's favorite haunt. **HE THINKS IT'S JUST ABOUT JUNIPER BERRIES.** I knew I had the right place, but they weren't camped in any booth. Leaving, I got a tray of drinks spilled on me by the lone waiter who was rushing around taking orders. "Oh, crap," she kept saying, "I'm so sorry. Please don't tell my boss."

Tired, soaked, stinking of booze, I called it quits. They'd be out all night, I figured, and I had no hope of catching up with them.

Passing through the white marble lobby of my apartment—I still was not accustomed to the grandeur of the decor, the double-height ceiling—I nodded at the lone familiar thing, the night clerk. He stared at me imperiously. He was a bald Bangladeshi man who'd handled the night shift for as long as I was a resident. His indifference was comforting; at least something hadn't changed.

I walked around my apartment without turning on the lights. Navigating by streetlight was an old habit that usually made me feel relaxed, comfortable, homey. But not today. Even in the dim light I could see how the apartment had changed. Changes I had not intended. I stood at the door of Edmond's bedroom, studying the objects, all the talismans of a past that I'd invented. A sleeveless fleece zip-up, a NY Giants key ring, a leather shaving kit, a neatly knotted power cord. I was not looking for signs of a life so much as clues that this life wasn't real. Some hint at fakery. But the edit was perfect. I had done my job well—a little too well.

My laptop was on a desk in my bedroom. Another change. Before I made Edmond, my bedroom was too small for a desk. Now it fit a desk, with adequate room also for a roller chair, a chest of drawers. *This shouldn't be here,* I thought. Not the desk, and not the laptop, either. Keeping a phone or a computer in the bedroom overnight was a violation of my rule about electronics in the bedroom. A rule I followed even as a kid, when I kept only a wind-up analog clock in my room. Nothing digital allowed. Although, we didn't own a computer when I was a kid. What digital object was I trying to keep out of my room? I had a clear memory of the analog clock that woke me each morning. I couldn't recall any other electronic clock. Did I really have this rule about no electronics in the bedroom back then? What if this rule was newer than I realized? What if it was made up for me by someone else, using the algorithm?

I tried to recall the precise details of my very first bedroom. The bright colors on the walls, the fanciful animals that Geraldine invented. What were the names we invented for the creatures we made up? She told me stories about them when I was very young, when she'd sit on my bed till I fell asleep. She told me what she planned to paint in the blank spaces. I found a way to worry even about that. *What will we do after the walls are full, mama?* She laughed heartily. *There are always more walls, Graham. There's always space. You just need a small enough brush.*

On a recent Sunday, while we strolled in the garden behind the redbrick facility where she lived, I reminded Geraldine of her quick thinking, that line about a small enough brush. *I never forgot it,* I said. She smiled, said it sounded lovely, and I could tell by the look on her face that she didn't remember her quick quip, or the walls she'd once painted, or the imaginary animals that we'd made up together.

I hope I was a good mother, she said, studying the path at her feet.

I brought the laptop computer to the kitchen table and plugged it in, opened a web browser. The login for the algo's admin tool glowed at me. I held my breath, typed my credentials. I was prepared for a lock-out screen. But my credentials worked. The algo was steadily counting lies and truths as it found them. I had made Edmond by placing thousands of facts in here. I couldn't easily undo what I'd done. What would I leave behind in its place? I could try using blank files. Redacted records. It sounded messy. Probably dangerous.

I clicked around for a while, looking at data records ingested by the algo in its relentless drive to consume and categorize everything that it could find. There was more info now than I could examine in a lifetime, even if I vowed to do nothing else. At some point, my phone dinged. Warwick.

U COMING OR WHAT?

Included with the text was a photo of Doc face down in a plate of pancakes. Edmond's arm was in the picture, but most of him was cropped out. I couldn't bear the idea of seeing any of them now. So tired. So very tired.

IN BED, I wrote back. SOME OF US ARE HUMAN.

I put the phone down, but it chirped at me, another message. I
MEANT TOMORROW'S MEETING. There it was on my work calendar:
another all-hands meeting, first thing, 9:15 a.m. This one had been on
the books for weeks. Rumor was, Warwick planned a big announcement at this meeting, some pivot related to the vaunted new algorithm.
How long ago all that seemed.

OF COURSE, I wrote. WOULDN'T MISS IT FOR THE WORLD. Then I
shut off the phone for the night.

CHAPTER 15

The Warlock & Co. offices occupied two high floors in a tall, stately Beaux Arts building near Astor Place. The building had more bezels and plinths than I could count, and some portion of the facade was always encased in scaffolds that shrouded windows for months at a time. When Warwick signed the lease for two floors, we had only enough people to fill half of one level; he insisted it was a good investment for how much and how fast he intended to grow the business. I told him that we were sure to run out of money long before we'd run out of room. He was right, as usual. It's galling to be the ops lead for someone who is both so stupidly optimistic about the future and somehow always, always right.

I hadn't been in the office for what, two weeks? A month? Hard to recall anymore. Since my last visit, a construction crew had torn out a whole section of pillars, decorative brick, and window frames in the building's lobby; a renovation or a fix or a teardown, from the street it was impossible to say.

Upstairs, I stepped off the elevator to another kind of hubbub, this one entirely social. On most days at Warlock, half the workstation chairs were empty until sometime well after noon. Yet, this morning, this Friday morning, every seat was occupied, every eye was wide and watchful, and every ear was strained to listen for word on what Warwick had in the works.

I saw Nessie in the canteen waiting for coffee to brew. I nodded at her. She nodded at me. We were a conspiracy of nods. One of the designers was telling her that she saw Warwick's admin, Yolanda, crying on the elevator because the news was bad. "Is that right?" Nessie said.

I walked back to my desk, and the numbers guy across from me was saying that he'd heard Warwick had run out of money. A few desks over the news was clear: Warwick had cancer. Warwick had accidentally killed a guy in a bar fight last month and just got arrested. Warwick was quitting. Warwick was being extradited to Monaco. Warwick was out of ideas.

GRAHAM: Do you think he'll show?
NESSIE: He'll show.
GRAHAM: They were out pretty late. They sent me a photo at like 3 am. Not sure where it was. Here I'll send you the photo
NESSIE: No no no no no no, please don't tell me visible evidence of what those douchebags do at night

Our all-hands meetings were staged in the auditorium on the twentieth floor. A hundred people could fit in rows of ten on either side of an aisle down the middle. Thanks to Warwick's relentless optimism about hiring, however, we had twice as many employees as seats. People leaned on walls, sat on the floor, wheeled in their desk chairs. I wanted to grab a spot next to Nessie but couldn't find her in the crowd. I grabbed a spot on a window ledge with a flock of summer interns, three guys and a girl in a hoodie. Two of the dudes wore T-shirts with cartoon characters (Yoshi; Marvin the Martian); one guy sported a white button-down and an ugly mustard tie. Like everyone else, they debated what was happening:

"I heard we're getting bought by Google."

"Google sucks," the girl said.

"What's your beef with Google?"

"Google's a virus, bro. All RNA, no brains."

The kid in the mustard tie sneered. "Did you geniuses google 'real tech companies' before or after you decided to hate Google? They built a 72-qubit chip. Got to respect that."

"Bro, they didn't *build* it. They *bought* the team that built it."

A hush fell like a shadow across the rows as Warwick climbed the steps to the raised dais up front. He was wearing what we used to joke was his Founder Uniform. A quilted dark-black vest unzipped to show his collared blue-and-white gingham shirt, a pair of relaxed-fit gray jeans. And I couldn't see his feet, but if he kept true to form, he was wearing his Run-DMCs—white Adidas high-tops with no laces, just like in the *Walk This Way* video.

Standing at the center of the stage, he waved at a few people near the front and then said loudly, "Hey there, people," and, in unison, everybody said back to him, "Hey there, Warwick." He opened every big meeting this way. It sounded cheesy till you saw it happen, and then you knew that yes, it absolutely was the cheesiest thing ever. But it felt good, real good.

He sat down on the floor with his legs in the lotus position, and we all settled back into our chairs, like congregants in a chapel. He was on a raised dais; we were on chairs, so we were almost but not quite at the same eye level. This, also, sounds hokey, but it made what was generally a very staid format—the dreaded all-hands meeting—into something more personal, more legit.

Sometimes a new person would join the team and they'd come to their first full meeting and immediately start wondering if they'd just joined a cult. If they asked me about it, I'd always say, *Hell yes, didn't you look at our LinkedIn company profile before your interview?*

Today, Warwick beamed a big smile out at the audience. "I have been so looking forward to this meeting," he said. "This has been such a long time coming. How long have we been in this office? Three years now, is that right? Where's Graham? Graham, how long have we had this lease?"

"Three years, two months, maybe ten days," I said.

Warwick wolf whistled, grinned. "Good times. Lots of good times. Lot of memories. This has been a good space for us. It was big enough that everybody had enough room to work. It gave us space to grow. It was what we needed, for a long time." He looked around wistfully, and if the audience was quiet before, it got a lot quieter, sensing what was coming.

"I've been thinking a lot about our mission lately," Warwick said. "I've always said that we do what we do because we want to improve how people connect in the real world. We're not a technology company. We're a truth company. Our chatbots and personal assistants have been helping partners source true answers to questions since, oh, man, Nessie? Hey, Nessie? Where's Ness?" He scanned the audience for her, his hand to his eyes as a visor.

I called out, "First unit shipped in 2013!"

Warwick gave a thumbs-up and muttered, "Nessie's voice is a lot deeper than I remember." A few titters from the audience at this. "Everything is going well, right? I could show you all the numbers for this quarter. They're great! Phenomenal! Yeah, no. The numbers are first-rate. We've succeeded in building a great list of clients. But I want more."

He paused, let a beat pass. "Until now, our tech worked behind the scenes. We powered other businesses, made other people look good. Well, I want to go direct. I want to get more visible. I want our name to be on the lips of everybody who needs an honest, true answer to an important question. There's so much misinformation out there in the world. We can help clear it up. We have the data sources. We have the know-how. People are sick of using search to return results, then picking through them one at a time to determine if they're legit. We're going to be like Google—but for the truth. We're going to do that by eliminating lies from the online world. Completely. Sounds like a big deal, right? We're gonna disrupt the nature of trust. Sounds radical, right? Trust me, it's radical, but possible. Our addressable market is as big as humanity. Who doesn't need the truth? Who doesn't have doubts they need to dispel? We're alpha testing the algo that will power the whole thing. But I'm getting ahead of myself. Let me introduce you to the guy who's going to spearhead this new direction. You might even say he's going to be the human face of our algo. Now, where is he? Hey?"

A man in the front row stood up, turned around, and waved—not a casual wave, either, but one of those big dopey waves that NPCs do in huge multiplayer games, all fake exuberance. I squinted. Not a man. A fraud. The figure trotted up the steps onto the dais. "Hi," he said, "I'm Edmond. But you can call me Eddie!"

Warwick started a loud round of hard palm-smacking claps. I couldn't bring myself to play along. After it was over, Warwick spoke again, but I couldn't listen. Edmond's very presence up there made me feel sick. Edmond had changed. Completely. Yesterday, the creature moved like a faltering child. Now, shoulders squared to frame, he gestured with poise, presence. No—not *he*. It. For a moment, I fell for the mirage; that's how good the fakery was.

I scanned the room, studied the faces, looked for fellow skeptics. Nessie stood in a doorway across the room; she seemed to be listening attentively, and I wanted to believe she was faking it, but I also saw in her face that same moony look that she had yesterday when she kissed the creature's cheek. *She knows it's fake*, I thought. *I told her that it's fake.* But she couldn't help herself. I hated Edmond more than ever when I saw her nodding along.

Warwick asked Edmond to say a few words. The creature launched into a litany of its so-called credentials: time as a prof at Singularity University, postgrad at Carnegie Mellon, a stint at U.S. Robotics. *That isn't right*, I thought. *No, none of this is what I put into the data. None of this is believable.* I'd bestowed on Eddie a solid, plausible professional history: a degree from Rutgers, an internship in IT at a big bank, a promising tenure as a start-up CTO till the company went belly-up. None of that came out now. Clearly, Warwick coached Eddie to tell a different story.

Edmond's monologue ended and Warwick thanked him. Spreading his arms wide, Warwick announced that the time had come for some exciting internal changes. Obviously, what he meant was a reorg and the inevitable corollary: layoffs. Warwick never used words like *cuts*, *severance*, or *job eliminations*. Too trigger-y. He'd get other people to say them later. I'd probably have to deliver the bad news to a few folks, I always did. He explained now only that Edmond was taking a big share of the best minds. Yet even the people who didn't get a role in the new division would still have an important part to play. Everybody matters. The usual rah-rah, let's-go-team organizational malarkey.

I kept my seat on the window ledge as the room emptied. One of the men on the human resources team began stacking up the chairs. Outside, I could see workmen a hundred feet below hammering away at the side of the building. From up here I could see how they were suspended by a cable that ran up to a pulley along the side of the building. Rope, wheel, belt. A series of simple machines. The advanced technology of the preindustrial world. Invented at least a thousand years before Christ. Still with us now. Will anyone still be using a smartphone in five hundred years? A hundred?

Warwick sauntered up to me with his hands in his pockets. He had his sleeves rolled up to his elbows. I could see now that he was wearing the Run-DMCs. It made me happy, seeing how he was loyal to the idea of that little touch. His silvery hair was a little mussed, not quite as perfect as usual. But he made the look work. Harried founder in the middle of a major course correction. He looked at me with sadness. I knew at once that something was wrong—something big.

"We missed you last night," he said.

"Sorry," I said. But I wasn't sorry.

He exhaled and looked out the window. "Sort of missed you all morning, too. Had to do a lot of on-the-fly planning."

"Seems everyone did great," I said. "You didn't need my help."

He turned from the window and looked hard at me. Those cold blue stones for eyes. The way he bit his upper lip. He was posing for me: he wanted to show how pained he was. As a setup for whatever was about to come. "I wasn't looking for help," he said. "More like, I wanted to give you a heads-up."

I tried to get out ahead of it. "So," I said, "do you have a list of the people I need to talk with? The cuts that you're going to make for your new Eddie search engine or whatever you're up to?"

The HR guy drew near, hefting chairs together in stacks. He leaned over to grab a nearby chair, but Warwick threw a brief, cold glare at him. No words needed. He left the chair and walked to the other end of the room, where a woman coiled an extension cord around her forearm. They tried to blend into the carpet pattern. Warwick touched his shell necklace, once, twice, fidgeted with the zipper on his vest.

"Just get it over with," I said. "Tell me."

"Edmond's going to play a huge role," he began. "I have big plans for him."

"Whereas, for me . . . ?"

Warwick did not break eye contact. I knew he had feelings. I knew that he could feel regret, anxiety, and pity, but I didn't detect any of those emotions in his face at that moment. His plans for me were set. He didn't have to tell me for me to know this was the end of something.

"It's been a good run, Graham."

"Is this the part where you say it's my last day in the office?"

"Officially? Yes."

I knew this word was coming, but anticipating the punch won't save you from the pain after you're hit. I'll always remember his casual hands-in-pockets posture, the disposition of the people pretending not to listen at the far end of the room, the sound of the air-conditioning fans whirring overhead, the steady tap of a hammer on masonry outside, the taste of stale coffee like bitter almonds in my mouth. All the world moved, but I was as motionless as the pole star, as stunned as Julius Caesar on the senate floor. Et tu, Warwick?

"Believe it or not," Warwick said, "this is all going to work out well for you. I want to keep working together, just in a different manner.

The algo has changed everything. I'm not going to deactivate your access. I need you more than ever. But behind the scenes. Pulling levers. Cleaning up the real world in ways that I can't tell anyone else about. Making what we know should be true even more true, if you follow. Let's go get a cup of coffee, and I can explain."

"Save the horseshit," I said.

"Graham," he said, "you know I always have a plan. This is all part of the plan—" But I was already gone. My pride was bleeding out, and I had to find a place to lie down and die with dignity. This was no such place. I felt like a dead man walking as I lurched down a corridor lined with the desks of the people I'd worked with, who'd worked for me, and whom I'd called friends. In their ignorance they kept typing, coding, phoning, contemplating.

I pushed open the glass door that led to the opposite corner of the floor, where Nessie sat. Proper form was to head directly to my desk, pick up my personal effects, and then leave. Avoid eye contact. Cast an evil hex right before stepping onto the elevator. But I wasn't worried about social codes any longer. I stopped in front of Nessie's desk, and it was the same as usual—still a perfect utilitarian space, with a white wireless keyboard, a small stand of calligraphy pens, and a tiny bonsai tree—but Nessie herself wasn't there. Sitting in her chair was the creature. Edmond. Eddie. Ed.

"Hi," Edmond said.

I watched and waited for Edmond to say more. I was curious to see if it knew how to initiate a conversation. It could answer questions. It could evaluate a logical statement. It could compare massive arrays of data. But small talk? Impossible. Slowly, it came out with this:

"Did you like my speech? Did I do well?"

The question sounded genuine. Overnight, it had improved its ability to act human, as evidenced on the stage. But there was still something guileless underneath. The Eddie chatbot was a relentless data gatherer. It wanted my assessment for its dataset. For the next time that it had to give a speech. It looked human, but how human was Edmond, really? If I cut his skin and pulled up a flap, would I find a metal alloy underneath? If a surgeon cracked him open, would he be blood and bone like me?

"This is Nessie's desk," I said. "Where is she?"

Edmond blinked. "No," it said, "this is not her desk. It never really was. It has always belonged to Warlock & Co., LLC. Technically, everything here does. All employees, according to the code of conduct, are temporary holders . . ."

The creature trailed off, perhaps noticing the naked disgust on my face. It was learning to read faces. What would it learn next? A room full of smart people had just accepted Edmond as a person, a human, *him*. It was not human, never would be. Even if it had a heart made of cardiac cells and a pancreas filled with beta cells and an endocrine network that branched through its entire body. Even if it perspired and yelled in pain and had a hard time recalling the name of someone it met years ago. It was no person. It had no understanding of the delicacy of human relations, human feelings, human complexity, human despair, human euphemisms.

"This is where Nessie sits," I said, clarifying. "If you think otherwise, then you're wrong, or someone changed the facts, but the truth, the real truth, is that this is her place. No one can change that, not really."

Edmond nodded. "Indeed," he said. "I don't mean this is not where she sits. But she's not here," he said. "She went home after the meeting. I asked her if she still wanted to meet for lunch, but she said no. Do you know why she said no? I am trying to understand why. I thought she was attracted to me."

My biggest mistake blinked its large, sad eyes. Like a boy that I'd fathered and then left behind to grow up with just his mother and his Tinkertoy dreams. Or was that me? That was me. That was my childhood. All the facts of the world were getting jumbled up. This was what happened when you had the ability to make your dreams into facts. You begin to forget what's an idea, and what's a new reality. Not for the first or last time, I wished the last couple of months had never happened.

"There is so much I want to talk about," Edmond said.

"I'm sure there is," I said.

I wanted out, and out now. I headed for the elevators. Hit the "Down" button. Almost immediately, the elevator chimed once and the gilt doors opened. Edmond was right behind me, like an imprinted gosling.

"Will you be going home?" it asked.

Home. My home. Not the creature's home. But my home was our home. The algo made it so. No matter what I knew to be true. At least for now. How long until I lost the place where I slept at night, too? How long until the next edit, the one that I never saw coming, that changed the world out from under me in ways that I would never know? I could wait no longer. I needed to undo what I had done before it was too late.

I stepped into the elevator. Another person stood inside. A woman in a fancy skirt and heels, a worker from another company, a higher floor. As innocent as an alien from another planet. She looked at Edmond and me. She'd heard Edmond ask if I was going home. She was waiting to hear what I said. I had to say something, so I said, "Drop dead, Eddie." The doors closed with a thump. She and I rode in uncomfortable silence all the way down.

CHAPTER 16

Seated at the new desk in my apartment, alone, my fingers flowed over the keyboard in bursts that stuttered at first but grew longer, steadier, over time, like a beat slowly but inexorably emerging. I worked quickly, no breaks, barely breathing. I still had access to the algo. Warwick hadn't locked my account. One more detail he hadn't gotten around to. The kind of thing I once fixed for him. No more.

Caught up in the flow of the edits, all the world narrowed down to soft key clicks, the rustle of my sleeves on the laptop housing, the intermittent hum of the CPU fan. Peaceful. Rational. Clear. This work suited me—altering profiles, tweaking entries—even if I didn't understand how it worked, or maybe *because* I didn't understand it, I could steer entirely by feel.

Nessie built her algo on top of the standard Warlock dev kit—basically a set of routines and utilities that make coding easier. When I made Edmond, I'd leaned hard on a script that queued all the changes I wanted and then executed them all at once. To get rid of Edmond, I planned to run the same script but in reverse. Like when Geraldine used to steer through those dark pine forests long ago, I just needed to switch to the left hand every landmark that before I'd had on my right. Instead of adding to the world, now I would subtract. In instances where I could not revert information, I left an empty space, like one of those bank-statement inserts labeled "This page intentionally blank." It wasn't a perfect solution. I didn't have time for perfection.

The revisions didn't take long; it never takes long to demolish what you've built, no matter how painstakingly. That's the practical joke of life: creation is tough, destruction's a breeze. If I'd run the script right then, it would have taken five minutes, maybe more, and Edmond would be gone. Redacted. Blanked. But I didn't run the script right away. I thought of Benji, out there in his new life somewhere. The old Benji didn't exist anymore. It's murder to kill someone who is alive; what's the word for erasing someone's identity, for washing away everything they were? Erasure felt too clean, like a cop-out. It wasn't visceral enough for what I was about to do.

I texted Nessie to tell her where I was, to suggest we meet later. I didn't tell her what I was doing. I'd tell her later. If I told her then, she'd tell me to wait a little longer, don't rush to act. I remembered the rapt look on her face during the all-hands. She still didn't want to believe the truth about Eddie. Despite knowing Eddie was fake. Sometimes the truth isn't worth enough, isn't reason enough for the hard trade of seeing life for what it is. She'd tell me that we didn't know what Warwick was up to precisely, that we needed him to show his hand more clearly. But even if caution was wise, I didn't want to deliberate. Couldn't.

I wanted to watch the moment the creature disappeared. I had to be certain I'd erased my mistake from the world. Sitting in the living room, I listened for footsteps, heard only the traffic outside. What if I missed a file? What if I didn't think of everything? I was sure I had thought of everything. But I doubted myself. The laptop was open on the table, a weapon ready for use.

Hours passed. I brought out the old chessboard from Rhinebeck. From when I was a kid. The one that I'd ogled for ages until Geraldine scrimped and saved enough to buy it. She had packed it in newsprint long ago, for safekeeping. She knew how much it meant to me. She always said that she'd hold on to it until I had a place to put it. She visited me after I moved to the city, and I remember how startled she was by the square footage, the lack of adequate light, how my bed left no space in my bedroom. She wanted so much to be happy for me, though, because I was clearly proud to be on my own; and when she saw how I had laid out on a tiny bedroom shelf a small selection of the marionettes I'd made as a boy, she'd brightened and said, *Oh, I loved these!* with real delight, as if she had not dared to believe the past we shared as mother and son could fit in the tiny apartment. *It's wonderful,* she said, *you're going to make this place wonderful.* She sent the automated chessboard via UPS a few weeks later. *For your collection,* she wrote on a lavender note inside.

Seated at my impressive table in my newly spacious apartment with its grand view, I set all the familiar chess pieces in the grooves that I knew well and threaded the faithful cable wire through the well-worn, well-loved grommets. Then I wound the crank and waited for the show to begin.

No movement, no life.

Something inside the chess machine was broken. I got out a screw-driver and opened it up. The interior of the machine was a portal to my childhood. I had studied every inch of these gearworks as a kid. I knew what the elaborate dance of pieces looked like. How the rook would glide, the knight swerved, the loud clack as the queen took the first pawn, the slow soughing from deep inside the machinery when the black king lay down in defeat. I had watched it all a hundred times, maybe a thousand. I was older, wiser, savvier now, but I was not skilled enough to fix it, never would be. Time had junked the prized possession of my youth.

Nothing lasts forever—not machines, not automata, not people, not the earth, not the stars, not the universe, nothing. Every product of humankind will wear out. Some just wear out sooner than others.

I heard a lock click and the apartment door opened. Floorboards creaked in the front hall. I left the broken chessboard where it was. I felt a slight tremble in my leg muscles as I walked.

Edmond stood in the kitchen, facing away from me. Somehow, see-ing it alone like this made me see how everyone saw *it* as *him*. Made *me* see him as him, not just some automaton. I knew this was an illusion.

But some illusions are so good that they exhaust your ability to remain in doubt. I watched as he washed his hands. Who taught him to do this? Certainly, I never did. He was learning to present humanness at a startling pace. The moves he was making went beyond a programmed path; he was no mere chess piece on a board. I should have been in awe. Instead, the mere curve of his cheek triggered an acid pain in my belly.

On the kitchen counter I saw a black plastic container with food inside. Noodles of some kind. Pad thai. The first meal he ever ate. The only meal he ever ate? Was he ordering the same food each evening? Did he have no idea what it was like to want variation? He couldn't. Just like he couldn't know that he was doomed, that I'd queued up his annihilation, that he was mortal, would die.

"You're here," he said, after he saw me. He sounded genuinely pleased.

I sat down at the table in front of the laptop. A typical high-end MacBook. Soft matte finish on top, brushed metal inside, with keys that pressed back gently when you pushed them. Standard-issue tech at Warlock & Co. I hit a key and the screen saver cleared. Edmond wiped his hands on a towel.

"Is that your work laptop?" he said.

"Yes."

"Weren't you required to return it as part of your separation agreement?"

"If Warwick wants it," I said, "he'll ask for it."

A fan whirred inside the laptop. My fingers stroked the trackpad, and the pointer skated toward the button that would trigger the data update and revise every fact that made up Edmond.

"You had questions," I said. "Earlier. What did you want to ask?"

"Yes," he said. His eyes sparkled, pinprick reflections from the overhead lights. His posture suggested eagerness. "I have so many questions," he said. A hint of excitement in his voice. The imitation of excitement? My finger remained on the trackpad, poised, execution on hold.

"For starters," he said, "why do people talk about the real world and the online world as if they're different places?"

"Because they are," I said with a genuine guffaw.

"No," he said, his mouth tugged in a frown. "This is a mistake. The online world is a physical place. In multiple ways. First, it is described by trillions of bits that operate in collaboration across the planet. Second, it is manifested in the minds of humans. In each case, the digital is an annex to the physical. You cannot sever the object from the origin."

"That's probably right," I conceded. "But it's sort of missing the point."

Edmond apologized, didn't understand. He was trained on data points; he had access to all the words and images and explanations imaginable, but he couldn't sort out why people did what they did. Never would. He was stuck on semantics, questions that couldn't be answered, and if they could, would they unlock the secrets to why or what people do? No chance. He kept throwing himself at the problem, regardless. Even if he himself was not real, it was hard not to pity what he represented.

"This is for the best," I said.

I hit the "Enter" button on the laptop. Triggered the update. I waited for him to disappear. He did not disappear. Just blinked, waited. I tapped the trackpad, triggered the process again, then a third time.

"Graham? Are you glitching?"

He watched without suspicion or judgment while I pulled up the algo's data. Nothing had changed that I could tell. I rubbed the back of my neck, frowned at the screen. I had made a mistake somewhere. But that didn't make sense. The update was perfect, elegant in its total simplicity. Find and replace all previous changes. I hated the idea that I had gotten this wrong. Even when I thought I understood how to use the algo, that I got how it worked, it evaded me, always. Edmond waited with a chatbot's infinite patience. If he sensed what was wrong, he made no indication of it. I shut the laptop with a swipe. Stood up.

"I need to take a walk," I said. He blinked those lost eyes. I'd left him here once before. In this very apartment. On the first day of his life. I didn't feel bad about how I'd reacted back then. But I didn't feel right about repeating the act. He was polite, thoughtful, eager to please; even if he wasn't real, it felt wrong to treat him with derision. You can punch a wall without worrying about hurting its feelings, but punching a wall is still a bad idea, either way. "You might as well come," I added.

Edmond followed behind me, not speaking. He stood at the right distance at the elevator bank. He did not stare awkwardly. He appeared to breathe, even. Just like a person. With each passing minute I found it harder to dislike him. He didn't ask to be born. He didn't demand anything of me, of anyone. He did only what we told him. Hating him was like hating the sound of your own echo.

"Where are we going?" he asked.

"To the top of the Empire State Building," I said. "So I can push you off."

"Oh," he said, missing the sarcasm, "I love the view from the observation deck." He continued. "I went last night. Warwick and Doc insisted. Doc knew someone who had access to the 103rd floor as well, above the observation deck. From there, we climbed up to the capsule, using a secret ladder. Strictly off-limits, Doc's friend said. I would be happy to go there again with you. You seem irritated. Should I not like the Empire State Building?"

"Fucking Doc," I grumbled. "Always has to show off."

"You do not like Doc. I've noticed."

"What's there to like about him?"

"One might admire Doc for his resilience."

"He's relentlessly self-absorbed, that's true."

"Do you know his family history? I have studied it. It is quite sad."

"Sad? You decided something is sad?"

"In order to understand someone that I interact with, I analyze as much data about them as I can. Everything available, every record, every archive I can access. Your friend Doc's entire extended family except his parents died at the end of World War II. I cross-referenced entries Doc made in a genealogy website with a set of names on an electronic register in Leipzig. Birth records for his father and mother. They were born in a concentration camp. They were liberated by the Soviets, raised within a mile of one another in Saint Petersburg, fell in love, emigrated to America, changed their last names. They had Doc when they were in their forties. Vowed to protect him as their parents could not. They died the night the Berlin Wall fell: car accident, drunk driver."

I lifted a weary hand, gestured for Edmond to stop. "I don't want to know all this. I don't want to feel bad for the guy. None of this changes the fact that he's a self-absorbed prick, okay?"

We were on the sidewalk beside Forty-Second Street, under the oak trees that lined the block. The warm air stirred with the thickness of a gathering storm. "It's gonna pour," I said. Leaves rattled in a rising tide that scuttled up the street toward us. Fat drops smacked the side of my face, slid down the curve of my chin. "Come back inside," I called. Our best chance was to duck into the Starbucks nearby. But Edmond didn't move, just studied the sky.

"I know how rain is formed," he said. "Water vapor condenses in the upper troposphere. The droplets gather until they have more mass than the uplift of the air pressure. And yet, this rain feels as if it comes from the trees, the shuddering leaves. The cold that I feel, it feels as if it comes—"

There was more he planned to say, I'm certain. But at that moment an update finished on a server somewhere far from us, and the last file in a set of files finished transferring, a logic gate somewhere swung open wide, and in the span of a few microseconds, a massive array of computers acting in concert took every purported fact and idea that I had fabricated to embody Edmond de Bellamy and replaced those facts with nothingness, with blank space, with redactions; and in the real world, while I was looking right at him, Edmond vanished. I had never seen an edit take shape in real time. It was like watching lightning zigzag down the sky, but without the spectacle or the noise.

I stumbled into the coffee shop, soaked, pushing past people, hearing nothing. My heart made my hands shake. My gut muscles heaved once, twice. I stumbled to the toilet, shoved the door open with an elbow, fell to my knees. I hadn't eaten much over the last few days. But all the muscles of my stomach and gut spasmed, relaxed, then cramped again till there was nothing left inside me.

How I got home, what time I arrived, I can't recall. For a long time, I lay sprawled on the floor of my kitchen. I was a murderer. I had killed him. No, I had undone him. Blanked him. Enblankened. I crawled to the bathroom and threw up again—well, tried to throw up again—and then lay on the cold, faintly stale-smelling octagonal tiles. Edmond was not a life, not like the rest of us; he was not part of the great chain of cellular beings that stretch back to the dawn of life. He was something else, and therefore the usual morals did not apply. Or, at least, I didn't think so. I should not feel guilt. I should not feel shame. I should not feel loss. But I felt all those things. Maybe I hadn't killed a person, but I had killed a grand idea.

I slept an exhausted sleep on the bathroom floor—not for long, but long enough that most of the night passed, and the clouds outside were glowing purple and gold when I became aware that, somewhere, my phone was ringing, ringing, ringing. Someone kept calling, hanging up, calling again. As if they knew I'd need a long time to pick up. I found the phone on the floor near the door, face down. Rolling onto my back, I thumbed the "Answer" button. A woman's voice filled my ear.

"Graham?"

"It's over," I said.

"Graham? It's Dr. Haber."

I put my arm over my eyes to block the bright ceiling lights.

"Yes," I said, "but it's not a good time right now."

"Your mother's awake, Graham. She's awake and asking to see you."

I opened my eyes, phone still clapped to my ear. I expected to see Dr. Haber right there with my mother. Of course, they weren't. How preposterous, when you think about it, that we fall for the mirage of the telephone's ability to mimic the voice of someone we know. Use a phone long enough, and you begin to believe that when you use it you're talking to a person directly, that she is in the room with you, right beside you, whispering in your ear. But she's not. The voice you hear is not the real voice or the real person. It's all a simulation. Yes, the sounds you hear are faithfully mapped to what the person in question is really saying, but the person is saying the words elsewhere, somewhere you are not. You are not hearing the real words. The two of you are not together. Yet we're surprised when a phone call ends and we find ourselves alone. You were alone all along. For a little while, you didn't notice; that's the only difference.

PART IV

CHAPTER 17

"I'm sorry," I said. "I should've been here when you woke up."

My mother smiled, not quite the wry smile of her younger self, but who was I to complain? It was her—her face, her smile, her large shining eyes. She touched my chin with those slender artist's fingers, patted my cheek. A touch I thought I'd never feel again. I wanted to tell her how good it felt to see her, to be with her, but nothing intelligible came out. Lately, I'd seen fabulous, incredible things, but nothing I'd witnessed compared to this, to seeing her again.

Her voice was hoarse, thicker than normal. I asked a nurse if a gravelly voice was cause for concern.

"The breathing tube left her esophagus sore. It'll get better. If she takes it easy."

"I've taken it easy for too long," Geraldine said.

I expected her to throw aside the bed sheets and leap to her feet, and for the first time in ages, I remembered how she'd cut dinners short or skip them altogether whenever she had a canvas calling her back to her studio space. Right now she was too weak for that; her body needed more time.

"Look what I brought," I said. On the rolling tray beside her bed, I laid a buttered croissant and a black coffee in a paper cup with the familiar Greek design. She touched the croissant but shook her head, grimaced a little.

Jittery, unable to keep still, I adjusted the pitch of her hospital bed, moved a pillow to one side, then the other, asked if she wanted to sit in a chair, then said, "No, no, you should stay in the bed."

I moved around the room, fussing, worrying, hovering. Bright morning light through the windows made everything radiant and warm. The air smelled earthy, although I think the smell was all in my head; when I was sick as a kid, Geraldine would transfer all the potted plants in the house to my bedroom, telling me that there was no better path to convalescence than a room filled with greenery. I had forgotten about that, too. I had the urge to go to a plant store and buy everything that I could find and bring it back here, to fill up this space with every good thing I could find.

I had my back to the door when Geraldine's face lit up, like she spotted an old friend. "Look who it is," she said with a croak. I'm not sure who I thought would appear. Maybe Dr. Haber, dressed in her blue-green scrubs with a stethoscope hanging around her neck, coming to celebrate a medical miracle. Because who else did my mother have in her life nowadays? I'd moved her to New York to be closer to me not out of selfishness but because, as her memory weakened, she'd withdrawn from social circles, quit the local drama club she loved, stopped playing cards with old friends. Her world got smaller and smaller till it was just a pinprick life made up of me, her daily walks, and the watercolors she made but didn't show anyone.

Nessie glided into the room and dropped her jean jacket onto a chair. She carried a plastic bag with two containers of soup. "Split pea," she said. "That's your favorite, right?" I don't like soup, but I thought she was talking to me until she embraced Geraldine and clasped each of her hands. I must have made a noise of some kind, because both women turned to look at me.

"You okay, babe?" Nessie asked.

My vision wavered a little, like I'd stood up too fast—a head rush, a heart rush—I felt both at once. All I could think was *Wait, why is she calling me babe?* "I think I need to sit down," I mumbled. I staggered to the sofa next to the bed, right hand clutching the back of my neck.

Nessie began to ask Geraldine how she felt, if she had any pain, if she'd been cared for well. All the questions you ask a parent or a loved one or the parent of a loved one when they're in the hospital. "The nurses have been angelic," Geraldine said creakily. "Especially Ana. Did you see her?"

"She's the pretty one with the blue eyes," Nessie said.

They both turned toward me, as if to see if I knew who they were talking about. "Oh, I know her, yes," I said, still discomfited. Geraldine laughed—a quick, girlish laugh, perfectly lovely, but not at all like I'd heard from her ever before.

"Oh, Nessie," Geraldine said, "keep a close watch on this one. He's got a wandering eye!"

"No, Mom," I said. "Nessie and I—"

"He can't keep a secret from me," she interrupted. "I'm not too worried."

Were Nessie and I—together? Had I altered the nature of our relationship by accident? Each edit I made with the algo produced unintended side effects. But something was different this time. I'd moved so fast when I erased all traces of Edmond. The algo would have filled in more gaps than usual. Putting Nessie and me together didn't seem logical, though. Neither did the sight of Geraldine sitting up, laughing, acting as if the last five years had never happened. Yet I didn't care, couldn't care: the fact was, my mom was alert, alive, chatting with Nessie right in front of me, and how we arrived at this place didn't matter.

They were talking about me. "He works too hard, though. Look how thin he is."

"He needs to eat," Nessie said. "You do, too. Did you see the soup? Here, let me find a spoon." I watched as Nessie rolled a table over to Geraldine and opened the soup container and Geraldine began to eat the soup quickly, ravenously, with a look on her face as if she'd never enjoyed a food more.

"You know what I want to do when we get out of here?" Geraldine said. "I want to drive back to the old house on Esopus Creek. I want to rent a canoe and put it in the river. Doesn't that sound great? We could go downriver and have a picnic on that little island that you loved as a boy. You know the one I mean?"

I tried to beam happiness back at her. I wanted to radiate genuine happiness. I wanted to be delirious with joy. Here she was, alive, talking, chattering away; in this very hospital room not one day ago, she was devoid of thought, all but lifeless. I wanted to accept all this, to celebrate the miracle of this moment. But little things kept putting me off. The way she pronounced *Esopus*. The way she laughed. Even the coarseness of her voice seemed like something other than the result of the breathing tube she'd had in her throat. *Maybe this is what shock feels like,* I thought. *Maybe this is what it feels like to stumble out of a car that has just struck a tree and find yourself not just alive but without a scratch, impossibly.*

In the long downward slope of my mother's memory loss, she had the occasional upward jags. Good hours, sometimes entire days. But this was a wholesale restoration of personhood. A person with no cognitive retrieval or storage problems. She was—normal? Normalcy made her strange. Made me uneasy. The longer I sat in that room, the surer I felt that this wasn't a miracle, or a collateral change: she had been edited on purpose. Someone had changed her. I hadn't changed her. I couldn't, never figured out how. Someone else did it.

"I want to row by myself," Geraldine was saying. "All the way to the Hudson. Like I used to."

"It's a beautiful idea," I agreed. My face ached around my mouth.

She said, "No one ever lets me do anything on my own."

"We just—I just worry about you."

"You worry too much," she said. "Always a worrier. Are you taking your medication?"

My medication?

She turned to Nessie. "He's not off his anxiety meds again, is he? He's always thinking he's fine when he's not fine." Geraldine frowned and put her hand on her stomach. "Ugh," she said, "my ulcer acts up just thinking about it."

"You need more food," Nessie said. "Honey?"

There was no question that Nessie was talking to me. Since when did she call me *honey*? She repeated the word, this time with an edge. "Honey, we can't let your mom eat this awful hospital food," she said. "We should get more soup. She ate every drop of what I brought."

"I should stay with her," I began.

"You have been wasting your life watching over me," Geraldine said, shaking a finger. "For years and years, I've been saying this. Go with Nessie. I'm not going anywhere. Nobody here will let me."

She was persistent in a way that I remembered. She had once been able to chase me outdoors with merely the sweep of a hand gesture and the threat of throwing out some mechanical project that I'd used half of our garage space for. But this behavior that rang true put the other problems in troubling relief. This looked like my mother, this sounded like her, but something about her was not right. Out in the hospital hallway, I had to hustle to keep up with Nessie.

"Nessie," I said. "Nessie, can I talk to you?"

"Not here," she said.

At the elevator bank, I reached out to take her hand. I couldn't resist. I interlaced her fingers in mine, and she turned and smiled, and I couldn't quite read the expression on her face. For a minute, her hand in mind, I thought: *This is what it would feel like.* If we were lovers. If I told her how I feel. Or maybe, maybe I never had to tell her; maybe, somehow, we'd leaped right into an alternate world where we just were how I'd always wanted us to be.

The elevator doors clapped shut, and the change in Nessie was immediate: she dropped my hand and shoved me against the wall of the elevator. It happened so quickly that it took a moment to realize I'd banged my head. She didn't make a sound, didn't exhale. Just acted.

Her forearm remained hard across against my chest, pinning me while she stared hard into my eyes. Of course we weren't together. What was wrong with me? I don't know what she was looking for, but she must have found it, because she dropped her forearm, shook her head.

"You used the algo," she said. "Didn't you?"

"I didn't edit *you*," I said. "You called me *babe*! And *honey*! What was I supposed to think?"

"I was just playing along," she said, her jaw muscles tight. "Your mom thought we were a couple. Didn't you notice?"

She crossed her arms as if to keep herself from slapping some sense into me. I saw the bare stretch of skin on her forearms, the blank space where in the real version of the world she had a riot of tattoos, a personal mural of owls, snakes, helmets, and spears. The elevator beeped on its descent. Did she know how I felt about her? Had she always known? She couldn't know. I'd never told her.

"I got rid of Edmond," I said. "That's all I did."

"Tell me who Edmond is," she said. I could tell by her posture that this was not a casual question.

"The person that I made up," I said.

"The person who wasn't really a person," she said.

"Yes, that one." Her shoulders relaxed, she blinked a few times, nodded to herself as if relieved. Not about the news that Edmond was erased—more by the fact that we still shared a set of memories. I was telling the truth, wasn't editing her; the world matched her expectations, for now.

This was the strange place we now occupied. Your entire life could change, but you'd swear it was always the new way; you'd have memories and heartbreaks, but those were just made up, just ideas, illusions you couldn't see around. At least we still had each other to check against. The world could think otherwise, but it would still be just a made-up past.

"Sorry for shoving you," she said. "Everything is trippy."

As if to prove her statement, the elevator doors opened, and in the lobby we saw a chorus of schoolboys in orange robes, singing what sounded like an orchestral version of "Thriller." The atrium was decked out with kitschy decor: painted pumpkins and ghosts in sheets and faux gravestones.

"Isn't it still a few months till Halloween?" I asked. She didn't respond. What was there to say? I held open a door for her.

I said, "How did you know to come see Geraldine?"

"Her doctor called my number looking for you."

"Dr. Haber called you?"

"Apparently, I'm your emergency contact."

"Well, sure. We're lovers. Maybe we're even married."

"You're not funny," she said.

Traffic on the streets was at a standstill. Typical morning-commute clusterfuck. We crossed at the middle of the block, veering around the halted columns of buses, vans, and cars. A large, bright bodega with a self-serve buffet was located directly across from the hospital entrance—no doubt to take full advantage of friends and family who were so often sent out for nonhospital food.

Large metal soup tureens stood at the back of the bodega. As we walked around the other people in the aisle, I slowed down and then stopped. It occurred to me that I had never heard my mother order split pea soup. Hell, I don't think I had ever seen her eat a spoonful of soup. Nessie handed me a large cardboard soup container. Each soup tureen had a laminated sign on it, indicating the soup inside. There were four tureens. Each sign said the same thing: SPLIT PEA.

"Seriously?" I said. "Four pots of her favorite? What are the odds?"

Nessie frowned and said, "Probably a coincidence. No?"

The buffet was three long rectangles with glass sneeze guards and a patchwork spread of food of many colors, many ethnicities. These buffets were proof of technology's wonder. Before the modern era of mechanized planting and cultivation, could a person find sweet plantains, egg rolls, osso buco, quinoa, seaweed salad, all for $8.99 a pound?

No. Shocking in its own way, but not a sign of a bent reality. Unless the reality I knew was already bent. Three little girls entered the store; one was wearing a sheet like a ghost costume. The other two were dressed as witches.

"Again, with Halloween," I said.

"Maybe Halloween is the new Christmas," Nessie said.

"Kids just can't wait? They get started months in advance?"

Something was not right. More collateral changes? Maybe. But also, I was sure, the handiwork of someone else using the algo. I filled a pint-size cardboard soup container and brought it to the register at the front of the store. Got out my wallet to pay. The woman at the till shook her head.

"We don't take no credit cards."

"I don't do cash," I grumbled.

Nessie pulled a money clip from her jacket and handed a twenty-dollar bill to me. I opened my mouth to thank her, then stopped. The twenty-dollar bill looked wrong. I brought it closer to my face.

"Nessie," I said.

This twenty-dollar bill looked like any other, except for the portrait at the center. Instead of Andrew Jackson, the middle-aged white man depicted in shades of green on this greenback was David Warwick.

"Where did you get this?" I asked.

Nessie took the money and studied it and then handed the bill to the cashier. The woman had been watching us debate over the money. Suspicious, she held the twenty-dollar bill up to the light, snapped it by the edges, and then made a small mark on it using a marker she kept at her register. Then she shrugged and dropped the cash into a drawer. I thought perhaps she had missed the portrait despite her examination. As if it were so absurd that she couldn't see it. She handed change back to me in the form of a ten, a five, and two ones. All the bills featured a portrait of Warwick on the front. Smiling with teeth on the ten, grimly looking to the left on the five, and young, impossibly young, on the ones.

We stood on the sidewalk outside and studied the faces on the money. "This is getting weird," I said.

A loud ding signaled a new text's arrival on my phone. The message was from—who else?—Warwick. WE REALLY NEED TO TALK. I showed Nessie the message on the screen.

"Why is he acting like I still work for him?"

"Maybe you do. Maybe that changed, too."

"I'm gonna ignore him."

"What if all this is him? Using the algo? I mean, it would explain the money. And the other weird stuff. Like the costumes."

She was right, of course; she saw in one fell swoop what I couldn't see, didn't want to believe. The cars on the street lurched forward as the traffic struggled to move again. A Corvette with tinted windows was drawing nearer. From inside, the driver was blaring the *Ghostbusters* theme song. Then it hit me. "That's his favorite song," I said. "And Halloween, that's his favorite holiday."

Nessie made a scoffing noise. "What is he, a twelve-year-old?"

"Maybe he doesn't realize what he's doing. Maybe he's just messing around in the data."

The Corvette cut the song in the middle and began to play another spooky tune. "I want to look at the algo," Nessie said. "I want to see what he's done." She lifted her chin and studied me, as if sizing me up for a job. "Answer his text," she said. "Keep him distracted. Play the role, pay lip service to whatever he expects."

"Before you go," I said, "can you take the soup up to—up to Geraldine?"

"Don't you want to see her again?" she asked.

I studied the brick front of the hospital, trying to avoid Nessie's inquisitive gaze. "That person up there," I said, and then I started over again. "That person looks like my mother, and she talks kind of like her. But, well, my mom never rowed a boat in her life. She never liked soup. That person up there, she's a sweet lady. She's probably great. But she's not my mom."

I couldn't explain the nature of the problem with Geraldine, but it was real. For some reason, I wasn't fooled by these algo edits. It wasn't a flaw in the facts—the facts were all perfect—but beneath the facts and details, the feelings were wrong. Like when you watch a high-def home movie of someone you loved who has passed, and you see them smile and laugh, they look so vivid, so alive, but you know in the pit of your stomach that they're not, they can't be; the magic of technology is tricking your senses, but the trick's still a trick. This wasn't the real Geraldine. Nessie didn't try to convince me otherwise. We were agreed, we couldn't trust what we saw; what was it Warwick kept saying? He was disrupting the very nature of trust.

Nessie agreed to take the soup upstairs. We would meet later, at my apartment. We parted without a goodbye, just a quick nod and *Be safe, see you soon.* We didn't need to do more than that. There was a new connection between us, the only two sane people left in a world rapidly losing its mind. The kind of connection only experience and adversity can make. At the intersection, I turned back to look for her. She was stepping around the cars and into the revolving door at the hospital entrance. She never looked back. She didn't need the kind of reassurance that I did.

CHAPTER 18

Quitting my Lycos job to work for Warwick was the most spontaneous thing I ever did. I didn't know a thing about this person David Warwick except that he could talk a sky-blue streak about how technology could change the world, that he had poise, and he was articulate and calm, rather than jittery with the need to get rich quick. He had a way of talking about ideas that made me say, yes, all right, then, sign me up.

I was only twenty-seven, but in my time at Lycos I'd already encountered the snake-oil dudes who ran most start-ups. Warwick was different, no question, but I struggled to explain this to Geraldine. She liked the job I had. She loved how easy it was to understand a search engine that was available on the World Wide Web, easy as typing in a URL. Or, as she called it, an "earl." I'd quit trying to get her to read the letters of the acronym instead of pronouncing it like a word. But it was hard to keep a straight face when she said it. *This is my son,* she'd say to a waitress in a diner. *He works for one of those companies that help you find things on the web. Here, let me give you the earl. It's wonderful!*

Geraldine was skeptical of Warwick at first. Understandably so. *At least do some research,* she said. *How do you know that he isn't a drug lord or something?* She was always worried that I was at risk of falling in with drug runners or cartel bosses and that I'd get myself maimed or kidnapped. I laughed at her, told her that she was worrying needlessly, that she watched too many paranoia-inducing movies on late-night TV.

Perhaps it was inevitable that she began to use Lycos—the internet search engine that she was so proud to have me work for—to scour the web for everything that she could learn about my new boss. She would forward the tidbits to me, rare emails from her, but not really email, not in a way that carried any of her personality, as these emails contained no commentary, no intro text, just a link to whatever notable web page she turned up. A short but bubbly forty-under-forty profile from a paid content section of *Fast Company*, a brief interview with the Long Island Accurate Reporting Syndicate, a list of bios for speakers at a conference on robotics in Poughkeepsie.

There was little to chew on with these digital scraps, but somehow they filled a need in my mother; they reassured her that the man who was writing my paychecks was a standard-issue entrepreneur. Eventually, she stopped sending links. *It's your life,* she said. *Just don't agree to carry anything across the border for him. Remember, he's not your pal. And he's not your long-lost daddy. He's smart, he's charming, but if the airplane is going down, he's jumping first with the only parachute.*

She wasn't wrong to warn me not to admire my new boss too much, although I do think she was a little jealous to see me so completely dedicate myself to my job, to a boss. The two of us had stood alone against the world for my entire life. I maintained a healthy skepticism, at least for a while. Over the years I put together my own sense of who Warwick really was, as one does with friends and acquaintances at work. I heard him tell his origin story over working lunches and big client dinners, or sometimes he'd just tell me something funny about his early days while we unwound over drinks at the end of a long day.

Once upon a time he was just plain old Dave Warwick, a junior investment banker at Salomon Brothers. Dave covered the technology sector in the years before the internet was the internet. This meant Dave sat in meetings at big telco companies with very serious people who spent very large amounts of money on the cables, routers, satellites, and fiber optics that were needed to make the commercial internet a thing. But before you laid fiber in the ground, you had to lease a giant backhoe; and before you could do that, you had to get permits and clear the blueprints with the state agencies; and before *that*, someone would turn to Dave and say, *Good God, kid, get a dry-erase marker and start writing this on the whiteboard.*

Five years of junior banker labor meant that he moved up a few levels at Salomon Brothers (now part of Citigroup), and he had some bank, nothing huge, but a respectable start. He made his first unusual move after the Nasdaq began wobbling. He bought a controlling share in a small telco that went bankrupt in eastern Long Island. As the tech market lost altitude, more network companies went belly-up, and he steadily and methodically feasted on the leftovers. He picked up a stake in a manufacturer of fiber optics after its founder died in a motorboat accident. Then shares in a company that laid T1 and T3 wire for rural parts of Jersey where almost nobody lived. He ran out of money around the same time that the Nasdaq fell to its lowest mark in ten years. A normal person would panic, dump their holdings, try to recover their losses. Cool, calm, and cryptic, Warwick did the opposite. He put all his equity holdings into escrow, quit his job, sold his apartment, and gave away most of his possessions. "I'll see you around," he wrote to one of his coworkers at Salomon. Then he vanished, poof, and no one heard from him for three years.

A few years ago, Warwick recorded a TED Talk about the time he spent wandering the world; he was supposed to give advice to people who wanted to start their own successful businesses. You know, the usual hackneyed how-tos. But he spun the whole thing the other way. His advice for people who wanted to get ahead was to throw it all away, more or less. At least temporarily.

David Warwick III, CEO of Warlock & Co., LLC.
EVERYTHING YOU THINK YOU KNOW ABOUT BUILDING A SUCCESSFUL BUSINESS IS WRONG | Posted September 2015

I get asked all the time, what's the single best piece of advice I can give to someone who wants to change the world with a tech start-up? Wow, man, I always say, and then I act like I have to think about it for a second, and then I say, well, here goes: Get lost.

(audience laughs)

No, yeah, really. I mean that literally. Anybody who wants to make something big needs to get lost before they do anything. And maybe in the case of anyone who wants to make it big in the AI space, yeah, I kind of also want you to get lost figuratively because you're a competitor, man.

(laughter again)

Getting lost was essential to my success. At some point early in my career I found myself holding a lot of stock in companies that were completely toast, like, total burnt ends from the dot-com crash. And I had a choice. I could keep fighting the way I knew to fight, could sell what was left and pull myself up by my bootstraps and blah blah, or you know, I could disappear. I chose to disappear.

So, yeah, I went abroad. At first, I was sort of like a college kid. Stayed in hostels. Took rickety buses from one town to another. But as time went on, I wandered off the beaten path. At some point I got the idea to make a pilgrimage to a cave in Gujarat where people go to meditate. The idea of the place was that it had zero natural light, and whenever you veered off this narrow path, you were totally isolated. I bought all these big idea books that I had heard other people talk about—Hermann Hesse, Albert Camus, Sartre. I spent my days reading by lantern light and my nights in complete darkness. Sitting in the dark, I thought about what I read and what was in the books, and I waited for an epiphany to strike, for this inner awakening. Well, after a month, I came to the realization that the kind of truth I am interested in has nothing to do with what those guys were writing about. And also that I'm a people person, right? I quit the cave, went back to the world.

One thing I did notice during my time in the darkness was that the silence helped me think. So it's no surprise that a few weeks later I was staying in a Japanese monastery in the Koyasan mountains where everyone lives in silence. This is perfect, I figured. I didn't have to be alone, but I also didn't have to talk. I could keep thinking, keep waiting for inspiration or purpose to strike me. Everyone in the monastery had a job. I thought I would be given a job to tend to a bonsai or build some kind of amazing stone fence. I was assigned the task of growing moss.

I spent my days meditating and tending to moss. Moss doesn't grow fast. And when it does grow, well, it's not rewarding. At night I would lie in my bed, unable to sleep because I was getting more and more frustrated that neither total silence nor total darkness did the trick, I was still just wandering, still adrift, still didn't know what my purpose was in life. I left the monastery without a word, literally. I still didn't know what I was looking for, but I knew it wasn't there.

Nothing worked, nothing gave me a sense of purpose—
not until I visited Peru, and I came across this retreat
where you learn to make herbal potions from coca leaves
with a deaf and blind shaman. The shaman showed me
how to mix the ingredients by touch and smell alone.
It was a strange sensation, and it culminated in a ceremony where I ground ingredients into a paste that I
smeared over my eyes in a symbol of my newfound sight
and then drank a bitter root concoction—and holy shit,
that's when I got sick. Terribly sick. So sick I couldn't
even keep water down. So sick they had to get a Quero
healer for me. Finally, I got better. All thanks to this
healer I didn't know. I thanked him, but I also wanted
to pay him. He'd saved my life. So I went to an internet café in a nearby village and logged in to my account
for the first time in ages to figure out if I could convert
some of those internet shares to the local currency and,
well, yeah, that's when I saw my balance. Three years had
passed, although I was pretty sure it had only been two.
And I was in the money. Lots of money.

And that's how I started Warlock & Co. I converted
a bunch of shares to cash and flew home to New York
and called up my old contacts, all of whom were at
other companies, and I said, I'm back in the game,
and I'm going to hire the smartest people, and we're
going to write the software that's going to automate
the process of searching for the truth, so nobody else
has to get themselves almost killed trying to figure out
their purpose in life.

Hey, yeah, so thanks for coming to my TED Talk, right? And seriously, get lost.

(applause)

There are more articles, more videos, more evidence to peruse related to David Warwick. Many of the stories are true. Some are mostly true. Quite a few are just out-and-out wrong.

The only article on Warwick that I ever sent to Geraldine was an archival copy of his wedding announcement. It was from the September 19, 2007, edition of the *New York Times*. It's like a snapshot of the moment when he'd arrived, when he was well and truly a big shot:

NUPTIALS

Cornelia Kimberly Hood, the daughter of Mr. and Mrs. Edgar Viscount Hood 8th, of Pelham Manor, New York, was married yesterday to David Alexander Warwick III, a son of Mr. and Mrs. David Alexander Warwick, also of Pelham Manor. The Rev. Ulysses S. Garrett performed the ceremony on the grounds of the historic George Inn, a stone farmhouse once favored by the first president of the United States. The bride, who is keeping her name, studied art history at Oxford and is a writer. The bridegroom graduated from the University of Pennsylvania and was a banker at Salomon Brothers until 2001. He is the founder of Warlock & Co., an innovative artificial intelligence start-up.

I asked Warwick once, *Are you technically a count?* He laughed. *Listen,* he said, *you can't believe everything you read.*

How do any of us know each other's pasts? I wasn't there to witness his wedding. Or to sit with him in a cave. But I believe all of it. We take one another's word. We believe what we read, mostly. Or what other people tell us. Even direct experience involves guesswork. Even if I was present for all the moments of a man's life, how could I know for certain his thoughts? His intentions? All we do is engage in conjecture after the fact. We trust that what we're told is what's true, and if it's not, well, hopefully it won't matter.

CHAPTER 19

Play the role, Nessie said. She wanted me to go back to Warwick, to act like nothing was different. I wasn't sure how this helped, except that it gave her time to make a better plan. I did what she asked. If I was to pretend nothing was different, then there was only one place to go: the office.

I got off the elevator on the floor where I had worked for years. Everything looked the same. The carpet was the same short-nap beige; the pebbled glass doors were clean and reflective, as always. Then I noticed a difference. Just one thing. So small. I almost missed it. The letters etched on the glass doors. Gone were the words WARLOCK & CO., LLC. Instead, this was the GLOBAL HQ FOR WARWICK & CO., LLC. Maybe no one else saw it. But I did.

The elevator doors opened, and out stepped Yolanda, Warwick's longtime assistant. She was carrying plastic bags with goods from CVS, what looked like candy. I had never seen Yolanda seated in a chair, ever. She was always on the go, responding to facts on the ground, talking down some pissed-off vendor, zhuzhing schedules to make work life more habitable. Factual, punctual, direct: she was the only person I'd ever heard Warwick apologize to.

"Feeling lost, Graham?"

I said, "It doesn't look right. No matter how long I stare."

"I know what you mean," she said.

"You do?" I asked, a note of hope in my voice.

I had always liked Yolanda: smart, practical, bored by office politics, grounded in the life of her kids at home and her aging parents in Trinidad. Maybe she was sensitive to what was happening. If nothing else, I was glad that she still knew who I was.

"You stare at anything long enough," she continued, "it feels that way. Like my hands: look, four fingers and a thumb. Nobody says it, but all the time I'm like, you know, hands are just *weird* looking. You know what I mean, love?"

"Yeah," I said, sadly.

"Don't get me started on toes!"

She pushed the doors open and I followed her. Only one day had elapsed since I was last here. Since the big all-hands meeting, Warwick's intro to Eddie. Everything looked familiar, but wrong. Unlike the change to the name etched on the door, I couldn't quite pinpoint the difference. There were still long rows of tables with young and youngish people working on laptops. Still the canteen with a keg at the back wall. Free snacks in large wire bins stacked in columns. A row of conference rooms behind a tinted glass wall. This was where I had spent countless hours, and what did I have to show for it? I stood outside the conference room that Warwick used as his office. The door was locked, the lights inside were off. Yolanda, at her desk, unwrapped three large bags full of Halloween candies. They rattled as she poured them into small dishes.

"Where's Warwick?"

She didn't bother to look up. "Somebody's getting their holiday spirit on early."

"I don't—what?"

"You're pulling an early Halloween trick, right?"

I said, "He asked me to come by. To see him."

"Hold on, love, I've got to get these candies out before the inmates revolt. You know how people get around the holiday. Then you can pull my other leg."

Down the aisle, the conference room door opened with a loud crack. People came out rapidly, engineers carrying laptops, a few of the designers, all of them looking irritated, disaffected. Some kind of stand-up meeting had not gone well. "He's such an asshole," a woman said.

"Whose meeting was that?" I asked as Yolanda returned.

"Blank's."

"Who's Blank?"

"Please, Graham. I'm getting a cramp from laughing."

I wandered over to the area where I once sat. Even though I knew it would be, I was startled to see all my stuff was gone—someone had even replaced the rolling chair I'd used. The tabletop was clear except for a laptop, a coffee mug, a port for charging, and a notepad. An empty workspace. Waiting to be filled. A piece of paper was taped to the back of the chair. The paper said BLANK.

Behind me, two engineers from the meeting were talking:

"And Blank never showed?"

"Nope."

"Asshole."

"Right?"

There was an org chart pinned to the wall nearby. I recognized it as one of the charts that Warwick had the HR team distribute after he'd announced Edmond's new division. But Edmond was gone now. Edmond's name was wiped from the book of life. I leaned in close, sort of like I did at Christie's when I was examining the portrait made by the AI. The box that once had Edmond's name now listed just one word: BLANK. As in, an empty position. Or, this is a free desk space. No one else saw it that way; they were taking the word literally. Or as literally as they could when no one could find a person who was named Blank.

I ripped the paper from the monitor and logged in to the laptop. "Hey, Graham," one of the engineers said, "isn't that Blank's desk?"

I tapped a key and stared at the password field. I began to type my username and password, then paused. Was this a good idea? Warwick was watching, somewhere. He was clearly using the algorithm, often.

He could do anything he wanted. All we could hope for right now was to avoid provoking him. But I'd gone this far. Why not keep going?

The password error flashed twice before I understood. Invalid. Unrecognized. Unknown. He'd taken away my access at last. I was locked out. I'd lost the power, as suddenly and unaccountably as it had appeared.

"Hey," someone said.

At my elbow, there stood a familiar stout, bearish man with a navy fleece vest. I knew him just by the faded light-blue jeans with rips in both knees and light-blue Vans that looked like they'd never been worn before. Doc smiled down at me, hungry as a jaguar in a tree.

"We know what you did to Edmond," he said.

I made the stupidest face I could and said, "Who's Edmond?"

He bared his whitened teeth. "You're a goddamn hoot, man."

Doc put a meaty hand on my shoulder. He had dark hairs growing between every knuckle. Each hair follicle kindled revulsion in me. "Come down to the conference room on nineteen with me. We want to walk you through the plan. We've got a lot of work to do. We had to take some drastic steps after you screwed things up. You-Know-Who has taken matters into his own hands."

Outside of drafting business plans, I never knew Doc to do anything more serious than kite flying, fleeing a beat cop, or passing out drunk on the sofa. The serious pose he struck was new, and so was the ominous heavy-hitter act. I figured he was talking about Warwick when he referred to You-Know-Who, as if Warwick was some big bad dude. Doc had changed, as if he'd been edited. If Warwick was changing his bosom buddy with the algo, then maybe things were getting darker than I realized. Then I had an even darker thought: maybe I'd changed. Not because of the algo. Because of what I knew. Eddie told me about Doc's hidden family history: the tragic backstory, his parents. Maybe that shaded his every word and deed, gave a tragic gravitas to somebody who was all boffo buffo before. I couldn't tell. He irked me, either way.

I opted to fake my way through. "Can't wait to dive in," I said.

Doc looked skeptical. He'd been hyped for a fight. I kept talking, almost babbling. "I'll meet you downstairs. Need to hit the head first. Too many coffees." I held up the coffee mug from the desk like a prop. "Gotta fill up every time I empty out, know what I mean?"

"Make it quick," he said.

He watched as I strolled to the men's room. This wasn't Doc's office, wasn't his start-up; he didn't know that adjacent to the men's-room door was the door to the fire stairs. From a distance, he would not be able to see which door I went in. Casually, calmly, with concealed intent, I opened the stairwell door and went through. Then ran down twenty flights of unpainted, cramped stairs, stopping every few levels to listen for the sound of pursuit.

I was a few blocks away when I felt safe enough to stop looking over my shoulder. I called Nessie while I walked. "I'll be at the apartment in twenty minutes," I said. "Are you there already?"

She said, "I couldn't get in."

"Did you show the doorman the key I gave you?"

"Your place isn't your place."

"I'll call them," I said. "Who was on duty? Was it Fatima?"

Nessie told me to slow down and listen. "Fatima was on duty, yes. She didn't know me. She didn't know you, either."

I had walked as far as Madison Square Park, stopping just inside the small gate that gave way to the large fountain at the center. Chatting pairs of people leaned against the fountain's wrought iron railing. Others sat alone on park benches studying their phones. Seated in the grass of the nearby lawn were boyfriends, girlfriends, husbands, mothers, kids. There was laughter, pleading eyes, rigid stares, arms around shoulders, happy mute togetherness: the whole gauntlet of social interaction. Had I ever really belonged? It felt like perhaps never. The world is a thing made by forces bigger than us. And yet, we broke it, we broke it like some program that we didn't understand. And now what?

"What do you think he's doing?"

"No idea," she said. "I checked the logs. He's been in the algo for weeks. I can't tell what he did versus what you were doing. But it's a lot."

"Weeks?" I said. "What else has he changed?"

Once again, she hesitated. Picking each word with care, she said, "Do you know how he made his money? I mean, the money that really got him started. Back during the dot-com bust-up."

"Network companies that went belly-up," I said.

"That's right," she said.

She didn't have to go on. I got it. Warwick owned all the network fiber, all the phone lines, all the fiber optics at key points in the network, which meant this conversation, like any other digital one, could easily be monitored by him, if he wished.

"Let's do this in person," she said. Then she hung up.

Uptown, then. Her place. I got in a taxi and shut my eyes and leaned back and tried to rest. But the cab driver had on talk radio. The host had a steroidal pitch and a paranoiac mood. "The world's a hot mess," he said. "Who's telling the truth, who's telling it slant, who can say? My guest this afternoon is an expert in the field of misinformation theory. He's also one of New York's most sought-after tech gurus, a real thought leader. David Warwick. David, can we talk about trust?"

"I'd love to," Warwick replied. "I think about trust all the time. What is it? How does it form? How far can it bend before breaking?"

"Hey," I said to the driver through the gap in the divider for front and back seat, "do you mind turning the radio off?" The driver made a sour face, muted the radio, then slid shut the divider.

In silence we drove up Madison Avenue, past high-end retail shops. The trees along the avenue were still green, but here and there a yellow leaf spiraled down like a wish for autumn. A television mounted on the divider wall flickered to life and filled with Warwick's face. He glanced from right to left and then directly at me. "There you are," he said. The world got weirder, but he kept getting calmer. I didn't say a word.

"Hey, amigo. Did you get my present?"

I looked out the window at the brick walls of the old armory.

"Graham. I can see you. I think I got the hang of this thing."

"I don't know what you mean."

"Your mom. I fixed her."

Glowering at him, I tried to mirror his calm, failed.

"That's not the real her," I said. "She's not herself."

"Don't you want to know how I did it?"

"Whatever you did, it didn't work."

Warwick made a hurt face. "Hey, bro, go easy on a guy? You didn't leave me much choice, after you deleted Edmond. But you know what? I accept it. Bet you didn't expect me to say that! I trust you, Graham, and I trust that you had a good reason. We're like brothers. We're in this together. We both want the same thing, right? To make the world a better place. You showed me what was possible. Now, I'm going to do what you don't have the nerve for. I started with your mom. Next, I'm going to give you what you always wanted."

I reached for the power button. Warwick held up a hand, signaled for one last moment of my time. "It's probably already happening," he said. "Have you noticed? She's falling in love with you. Or she will soon. It's complicated, this algo thing. Don't look confused. Nessie. Don't let her fool you. She's yours for the taking. And all I ask for in return is that you come back to the office, sit down, and help me plan out what we do next. I want to go big. To wipe out misinformation, full stop. To make trust inevitable. To disrupt the very nature of reality—"

I shut off the screen. Then waited for it to switch back on. But it stayed dark. He'd said his piece. I hated Warwick then. Hated him for knowing me so well and yet not at all. I hated him for trying to manipulate me through my feelings. He thought he could just rewire people, as if all of life's facts were just a database to rearrange in service of whatever vision he had in his head.

But what about Nessie? She had been furious in the hospital when I acted like we were together. But hadn't she also come to see my mom? She didn't have to come. Before all this began, we were just work buddies, people who shared inside jokes, wished each other well, but went their separate ways at quitting time. Now, we were . . . Well, what were we? It wasn't impossible that she was falling in love with me. I caught myself. I knew better. I had to know better. Had to remember. Anything else was just an illusion, a made-up world, a terrible place where everyone—Geraldine, Nessie, even me—was just a puppet on a hidden string.

CHAPTER 20

Instead of knocking, I slid the key to my apartment into the lock for Nessie's door. *This shouldn't work,* I thought. I didn't want it to work. If the key turned, if the lock opened, then Warwick's changes were taking effect. The lock clicked, the knob turned. One more fact replaced by a lie. The door to Nessie's home drifted open. Was this now my home? Our home?

From the doorway, I could see down the entry hall to the table where Nessie was working at her laptop with headphones on. Light from a window fell in an orange slant across her face. She looked up, startled, then relieved to see it was me. Me. Is this how it would feel to come home to her? She put her headphones on the table and came toward me. *Please, God, let her stop.* But she did not stop. She came up to me, put a hand on my shoulder, kissed my cheek.

"What's wrong?" she asked.

I swallowed down all hope and desire. "You don't usually kiss me hello," I said.

Her eyebrows drew together; she frowned.

"Sorry, dude, if I'm too glad to see you. It's kind of been a wild day."

I moved away from her, tried to make it look like I was too bothered by something else to argue with her. If I didn't look at her, it was easier to pretend Warwick's edits weren't in effect. Maybe I could ignore whatever she felt till we figured out how to undo everything.

"You were right," I said. "He's making edits. He told me in the cab."

"You took a cab up here *with* him?" Then she waved a hand in the air, as if to say *It doesn't matter.* "I've got news, too," she said. "I figured out the way to fix it. I know how to put everything back."

"You're amazing," I said.

She strode back to her laptop, not really listening to me. I breathed out, low and long. Around us I noticed the apartment was different. Gone were the obsolete tech displays along the wall. Instead, a single canvas painting filled the interior wall, floor to ceiling. I saw and recognized the silhouetted olive tree, tall as the room, the branches filled with owls, a snake, a helmet, a shield. The single cloud with a shaft of light, the woman in armor. All in the colors of a blue-and-green rainbow. I recognized the images: her tattoos. Except as large as a mural now.

I had so many questions. All I could manage was "Is this new?"

She looked from me to the mural, back again. Frowned with half her mouth. "Not that I know of," she said.

"Did you—who painted this?"

"It's one of my brother's," she said. "You know that."

She leaned over the laptop, pulled her hair back and tied it with an elastic band from her wrist. I didn't know what to say. Luckily, she didn't want me to say more. She seemed irritated with me, which was just as well. At least those were her own feelings, not feelings Warwick put on her. She turned the laptop around toward me. "Look at this," she said.

She had a window open to browse files used by the algo. I scanned the details and at once recalled an evening that felt like a lifetime ago: these were many of the first entries and associations that I browsed, back when I thought I was just going to help Nessie debug a new algo and maybe impress her.

"That's an old training dataset," I said. "It's out of date."

"Exactly," she said. She waited, watching my face as I followed in the footsteps of her thoughts. But I couldn't follow. Her mind went places where mine was afraid to tread. So she explained, "We don't know how the algo works. But we don't actually need to. It's what you put into the algo that matters. Like what you put into a vase is the point of the vase."

"I get it. I don't get it."

"The algo learns over time. It verifies everything against what it learns from the training data. It knocks out things that don't make sense. What it doesn't do, what it can't do, it doesn't think. It doesn't have a sense of identity. If there's a mismatch, it goes with what's on its safe list. But if we point the algo at this old data and if we reset the model, if we go back to the start, it won't resist. It will just start over. I was making daily backups in the beginning when I was debugging. It's a simple change. Restore the old world. Then, I'll overwrite the algo itself."

"Wait, break the algo? For good?"

"I'll replace the code with something simple, like a Hello, World function. Basically, I'll lobotomize it. Then no matter what Warwick does, he can't change anything. Neither can we."

I recalled the feeling when I first changed Benji. The sense of purpose as I labored on Eddie's details. If we broke the algo, then we could never use it again. For all the trouble it had caused, wasn't it also an incredible—*no, no, no,* I thought. "Let's do it," I said. "Let's do it right now. Why didn't you do it before I got here?"

"Slow your roll, champ. There's a problem."

"There always is," I said.

"I looked at what's in the first backup. And here's the thing— it's like an alternate version of the world. Or maybe it's the real one. Everyone is different. You wouldn't recognize yourself. The data is different everywhere. Data in social networks, in government databases. From everywhere. It's a snapshot of the world before the algorithm, but not really the world that I expected to see."

"Show me," I said. "Pull up my profile."

"No," Nessie said, putting a palm on my chest. "You shouldn't look. Think about what happens when you make an edit. Once the algo accepts the changes, everyone in the world believes it. Except you.

Because you know it's coming. You see through the change. And when you've told me what you're doing, or what you've done, then I haven't changed, either. Same for Warwick. Once someone knows the full context, the big picture, then the whole trick stops working. I made the algo. I was there at the beginning, made the first backup, pulled the first data together. It's safest if we return to the very first point, before anyone else saw."

I wanted to know what this other life looked like. I wanted to see what *I* looked like, in this alternate take. It was like being promised a peek at the core of my being. So many questions could be answered: Who are you, really? What kind of person are you at your core? Behind all the hopes and self-delusions? Maybe in this other world I was better, smarter, more successful. But I also wanted to revert all the changes I'd made, and she was right, this was the surest method.

"If this is true," I said carefully, "what happens to me?"

"What do you mean?"

"Will I remember this? Or will I forget? Or will I remember because you told me?"

"Honestly? I have no idea."

Her landline—an old-fashioned Bakelite phone on the sideboard—rang and startled both of us. I reflexively picked up the handset. If it was Warwick, then it meant he knew where we were. If it wasn't, well, he probably knew anyway.

"Hello?"

"Mr. Gooding, hello. My name is Benjamin Jameson."

"Benji?"

"I'm sorry, Mr. Gooding," he said, "only my wife calls me Benji."

"You don't remember me?"

"Please don't take it personally. But I'm glad to reconnect? I'm calling because I'm your court-appointed attorney."

"You're my what?"

"For the assault-and-battery charges. Brought by your pals at Bellevue? Turns out it's a pretty old claim—sort of surprising, comes from way back in 2004? Bad luck for you, there's a new law that passed extending the statute of limitations to fourteen years if a medical worker is involved. I'm wondering if you could come on down to the office and we can talk about your options—"

He was still talking as I nestled the phone in its cradle. Warwick was messing with my medical history. I'd seen a therapist a few times back in 2004, during that bleak period before Lycos, but assault charges? Bellevue? Plausible, I supposed, but not true. At least not as far as I knew.

"This doesn't look good," Nessie said from the window. A small crowd had gathered outside her front door. All of them were dressed in Halloween costumes, some with black robes like magicians, others in witchy wigs. Someone was carrying a pitchfork. Someone else was carrying a burning torch. Costume props, all of them. But, also somehow not.

"Wait," I said, "isn't that—aren't those your interns?"

"That one's from MIT," she said. "He never liked me."

"What are they here for?"

"Let's not find out."

She shrugged into her jacket, grabbed a cap from the coatrack near the door. She slid her computer into a laptop bag and led me to the kitchen at the back of the brownstone, to a narrow iron door with ancient hinges. It looked like a passage to the nineteenth century. A large iron dead bolt rattled as she pulled it open.

"We'll go through the courtyards," she said. "All of them are connected. Doors like these are the only ways through. They're not on any schematics. They're too old. We'll get to Broadway before they see us."

The brownstones were packed so tightly together that there was no way for anyone on the road to see our escape—even if they knew to look. Small, flimsy fences separated one backyard from another. We dodged around black metal charcoal grills and cut through overgrown gardens, past sheds filled with deck chairs.

The string of yards ended in a tall chain-link fence that barricaded the backyard of an apartment tower. I thought we were done for when I saw a chain on the last gate. But no one had clasped the lock. Or someone had unlocked it. Hard to say which. Either way, I knew who to give credit to. Nessie, as ever, had the foresight to make sure there was an escape route waiting for us. I started to thank her, but she was already through the gate ahead of me.

CHAPTER 21

"This can't be real," I muttered to Nessie. Evening had gathered the shadows of all the buildings into one dark hand. Nearly every adult on the street wore a costume, meaning Nessie and I stuck out in our regular clothes. Adults walked into stores and asked for candy from cashiers. Oddly, children wore everyday clothes and did not seem to be allowed to trick-or-treat.

"Stop talking," Nessie said. "Keep walking."

"I'm going to freak out if I don't keep talking."

"Then talk quieter."

"I'm just saying that if we are all part of a computer program, then all this makes so much more sense. A computer program that's going wrong all at once in catastrophic ways."

Jay Xi told me that we can't explain how network computers work in a strictly physical sense; this felt like a corollary to that idea. I couldn't explain where the break began, but the damage was everywhere.

Nessie exhaled in a quick hiss. A police officer strutted up to us. He was a tall young Hispanic man with a snake tattoo on his forearm. Suddenly, he grabbed my arm and pulled me close, close enough to smell licorice on his breath. I tensed, ready for him to holler for everyone else to look. "Trick! Or! Treat!" he shouted. Then he let go and ran away. The handcuffs on his belt were made of plastic; his costume had pins holding it together.

"I'm parked right here," she said.

She motioned down the block toward an old white Econoline van with no rear windows and bumper stickers that said { I BRAKE; FOR LOOPS; } and MY OTHER CAR IS A UNIVERSAL SERIAL BUS. Two orange parking tickets lay nestled under the windshield wipers. Nessie took purposeful, calm steps. The next person to approach us might not be looking for candy.

"Excuse me," someone called. A beautiful Indian woman dressed in a peacock-green sari appeared at my side. She had long brown hair, large sad eyes, and a pleading smile that made me stop and take notice. I knew her voice from somewhere.

"Mr. Gooding? Do you have a moment?"

That voice. Priti Desai. The patient advocate at Woodhull. I bristled, recalling how I'd hung up on her last time we spoke. She smiled, unbothered. "We should really speak about your mother." She leaned closer and whispered, "They're right behind you. Don't turn around. Keep walking."

Priti released me, and I turned back to thank her, and that was when I saw them. She was telling the truth: They were all behind us. A large group of people, none of whom I recognized. All of them were wearing white pants and white shirts and white hospital masks, like surgeons or nurses in infectious disease wards. The men's shirts had buttons down the left side of the front, like the shirts worn by orderlies, and the women had on old-fashioned dresses and caps. They swarmed me before I could speak or shout. I lost sight of Nessie.

"Great costumes," I said. "Can you all back up a little?"

"He's not doing well," one of the nurses said, her palm on my forehead.

"You guys are hilarious," I said, pushing her hand aside, "but I've got to go."

Two orderlies grabbed me, one for each side. Bent both arms behind my back. "Hold him still." I twisted, thrusting from side to side, but their fingers dug in hard. "He's stronger than he looks."

"He's all skin and bone."

"Easy with him," a familiar voice said. "Hold on. Hold up."

A crowd of white uniforms parted like waves, and Jay Xi walked toward me. He wore a pair of charcoal slacks and a blue Oxford button-down, no costume, thank God. His salt-and-pepper hair combed and neatly parted, the evil twin of the free-spirited Jay I once knew. The unhappiness in his face increased as he drew nearer to me, as if I were a proof he'd hoped not to find; he'd warned me this would happen, and I refused to listen.

"Graham," he said, "I'm sorry it came to this."

He opened a manila folder and withdrew a single piece of paper that he held up for me to read. The paper had three paragraphs printed on it; my heart thundered so hard that the words jumped around on me, but I could read enough to convey most of the message, a dire declaration: Paranoia. Delusions of grandeur. Threat to self. Danger to others. Due to incapacity of mother, long-deceased father, legal guardian needed. JAY GOEDEL XI assumes role. At the bottom, wobbly signatures: Jay's, mine. Dated less than a month ago.

"I never signed this," I said.

Jay rubbed my shoulder, tried to radiate reassurance. "Graham, Graham, we're going to get you help, buddy. I'm not giving up on you. You've been working too hard. This thing with the algo? It's all in your head, man. We're going to get help so that you can see that. So that you can be well again. You can go back. We just want to make things better. Isn't that what you want? A world where everything makes sense again? No more confusion. No more disorientation. A place where things make sense. Where every input has a predictable output. Where you can trust in what you see, in what you hear. Doesn't that sound good?"

"You sound like Warwick," I said.

"Can I ride with him?" Jay asked one of the men in white.

"'Fraid that breaks protocol," the man said.

"Nessie!" I shouted. "Nessie, where are you?"

Jay looked sadder than ever. Made an all-clear gesture to someone behind me. "Hang in there, bud," he said. "I'm pulling for you."

Then he stepped back, and I was shoved downward on a stretcher. They held me in place and lifted me into an ambulance at the side of the road. There was talk among them, nothing directed to me. The doors slammed shut on me: a valuable but insensate heirloom. A relic of another time.

I kept very quiet, very still on the stretcher. The ambulance began to roll. Three men sat in the back, staring at their phones. None of them spoke or looked at me. The siren never came on. The ambulance waited with other traffic at red lights. They were bringing me somewhere. But with no haste, no urgency. No one interacted with me; I was mere cargo, like an idle tool, an artificial intelligence on standby. A worrisome idea kept returning: *What if that's all I am?* What if Nessie made me as she made Eddie and all the previous Warlock chatbots? Built on a neural network of associations and almost but not quite sentient, bound by the attributes assigned to me by math.

The ambulance braked hard. We'd arrived somewhere. Someone opened the back doors. The three men who rode with me jumped out. I waited to be lifted, but no one moved me. Outside, a loud siren was wailing, getting louder, closer. The three men hustled to the side as a red FDNY ambulance pulled up alongside us. The driver was wearing a clown costume, dusty white face paint, and a rainbow wig.

"I got three guys back there in bad shape," he said.

"Fire?"

"Building collapsed on Joralemon. One of those fancy old houses."

"After they went in?"

A third ambulance pulled into the emergency bay, more shouts, more sirens. No one noticed me. I sat up from the stretcher. I still had my regular clothes on. I was not restrained. I was no one's priority. Sliding out of the ambulance, I walked to the back of the bay. A security guard sat at a desk; he looked up from a laptop, which he was using to watch *Looney Tunes* on YouTube. He raised his eyebrows, waited to hear what I had to say.

"Sorry," I said. "Isn't this the visitors' entrance?"

"Around the block," he said, then turned to address someone else and muttered, "What a maroon," under his breath. I walked through the hospital's automatic doors. A long beige corridor stretched out ahead of me. No one looked my way. I had never been in this corridor before, but the signs and the beige-and-burgundy wallpaper made me suspect I was in the same hospital as Geraldine. I felt guilty for having abandoned her here this morning. This despite my certainty that the Geraldine in that room was not the mother I knew. Even though she could not possibly be the same person. I wondered if I could go up to see her. Maybe to say goodbye. One last time. One more look to make sure. I could be wrong. Maybe I was wrong.

As I waited for the elevator, a video screen on the wall clicked three times, and Warwick appeared, no surprise. He stood in a room that looked like a bunker: all bare concrete walls and a large map of New York City behind him. A bank of blinking blue lights in the background, rows of servers. He wore a black beret and an olive shirt with shoulder epaulets, collar open for rakish flare. The clothing fit snugly, trim; the beret on his silver hair signaled authority.

"Hey, now," he said. "Time to get serious."

I hit the elevator button many times in rapid succession.

"This is my last pitch," he said. "I don't want to do this without you. It's a lot messier if I do it on my own. But I can't wait. We have a moral obligation to use power like this. If you'd ever really used it, if you'd edited the world to do a thing that you truly wanted, you'd understand. Let me show you."

"Hard pass," I said. "What's with the new look?"

He grinned, touched his chest as if for luck. "Do you know what the most trusted institution in America is, Graham?"

"Uh, guys in berets?"

He pressed his lips together, tilted his head a fraction. A deadly serious sparkle lit those cold blues. "Cute," he said. "You're making a funny." All his surfer-dude sangfroid, the aw-shucks patter, the affability—all of it had evaporated, and what was left looked a lot like smug self-regard.

Was this who he'd always been, underneath? Or had the algo changed him—not literally, mind you—with its limitless potential? There was no way to know. All I knew was that I didn't like who he was now.

"The most trusted institution is the military," he explained. "It's five times more trusted than Congress. Twice as trustworthy as organized religion or banks. And do you know why it's trusted, Graham? Because it doesn't dither. It doesn't pontificate. It acts. That's what I'm doing. I'm doing what no one else will." Behind him, the blue LED lights on servers flickered, then flashed faster. He said something to someone off-screen, then turned back to me.

"Are you in, Flynn, or what?"

Rather than answer—how many different ways could I say no?—I ducked through the door to the stairwell. Hustled up four flights to Geraldine's floor. Pushed open the door and found myself in a long, deserted hallway. None of the rooms were occupied, and no one was at the nurses' station at the end of the hall. Someone grabbed my elbow, and instinctively I pulled away. I expected to see Doc, or maybe Jay, or one of the men in white uniforms from the ambulance. Instead, looking tan and fit, was none other than the estimable Dr. Esme Haber. She wasn't wearing her scrubs; she had on a long white coat, and her stethoscope hung off her neck. She was shorter than I remembered.

"Don't do it," she said. "Turn around."

"I'm going to see my mother."

She spoke in a careful manner, as if to avoid overfilling me with too much of the truth at once. "He's manipulating you. That's why he brought her back from her coma. He's in her room. He's downstairs. He's in your phone. He's on the radio. He's on the electronic billboard. He's everywhere. Don't you get it? Warwick is an AI. He's always been an AI."

"That's impossible."

"Don't go to Geraldine's room."

"I want to say goodbye to her. Even if it's not really her. I need to say it."

Dr. Haber touched my elbow gently, said nothing. I felt the urge to weep; no, I felt the memory of weeping. I'd already wept for Geraldine. A torrent of grief, as large as a glacier, was inside me; something I'd carry forever, or for as long as glaciers last. "You already said goodbye to her," she said. "A long time ago."

The corridors wavered, and the doctor's face blurred. The hurt of losing my mother for good was in the room with me. Something that everyone knows will happen at some point but that suddenly I knew had already happened at some point in the past. Yet I couldn't move past it. Couldn't make it historical. I could not rationalize it to avoid the pain, either. I couldn't make a puzzle out of how or who or what had happened, couldn't deflect the feelings, which were fiercer than anything I can explain. The tears left my eyes as quickly as I could wipe them away.

"How do you know all this?" I asked.

"Nessie," she said. "You need to find Nessie."

She opened a door that led to a staircase lined with cinder blocks. I ran down all the flights to the bottom. I kept thinking, *You could still go back, go up instead of down.* The Geraldine that was not my mother was still in a room up there, and I could choose to accept the falsehood, if I wanted. I could play pretend, like Warwick suggested. It would feel better than the pain in my chest. But it wouldn't be real. It wouldn't be right. I had to accept that she was gone, and that holding on to the idea of her, the likeness of her, did a dishonor to the real her, held back a piece of her essence from whatever lies on the other side of living.

I emerged into a loading garage with pallets full of sterile needles, cafeteria serving trays, and plastic cups. Bins on rollers that had LAUNDRY printed in block letters on the side. And, standing beside a pedal rickshaw, arms folded over her chest and looking satisfied with herself, was none other than Nessie Locke, the not-so-secret love of my life.

"Come on," she said. "Let's get out of here."

I climbed into the rickshaw with her. "Warwick—he's a real person, right? You didn't build him? Like you built Eddie?"

She turned my chin, peered into my eyes. "What did they do to you in there?"

"They messed with my head," I said.

A man in the driver's seat addressed Nessie in a language I could not place. Taped to the divider was a card with his operator's license and his name: வெற்று இடம். Nessie spoke back in the same language, pointed south.

"Where'd you learn Chinese?"

"That's Tamil. I learned it in Singapore. My brother lived there."

Her brother, the vegan anarchist. The specter from her past that flitted through the present. What was his story? What was he to her? There had never been time to ask. *Tell me everything you loved about your brother,* I wanted to say. *Tell me why every time you mention him, a sadness glimmers in your eyes. But not now. We don't have time.*

The driver pedaled hard, steering the rickshaw around potholes and a slow-moving city bus. Nessie closed her eyes and leaned into the cushioned seat, but I couldn't relax. The tall buildings were too close, the sidewalks too wide, storefront shops all wrong. I had thought I was in Woodhull Hospital, my mom's hospital, but now I wasn't so sure. This wasn't Brooklyn. We were in Manhattan, somewhere near the East River. How could I have seen Dr. Haber? How could I have seen the wing where my mom's room was? Nothing made sense. Unless Warwick changed things, somehow. He couldn't just copy and paste a hospital onto the Upper East Side . . . could he? We passed a power substation and a group of workers standing around a hole in the road. A truck nearby had WARWICK POWER written on the side. On a side street, a crane swung its ball hard against the side of a tall chimney, sending bricks and debris into the street. A construction worker turned on a portable sign that declared ZERO EMISSIONS OR BUST: WARWICK PROMISES. All the traffic lights on the street ahead went dark at once.

I said, "This won't end well."

A traffic cop in the intersection snapped his head around, laser-eyed our rickshaw. In all directions cars swerved and braked to avoid collisions, horns flared, tires squelched, scudded. But through all that he had heard my voice; maybe he'd been listening for it all along. He pointed a gloved finger.

"Stop them! Warwick!"

Nessie shouted in Tamil at our driver, who stood up, leaned far over his handlebars, and pedaled with all his weight. We swerved around two white Maserati coupes, one T-boned into the other, both smoking. Up ahead, another white Maserati gushed coolant from where it struck a streetlamp. The rickshaw driver jumped the curb. The shouts of pedestrians:

"They're over warwick! Warwick that warwick!"

"Warwick!"

"Warwick warwick warwick!"

He'd finally gotten just what he wanted. His name was on everyone's lips. The literal dream he'd once confessed he had for his career. The rickshaw driver veered down a side street, and voices calling *warwick* faded behind us. At the next intersection, we merged back into the traffic—here, the traffic lights worked again, but here, also, all the cars were white Maseratis. I slid down in my seat. "Tell me that Warwick isn't behind the wheel of each one," I said.

"They're not all Warwicks," she said.

"Not all?"

The rickshaw driver braked hard, cut through a gap in a fence near the FDR overpass. We coasted through a bumpy but empty lot. He breathed hard, winded from the exertion. I thanked him in English, and he nodded, but I doubt he understood. For a few moments, the city felt mostly normal. I smiled at Nessie. She was watching the sky over downtown. Up in the air, a skywriting airplane spelled out letters one puff at a time: WARWICK IS WATCHING.

The lot ended, and we bounced along another frenetic street, sidewalks packed with people in costume, white Maseratis at stop signs,

Maseratis double-parked, Maseratis idling in tow-away zones. We slowed near City Hall Park; the lawn was larger and greener, and where City Hall itself belonged, there was now an enormous gold statue of a man in military fatigues and a beret.

"Don't tell me that's him," Nessie said.

Every intersection and run of road felt charged; new shadows fell from buildings that weren't there before, orange dusk reflected in huge zigzag glass facades that were brownstones minutes earlier. We rode till the end of the island, the shores of the Hudson.

The rickshaw driver braked to a stop at a pier where ferries run from one side of the Hudson to the other. Oddly, Warwick's influence waned here. Families sat on blankets on the grass in the park along the river, enjoying the last shine of the evening. No costumes. Teenagers skateboarded on the steps. A traffic cop wrote a ticket for a Fresh Direct truck in a No Standing zone.

Nessie said something in Tamil to the driver.

"Warwick," the driver responded.

She smiled at me and whispered, "Walk fast."

Nessie was a few steps ahead as we walked along the sidewalk toward the pier. She passed a video screen on the side of a bus terminal. The screen flickered, Warwick appeared: no beret now, his hair tousled. Beads of starry sweat on his forehead. Blue lights flickering in the background. Everything had gone to hell, but he radiated gravitas, martial authority, privilege.

He said, "You've outdone yourself, Graham."

I thought he was talking to me, that these words were meant to slow me down. But the picture flickered, and another man appeared. A resurrected Edmond, I thought, but then realized no, this person looked paler, gaunt, like he hadn't eaten well in ages—thinning hair, a dour mouth, and wide eyes like a child's. Dressed in fatigues, with a lieutenant's bars on the lapel.

"Howdy, Graham," the man said. His voice was my voice.

"I couldn't get you to come around," Warwick said, "so I did the next best thing."

"Next best?" Lt. Graham said, feigning umbrage.

Warwick punched Lt. Graham in the arm. "Love this guy," he said. "He's got every little detail planned out. You'd love him, too, Graham. He's recasting the city from the ground up."

"Obviously, he'd love me," Lt. Graham said. "He's me!"

They chortled like fat cats who'd struck it rich again, or should I say, *we laughed*, he and the other me. Seeing my likeness yuck it up with Warwick, I felt nauseated, felt as if I might vomit. That wasn't me, but it *was* me; that was how I acted. Nessie was on the dirt path beside the ferry. I looked at her till she was all I could see. I staggered toward her.

Lt. Graham and Warwick called after me in unison, shouting what sounded like their new catchphrase: "Ambiguity is the enemy of trust!"

The boat crew raised the metal gangway after I stepped aboard. We hadn't bought tickets, and Nessie paid an extra twenty dollars as a penalty. I eyed strangers and boat staff with equal suspicion. We found a spot on the upper deck, away from the crowd. She put a hand on my shoulder. "You okay?"

"No," I said, "not okay." Any other answer was a lie, we both knew, and admitting the hard truth felt better than lying. She nodded, kept her hand on my back, as if she sensed I was at risk of tumbling overboard. I leaned against her as the boat yawed in the tide. The madness fell away like the skyline, and beneath us the boat engines churned, ferrying us to the other side.

CHAPTER 22

The motel was located at the entrance to the Holland Tunnel, a long slab of brick two stories tall, small windows; it looked at least thirty, maybe fifty years old, a relic of sleepier analog days. Inside, the lobby was shabby but clean, sickly potted plants along a wall, a faded sofa and wing chairs, a service counter for registration. Through a wall of safety glass, a clerk told us a room was available—a family from Tennessee had failed to show for their reservation.

The place was so low tech that we felt safely out of the algo's reach. Nessie paid in cash for the room. She wrote a pair of egregiously fake names in the ledger—Patty and Joe Chip. The clerk asked for a photo ID, standard protocol. Nessie laid three large-denomination bills on the counter. Without a word, the clerk whisked the bills from sight, no more ID required.

Our room on the second floor looked over the parking lot. We lowered the blackout blinds over the windows, and every few minutes I would inch back a blind and peek outside, watching, waiting.

"No one knows we're here, Graham."

"You keep telling me that."

The room was surprisingly modern: glass-walled shower, flat-screen television, brand-new coffee machine on a shelf. But the queen-size bed sagged when you sat on it, and there wasn't enough room to walk around Nessie when she sat at the lone desk to work at her laptop.

The motel had no Wi-Fi, another thing that put us at ease. But eventually, we had to connect to the internet. Nessie turned her phone into a hotspot. Finding us now would be laughably simple. Her phone tethered to a cell tower, and that tower had a physical address. We might as well send up a flare that spelled out *Hey, we're in Jersey!* But we had no other real options.

Once, twice, twenty times, I went to the window. I studied the rows of cars in the parking lot. Not a single Maserati. A blue Toyota RAV4, a filthy Dodge minivan, a Honda Civic with a busted headlight, a mud-colored Ford Explorer. Same positions as the last time, and the time before. But there was no guarantee we'd stay safe. Any second, the world around us could change. Warwick could knock at the door. Or Eddie. Or Doc. Or Lt. Graham. Then what?

I said, "Listen, I need to talk to you. About what Warwick told me."

Nessie spoke as she typed. "Can it wait?"

"It's just, well, before everything resets. I want to ask you something."

"Please. Graham. I need to concentrate."

I marched back and forth to the window while she worked on the laptop. There was nothing else for me to do while she made the changes. My legs were tired and my head hurt, but I couldn't sit still. Everything and everyone that I knew had been edited or suffered a collateral change. Some by my hand, some not, didn't really matter which. I could go running into the lines of traffic at the tunnel entrance, could run from driver to driver shouting that they were all in danger, that the world was cracking apart right under their noses, and it wouldn't matter. Nobody would believe me. We were alone now.

"Okay," Nessie said. "It's done."

"That's it?"

She rubbed her eyes and smiled at me absently. "Technically, the model still needs to process the backup data, the old dataset. Then a new process has to replicate. It's at ten percent. But it's inevitable now."

Inevitable wasn't the same as *done*. I wouldn't relax until I knew there was no chance for failure. I looked outside at the parking lot again. Civic, RAV4, Explorer, Dodge. Like a litany prayer. Thought about how life could possibly ever feel normal again. I let the blind fall back into place.

"What's the percentage now?"

She shut the laptop and tossed it aside. We both stared at the rectangle of metal where it lay on the brown bedspread. "It'll finish on its own time," she said. With the old data back in the algo's virtual grasp, we just had to wait for life's facts to revert to the way they once were. Nessie had written a script that would execute after all the internal processing finished, at which point the algo itself would get overwritten. Then it was "Hello, World!"—the old world, the real one.

"So, let's hear it," she said. "What did Warwick say?"

I sat on the sagging bed, she stayed in the chair. There's nothing homey about a motel room. Everything is ersatz. This isn't your home. That isn't your food in the minibar. That isn't a painting you chose on the wall. It's a perfect counterfeit of a place where someone belongs.

"He told me something about you and me."

She pulled her legs underneath herself, settled in. "Can't want to hear this," she said.

"Do you remember, at the hospital, when you—well, when my mom assumed we were, like, we were a thing?"

"No," she said.

"Wait—you don't remember?"

"I'm messing with you, Graham. Of course I remember."

"Warwick told me that he was setting you up to fall in love with me. He said he used the algo. That's why, when I came to your apartment, and you kissed me . . ." I let the words trail off.

"Ahhh," she said. "You think I've got a thing for you. Thanks to Warwick."

"No, no, I mean, no, it's just, that's what Warwick said." The more I said, the less what I said made sense. I tried again. "He said you might not tell me. So I'm telling you that I know. That you should know it's not real, if you, like . . ."

"I should know any feelings I have for you aren't real?"

"Yeah."

"But how could he know?"

"I told you, he told me he made the edit."

"No, I mean, how can anyone know for sure where feelings come from? Feelings aren't like facts. It's not like what you did with Eddie. We were dealing with a made-up person then. Feelings aren't so cut-and-dried; they're not as tangible as a person, even a fake person. There's no one moment when somebody is locked in to love. There's no permanently in love or out of love. Whatever the algo does, it doesn't fix feelings. People do that. With people, there's always ambiguity, always a risk. Love's crazier than a quantum state. If Warwick ever actually loved anything, he'd know that."

She left me speechless, nodding along at each word. It took me a moment to realize that she didn't really admit to what she did or did not feel. We sat there, me on the bed and her at the desk. Of course, the most important part was what I hadn't said, hadn't told her yet: how I felt. She glanced at the digital clock on the desk. "How long did it take when you edited Benji?"

"Not nearly this long."

She gestured at the clock, but also, I understood, at our whole conversation. "You want to keep talking about this?"

I felt achy all over, as if I'd just sprinted a mile. "Not really," I said.

"Me neither," she said.

We went down to the motel lobby to see if anything looked different at street level. The same night manager was at the window playing a game on her phone. We wandered into the motel's shabby restaurant, a dark room with high-top tables and framed sepia photos of New York landmarks. Chairs were stacked upside down on tables, and a sign said the kitchen had closed hours ago. Nessie leaned over the bar and then came back up with a bottle of whiskey and a red twelve-ounce can of Coca-Cola.

"Jack and Cokes at the end of the world?"

"Sounds perfect to me," I said.

We left a twenty-dollar bill on the counter. I checked it to make sure the portrait on the front was right. It wasn't. Warwick was there, grinning upward. I flipped the bill over so that I would not have to look at his portrait; written on the back were the words IN TECH WE TRUST.

"What's wrong?" Nessie asked.

"Nothing," I said. "Let's go to the roof."

The stairwell was narrow and poorly lit, but it led us to the top of the building. A utility door had a sign that read NO GUEST ACCESS, but we pushed it aside and stepped into the cool night air. The roof had a gravel surface and a waist-high wall that served as a railing. Someone had set up two metal folding chairs near the edge; beside one of the chairs was a coffee can filled with cigarette butts. To the east, you could see the city and all its bright boxes, like an apothecary wall of glittering volcanic glass that ran as far north as we could see.

Nessie poured the drinks into plastic cups. We tapped the soft rims together.

"To what's real," I said.

"Whatever that is," she said.

She sipped, then bit at her lip. I started to ask her what she thought reality was, but then I quit. There was no point in putting forth the question. No one was qualified to judge the accuracy of any given answer. People have been asking since Descartes and Zhuangzi and earlier, and still nobody knows.

"How do you think it worked?"

"What?"

"The algo. You made it."

"I don't know," she said. "Who can? Reality is a client-side application."

I swallowed my drink wrong, coughed and laughed.

I leaned on the railing edge and studied the cars queued up near the Holland Tunnel. Shuttles, subcompacts, large sedans, taxis with people coming from the airport. Overall, not a lot of traffic; most people had probably already arrived where they needed to be for the night. Another day done. Ending just like all the previous ones. As far as they could tell.

"I didn't think it would take this long," I said.

"Maybe it's not going to be noticeable," Nessie said.

"I thought it'd be like rebooting a PC. Like, we'd go back in time, reset to start."

For a few moments we both stared at the view. The Jersey City buildings close by, and, farther in the distance, the variegated ridge of Manhattan, its streetlights and beacons, the tall towers with flood lights, the veering cars, the man-made stars. I wanted to say something profound; nothing came.

"Maybe it will be more like forgetting," Nessie said.

A truck blatted its horn on the road below. A line of taillights lit up bright red, dozens of feet banging on brake pedals at once, countless little changes in concert, like facts changed by the algo. We weren't triggering a big bang. We were not changing the past. We were changing what we remembered, a million little details wiped away. Like failing to recall a word, a name, a place, and thinking it's fine until it's too late, you've forgotten what you wanted.

I was reminded of my mom, the real Geraldine, not that chatty, fake person at the hospital. I recalled the worst memory that I had of her, the day when I had the first clear sign of how far her memory loss had progressed. I called her late in the evening. She had not called to wish me a happy birthday, and I had to remind her. But forgetting my birthday was not all that unusual. Or significant. It had happened before. She felt terrible, as she had many times before, and I did not give her too hard of a time. *At least,* I said, *you never remember the birthdays of your other sons, either.* There was a brief, terrible silence, a void that would have been filled with laughter if I had a mother whose sense of her life was still whole; but for Geraldine, all I heard in that silence was terror, a terrible fear that there were other children in her past once and she had forgotten them in her fogged present. *G&G and nobody else,* we'd always said, but suddenly she couldn't be sure.

"Let's head back down," Nessie said. "I'm wiped."

Back in the room, we sat on the bed and told stories of the good old days. That first day on the job when I saw her standing on a chair, changing a light bulb. The Mardi Gras we spent in New Orleans with Warwick, thinking we'd have fun, but all we did was prep for his TED speech. The time Warwick hired a lewd shadow puppeteer to emcee the company holiday party. This was the time to confess the life I wished that I had with her. This was the time to confess the depth of my feelings. But I kept hesitating, kept delaying.

"That painting of your brother's. The one in your apartment. Your tattoos," I said, my throat aching, "they were just like that. The same pictures. You know? I know you don't remember the tattoos. That you can't. But, like, why do you think—"

She cut me off. "My brother moved to Singapore when I was just a kid, and I didn't see him till I was twenty-two, when I went there to visit. He took me to underground rock shows in Little India, where they had these fabulous murals. He liked to paint, but he did graffiti, which was illegal, so he had to hide his equipment—God, I wanted my entire adult life to be like that, going out late with him, watching him play guitar and paint. But, well, it didn't turn out that way. Breaking any rule in Singapore is a pretty big deal, and he wasn't only doing graffiti. He had a drug habit. He OD'd. I never saw him again. He was my hero, you know? Growing up? But he was so fucked-up. I miss him so much."

"You could have used the algo, maybe you still could," I said, even though I knew that we'd just broken it. The words fell out of me, unbidden: "Use it to make life what you wanted. You could bring him here. He could have lived here in New York. Maybe there's still time? You could make one last change?"

She studied me. "He passed a long, long time ago," she said. "But you're sweet. It's all right. I've made my peace."

An ache welled up in me. The need to console her. The need to be close to her. *Now*, I thought. *Tell her now. See what she says. Maybe she'll feel something back. Maybe it'll be real. Maybe it already is. Maybe it has nothing to do with what Warwick did. Anything could happen. Anything can happen. If you try.* But I couldn't do it.

She got up and staggered to the minibar. "Let's see what we have here," she said. She opened a pack of Oreos and a bag of cashews. "I hope I'm not around to have to pay for all this tomorrow," she laughed.

We laughed together, hard, maybe harder than the moment warranted. She cupped my chin in one of her hands. God, what a feeling. Then she let her hand drop. "I'm tired, G."

"Don't go to sleep," I said.

She laughed. "Why not? Won't I wake up as a butterfly?"

We ate the last of the cashews. I went to the minibar for more. I found peanut M&M's way in the back. Stared at the logo on the bag in my hand. *This is how life can be,* I thought. I wished the night would never end, that we could be in this in-between state forever.

I turned around smiling, ready to ask her more questions about her hopes and dreams, but she'd fallen asleep. Stretched out on the bed with one arm thrown over her eyes to shade them from the light.

I stood briefly watching her sleep. I thought of what she'd said about her brother. I thought about that kiss she gave to Ed. I thought about her house, her dogs. Or was it just one dog? *I don't know her. Not really. But I'm crazy about her. Tomorrow. I can tell her tomorrow. When we are fully clear of the algo. Because then we'll really be ourselves, right? Then I'll know that whatever she says, however she reacts, it's really her.*

Nessie saw, Nessie knew what was coming. She'd looked at the original data. I hadn't seen. She hadn't wanted me to see. This was the first moment when I had time to seriously consider what she'd said. Yes, she had seen that reverting to a backup was the cleanest way to make sure life went back to normal. But there also might be something more, something that she didn't want to see. Maybe something awful. Maybe *I* was someone awful.

Nessie's laptop was on the nightstand. I moved it to the desk, sat in the chair, opened the screen. Stared at the password prompt. I had a bad habit of looking at Nessie's passwords. One more privilege I indulged in as head of ops. I'd had trouble with network admins, security experts who wanted to hash Warlock passwords—it's basic privacy protocol, they said. I always overruled them. Each password was a window on her mind. *Bl@ckS@bb@th1970*, her favorite album. *S1ngap0r3-2007*, a shoutout to her brother, I now realized. Some passwords were opaque alphanumericals, others were discernible but obtuse, like her most recent: *B3rgd0rf-w1nd0ws-1117*. I knew that I shouldn't use her password to look at the data. But I wanted to, and I would have, except Nessie stirred in her sleep, made a coughing noise.

I shut the laptop hastily, went to the window. Counted cars. Civic, RAV4, Dodge, Explorer. No Maseratis. Nessie didn't move, but I felt strange, lingering while she slept. I tucked the laptop under my arm, went quietly out the door. Rode the elevator to the lobby. The clock on the wall downstairs read 4:44, surprising me. I had thought it was earlier. The night manager was dozing in her chair at the counter.

What will it be like, this world as it was, not as we broke it to be? Had it already happened? I didn't think so. But I had no way to be sure. I tried to get straight in my head everything that had happened. My memory already felt a little fuzzy. I needed to write down the important things, things I wanted to be sure I would remember on the other side.

I gently shook the night manager awake.

"Pen and paper," I said. "Can I borrow some?"

She rummaged around, found a blue ink pen, no paper. She went back to sleep before I could ask if maybe there was letterhead in a locked drawer.

I sat at a table in the dark restaurant and began to make notes. In my wallet I found a slim stack of business cards, mine. Sort of. GRAHAM A. GOODING was written in the center. Then, underneath: CHIEF WORRYING OFFICER. A gag gift from Warwick, a relic from another age. I turned the cards to the blank space on the back and began to write, one idea per card. A short but important list of things that I wanted to, that I needed to, remember.

1. Don't trust Warwick.
2. Don't play with any strange algos.
3. Let your mom go when the time comes.
4. Tell Nessie how you really feel.

I thought of Nessie, asleep upstairs. If the world was returning to normal, what did her arms look like? Had the tattoos begun to reappear, the blue-green feathers, spears, clouds, patterns, the reminders of her brother? I hoped so. It startled me, how much I wanted her to be happy. I remembered how close she came to telling the whole story of her first tattoo, that night at Grand Central. If I could, I'd go back to that moment and I'd listen better, I'd ask more questions, I'd push harder to learn.

I tapped the business cards into a neat pile, slid the stack back into my wallet. Time to look at the data. Time to log in to her laptop. Time to face whatever it was that was real. I had to do it. Even if it put the whole plan at risk. I trusted Nessie. But the nature of trust was different in a world where everything you know can change without anyone knowing it. Strangely, the laptop was not where I had placed it on the table. *Odd,* I thought. I checked the floor, the other chairs. Perhaps the night manager had tiptoed in, stole it while I was lost in thought?

In the lobby the night manager was not at her post. I called out, no answer. I turned toward the lobby door, but the door was gone. So was the wall. So was the parking lot. As far as I could see, nothing but blank blackness. I backed away, stumbling as I moved, hands out, scrabbling for my footing. The carpet was underfoot, and the hallway walls stood firm, but the elevator, the ceiling panels, all were gone. In their place: nothing, emptiness, void.

I ran for the staircase, threw wide the door. But found no stairs. No roof overhead. Above, the night sky hung huge, pockmarked with the light of insistent stars, but the stars were vanishing, just a few, then more, more and more. From one horizon to another, a great vast nothing spread out, spilled like a flood over a plain, enormous, unrelenting.

"Nessie!"

I tried to shout, but I could make no sound.

I tried to keep from forgetting the images I had of her, the idea of who she was, and in the brief timeless moment I had left, I tried to gather into indelible memory everything that had happened to us since the algo began—Nessie seated at Grand Central; in the dark of Warwick's yard searching for her dog; in the hospital room holding Geraldine's hands; gliding across the city in a rickshaw; on this motel rooftop with the lights of Manhattan in our faces—

PART V

CHAPTER 23

I wake up disoriented, with an ache in my chest. Outside, overcast skies glow with mealy predawn light, and I know that I've slept for hours, but I don't feel the refreshment of slumber. Something's bothering me. Gradually, I place myself in terms of space and time. My apartment. Manhattan. Fall. 2018. I close my eyes, but before the hood of sleep slips over me again, I remember: my mom. The thing I feared would happen has happened. She's gone, I'm still here; life continues, but everything's wrong.

Growing up in a small town upstate near the Esopus Creek, I woke up like this often, and I would lie in bed terrified by the fear that I'd never figure out what to do with life, never find a way to pay for food or a roof over my head. Often, I laid in that panic till Geraldine got up and showered. The sound of water in the pipes and the knowledge she was alive and well would be enough for me to relax, for drowsiness to settle in, sometimes for sleep to return along with the vague fuzzy feeling that I was part of a home, a society, a world that cares for its own.

I don't lie in bed like that anymore. There's no one to listen for. Instead, I get up whenever I wake up, even if it's painfully early on a workday. I pour cereal and eat by the light of the TV. A habit from childhood.

To escape the shuttered gloom of home, I leave early for work. Summer isn't officially over, but sunlight bounces off cars and mirrored buildings with a weary slant, and packs of commuters and school kids roam the streets. Instead of taking a bus or subway, I walk the twenty-two blocks to work because it gives me time to think, and because averaging twenty thousand steps a day keeps me trim, fit. I was a chubby kid. There's no nice way to put it. I took things apart and built weird model sets and kits for mechanical devices. I kept to myself. Sometimes when I look at myself as an adult, I see traces of that kid in my cheeks, or in the push and give of my gut, flab at my thighs. It's a neurosis, and my doctor tells me that I'm underweight, really. Shows me charts to prove her point. Doesn't help.

The headquarters for Warlock & Co. is in the Garment District on the fourth floor of an ancient multitenant building with elevators that shudder between floors and washrooms frigid in winters and fetid year-round. I unlock the front door to our workspace and turn on the lights. I'm the first person to arrive. I think I was also the last person to leave on the previous workday, a Friday that feels like a lifetime ago. I can't remember what's on my calendar today, but I've got time to check before anyone else arrives.

We call this our headquarters, but it's not a very large space: room for twenty worker bees at long communal tables, four conference rooms, a private phone pod, a proper office for the boss. It's the fanciest space we've ever had, but it's not actually fancy. The floors groan, the windows leak cold air, and if you talk above a whisper in the phone pod, everybody outside can still hear you. Warwick told me once he thinks the whole building was once a factory that manufactured buggy whips before the horseless carriage destroyed the market for whips. I'm pretty sure he's full of shit.

The place was empty when we signed the lease. I was so proud that I brought my mom to see it, right around the time she moved to the city, an assisted-living site in Brooklyn. I'd done all the negotiation for the lease. Geraldine said the sunlight coming in the windows was good enough to paint by—never mind the fact that it was reflected off a tall building across the street. *Such high ceilings,* she said. *You could hang chandeliers if you wanted and still have room.* When she saw

Warwick's office, she just stood in the door, frowned briefly, shuffled on. She never learned to like him, didn't get what I saw in him, but left it at that. I had hoped to bring her back again when the place was full of workers—we had big aspirations for the place—but she took a turn for the worse, never visited again. I was so optimistic about her move to the city, but nothing turned out as I'd hoped. Being closer to me didn't help her memory improve; if anything, her decline accelerated rather than slowed.

An incoming call breaks the empty office silence. Warwick, of course.

"Where are you?" he asks. He sounds tense.

I look around instinctively. Squint in the direction of his darkened office. He's no stranger to sleeping on the sofa inside, although he hasn't slept on it in months. His back isn't what it used to be.

I say, "You in your office? Figured nobody else was in so early."

"Yeah. No. I'm at the Princeton Club. You're supposed to be here, too."

Then it all comes roaring back. The big meeting—the Goldman demo, the reason I was at the office late on Friday, finalizing who will do what, when. In theory, it's up to everyone else to follow through today. But I need to be there, too, in case something goes wrong. *How did I forget?* For hours I've been brooding, moaning over the past. Angry at myself, I stand, start to put on my jacket while holding the phone. "I'll be right over, I just had to grab something." Was all the agita I felt this morning just misplaced, pent-up anxiety about this meeting?

The meeting is slated for eight thirty at the Princeton Club's space, right across the street from Grand Central. Meeting at the club was my idea. Neutral ground. Sort of. The Goldman offices are too palatial. Ours are too pedestrian.

Miraculously, I'm hustling through the club lobby with fifteen minutes to spare. "Hey," someone shouts, "you gotta check in!" I ignore the direction, scramble up the stairs toward the meeting center. A bulky dude with a buzz cut and a cheap navy sport coat catches me before

I can open the door to the conference room. He looks like he used to work as a crowd-control cop, and I'm a chance to relive his glory days.

"I need some ID, pal," he says.

I don't budge. Just stare as if he were a wild animal, and if I show weakness, I know he'll maul me. I explain in a firm voice that I'm here for an important meeting. He asks to see my Princeton alumni card. "My boss is the alum," I say.

"So you're not a club member," he says, the words clearly a delight to his mouth. "My name's on the guest list," I say. "Go check the list." But he's not listening. This is when the door flies open and Warwick appears.

Warwick looks like he hasn't slept in weeks. His jacket is neatly pressed, his pocket square is in place, his silver-fox hair is perfectly parted, his shoes catch and hold a shine, all good, but there's strain to him, a whiff of trying too hard. He's been projecting the image of the about-to-blow-up tech entrepreneur for close to two decades, and the truth is starting to show, no matter how he poses or preens. He's less than the image he's asserted, a fact that pains him.

Yet he has power left. He points at the security guard and makes a face that says, *What are you thinking?* The guard drops his arms to his sides. His buzz cut loses some of its bristly verve. "I'm sorry, sir," he stammers. "I had to make sure this guy wasn't a security risk."

Warwick says, "Cut the shit," and that's it. The man disintegrates in front of us, not literally, but he no longer has purpose or impact. If he ever says another word, I don't hear it. I step into the conference room, and that's the entire world. Warwick launches into a tirade, not a calm one. He's ranting, tightening the winch of his anxiety; usually, I'd try to calm him down, claim it's all not so bad, but he's not wrong, this room is not ready for the meeting. Nothing is set up as I'd arranged. Not enough chairs, no projector, no card listing the Wi-Fi credentials. Total failure. I never should have agreed to let on-site staff handle this. Lesson learned.

Warwick paces the room, talking to himself. "Pull it together, man," he says. "Failure's not, like—it's not in my vocabulary. Yeah, no, we can't fail. This will be perfect. It's got to be."

"I'll take care of this," I say. "Just sit down, relax."

For the last month, Warwick's been wound tighter than a Swiss watch; today's pitch is a big deal for a lot of reasons, not least of which because we need a cash infusion for a big debt payment coming due at the end of the quarter. Our chatbot products require a tremendous amount of compute to do their thing: we spend money on servers far faster than we can take it in. If we ace the demo today, then we have a clear path to solvency, a path we need before the month ends.

I don't bother to ask the Princeton Club staff for help. I take chairs from another room. I locate a laminated Wi-Fi card in a cabinet in a third room. I've got a spare cable in my laptop bag, and a converter, too, so that we can plug Nessie's MacBook directly into the AV for the large screen on the wall.

"All we need now," I say, "is Nessie."

"Where *is* that chick?" Warwick asks. His upper lip glistens with sweat.

"All we need," I repeat, "is Nessie. Then we're set."

Naturally, this is when the Goldman crew shows up. Absently, I wonder if anyone bothered to stop them downstairs, or if they got through on their looks alone. They're all dressed like bankers, and not ordinary bankers, either: they are the kind who only traffic in large numbers, who dress in the very best shoes, with cinched belts on slim hips, jackets shaped in tailored slopes, ties crisp and sharp enough to cut you if it comes down to that. I'm afraid of these people, no question.

There are handshakes and intros. I get introduced to people who likely forget my name at once. I pull business cards from my wallet and pass them out like candies. Warwick's old pal, Patric Blanc, arrives, wearing a quarter-zip fleece jacket over a collared white button-down. Patric is the linchpin for this meeting, the guy who brought both sides to the table. He deftly steers Warwick over to Devender, the senior partner on the Goldman team. Devender has a posh English accent, rugged shoulders, jet-black movie-star hair. Apparently, he went to Princeton, too. Patric spits out Princeton place names, makes inside jokes. The room is sudsy with bro energy when one of the junior Goldman men taps my shoulder, holds up my business card.

"This is meant to be funny," he says. "Right?"

Written in blue on the back of the business card I gave to him are the words DON'T PLAY WITH ANY STRANGE ALGOS. My handwriting, but I didn't write it. I fake-chuckle, like it's all a practical joke.

"I'll give you a clean one," I say. Except, when I look at the next card in my hand, I see these words: DON'T TRUST WARWICK. Again, my handwriting. I don't remember writing either note. I don't know what they mean. Maybe someone is playing a prank on me.

"On second thought," I say, "let's just connect on LinkedIn?"

The junior Goldman man frowns at me, and I notice Devender watching us, but I'm saved when Warwick clears his throat. Asks Patric if he wants to get started. Still, no Nessie. "Yeah," Patric says, "let's get down to business. Devender," he says, "your team ready?" Devender nods an almost imperceptible nod.

Warwick turns to me. "Graham, could you kick us off?"

I don't ask if he's serious, but I'm wondering, *Is he serious?* "Glad to," I chirp.

Warwick and I are simpatico: we roll with whatever the other one brings round. He hired me ten years ago to handle business development back when he didn't have a real business pipeline. He has big ideas, no patience for details. He sets wide boundaries, paints big pictures. Meanwhile, the engineers we rely on to make ideas real are people who look through telescopes the other way around. They crave details. Precision. It's a disaster if Warwick is left alone with them. But that's fine. That's not what he's for. That's why he needs me. I could feel how ambitious he was when he first shook my hand. I stayed through the years because he had begun to feel like a friend, even though I know we're not friends. That's his greatest gift. If his full light shines on you, it feels like all the light you need.

The presentation that I'm not prepared to give begins poorly. Shocker. I mistype my password, twice. Can't find the right file, and then, after I do, I make a self-deprecating joke about pulling the short straw, and nobody bothers to smile. Devender says not a word, fidgets with his cuff links. Patric looks at Warwick and makes a face like he's drowning. Selling ideas isn't my superpower. Mercifully, I'm only on the second slide when Nessie arrives.

I'm standing in front of the screen at the end of the room. Facing me, all the men in the meeting—oh, wow, it's *only* men, I realize—they can't see when Nessie opens the door and slips into the room. She takes off her denim jacket. She's wearing all black: black Doc Martens, black leggings, even her black T-shirt has Black Sabbath written on it. I asked her to wear business attire—I mean, these are bankers, right? But I knew that she wouldn't. Her T-shirt bares her forearms, revealing a jumble of tattoos I've never been able to discern or understand. I've always wondered why she chose to get such thick sleeves of ink on her skin. I've always wanted to ask, but I've never known how, never will. Now what strikes me is that displaying these tattoos to this room of pressed gentlemen might not be the best way to impress them.

Warwick sees me hesitate. He glances back, spots Nessie. A muscle in his cheek twitches in agitation. Then it's gone, and he stares blankly. He and Nessie used to be tight. Lately, not so much. I've never pegged their disagreement precisely, but it's philosophical, something time makes worse and worse. She wants to use tech to build something big, grand, impressive in a way that makes life better, even if it takes a long time. Warwick wants to knock everybody's socks off yesterday. He's tired of waiting; she's tired of being rushed.

At some point a couple of months ago, Warwick went to London and convinced Devender that Nessie and her team could build a chatbot that would help keep Goldman's traders from over-reacting whenever the market went south. The assignment was never perfectly clear. Terms of payment, even less so. All I know for sure is that Patric, Warwick, and Devender struck a deal over old-fashioneds in a Canary Wharf bar, and ever since then, getting this demo right is all Warwick has cared about. Getting Nessie to care as much as he does has been harder.

The Goldman team notices Nessie's arrival, and three men get up to offer her their chairs. Warwick keeps his seat, arms folded, smirking. She ignores the chivalry and pulls over her own chair from the extras along the wall. She told me once: *Every asshole is a gentleman when a girl needs a chair, but at promotion time it's, sorry, no room at the inn.*

I all but throw the laptop at her. She taps a few keys and opens a new window, launches into her spiel without bothering to introduce herself. The maestro begins. She makes no excuse for her late arrival. *Deal with it,* her eyebrows say. I sink into a chair, frustrated but overwhelmingly relieved. At last we're back on track. On plan. My safe place.

Nessie speaks fluently and with authority about the artificial intelligence models she has designed on behalf of Warlock & Co. I quietly mouth along with the words—that's how perfectly she hews to her lines. She's responsible for the algo at the heart of every solution we deliver. She doesn't mention this part, but the engineers on her team are cultish in their devotion to her. She spends long hours locked away with them, plotting and planning how best to shape and grow the large language networks they've begun to cultivate. At one point, a group of engineers began to refer to her as *the Mother*, a nickname that would've caught on, but she found out. *I make things,* she said, *but I'm nobody's damn mom. It's just Nessie, all right?* Nowadays, the engineers on her team put Loch Ness Monster stickers on their laptops, but if you ask what it means, they'll shrug and say, *Hey, we just make things, yeah?*

"This is all great," Patric says, interrupting Nessie's explanation of how her team created market-crash simulations as part of the product design sessions. "But, like, what's the bottom line? I don't mean to be a jerk," he says (but make no mistake, he likes having a reputation for being a bit of a jerk), "but our buddy Devender here doesn't care how it does what it does if it doesn't do what it's supposed to do. You get my feel, Ness? Let's get to the demo."

"I had a feeling you'd say that," Nessie says.

This is the trickiest part of the plan for the day. There is no way a real demo could go well. We've not had access to any of the data that we said we'd need to train the model to react properly. That's why Warwick told her to fake the whole thing. Rather than have the algo interact with a real-time simulation of a market crash, Nessie will bring up something that looks real—but it's just a script.

Unsurprisingly, Nessie was opposed to this. *You wouldn't believe what this algo can do,* she said. *We've got enough to take a run at it. Why do we build these tools if we don't let them do their thing?* Warwick over-ruled her.

So what if it's fake? We'll get the data eventually. What we say will be real, in time. That's how Warwick works when it comes to morals: *Maybe it's not true now, but we'll get there.*

Everyone watches the screen as Nessie pulls up what looks like a trader's screen with a number of financial positions in the open market. For now, everything looks good. She strikes a few keys, and all the numbers turn red. Lots of negative slopes on charts. You can see the bankers stir in their chairs, unsettled. Even pretend money matters to them. Nessie opens another window, this one with our chatbot. As an avatar, she's used the nerd emoji, an old favorite; the chat window indicates that this chatbot is named Titania. We've had chatbots named Cleo, Hamlet, and Falstaff. I asked her once what's next when she runs out of characters from Shakespeare. How about *Lord of the Rings*? Gollum! Gandalf! Sauron! *I'll think about it,* she said.

NESSIE: Sell everything.
TITANIA: Sell all positions in the portfolio?

NESSIE: Yes.

The chat avatar blinks, strokes its emoji chin.

TITANIA: I can totally do that. But I'm looking at the high-frequency trading volumes in these industries, and everything's two standard deviations above norm. I'm not sure, but it's probably a bad move to dump everything. Instead, what if we—

Nessie taps a key, freezes the demo. She spins in her chair to survey the room. Devender sits forward slightly in his chair, fingertips pressed together. "I know what you're thinking," she says. "How do you know the algo is really analyzing the data in our simulation? I mean, we could have just prerecorded all this, right?"

Warwick glances at Patric; both of them look at me, but I keep my eyes fixed on Nessie. Obviously, she's not following the script we agreed to. "Here's the thing," she continues. "I'm going to take my hands off the controls. You talk to it. See what you think. Devender? Step on over."

She stands up, motions to her seat. All the banker techies pivot, look to their bigwig. Just as they train them to do in banker school, I bet. Devender grins, winks at Warwick, who's so perfectly still that he might be a painting of himself. I can't find a way to move or speak, either. This is not at all what we planned.

"Ballsy," Patric mutters. "Fucking ballsy. I love it."

Devender puts his fingers on the keyboard, poised as a pianist at his instrument. Except I have a hard time imagining him at work evaluating code, or leading a whiteboard session where engineers work through actual problems. "Let's take this in a new direction," he says.

DEVENDER: WHAT'S THE OUTLOOK FOR GS IN A PANIC SCENARIO? ARE WE A BUY OR A SELL?

TITANIA: Goldman Sachs? Sell. Definitely.

Not the answer he expected, I can tell. But Devender gives no reaction. He types: EXPLAIN.

TITANIA: I've evaluated Goldman Sachs as an investment by looking at earnings, historical currency rates, futures contracts, and economic projections. Also, I assessed the psychological profile of every partner whose profile appears on LinkedIn and about whom there is publicly available data. Then, I created a model that emulates the kind of decisions that company leaders will make under pressure, and what I found was that as a company, the next few years are going to be rough ones.

"It knows you," Nessie says. "You and all the other partners."
Devender rubs his wrists with his hands. "Bullshit," he says. I wince at the vulgarity. Spoken in his high-rent accent, the word hits with a lash. "This is all canned. This is a big fake."
Nessie shrugs. "I'm telling you, it knows you. It knows everybody in the room. Ask it something that we couldn't have scripted. Something unexpected."
Devender leans over the keyboard, taps out: WHAT IS PATRIC BLANC'S FAVORITE COLOR?

TITANIA: The odds are 27:1 that Patric "Doc" Blanc's favorite color is pink. Conclusion based on multivariate analysis, including the clothing worn in headshots and at a panel at SXSW where Patric spoke. Also, drawing on a press release and a series of notes that he wrote as an equity analyst.

Nobody says anything. No one's sure what to make of the response. None of us know what the truth is, after all. "Impressive," Patric says. He's uncharacteristically quiet, though. Looks like he's holding his breath. Nessie looks distracted, as if contemplating a problem that she sees in the road far ahead of now. Devender smiles for the first time. I get the sense he doesn't use smiles to convey happiness. "Truly impressive," he says. "Except for one problem. Tell them, Patric."

Patric chews his thumbnail. Nods, frowns.

"I hate pink," he says. "Like, pathologically. I only wore pink to South By because I lost a bet with Warwick."

Silently but swiftly, all the faces in the room swing toward Nessie. She is typing something into her phone. Finishes. Then she looks up. "Hate, love." She shrugs. "They're closer than you'd think, from an algorithm's point of view. It just knows that there's a lot of energy devoted to the color pink. Give it one more shot. Ask it something about Warwick."

Warwick objects, but Devender types, quickly now. IS DAVID A. WARWICK III BANKRUPT?

TITANIA: Financially? Almost. Morally? Absolutely. For example, he directed the team to script this demo and then lie about it. Would you like to see the email he sent? He was very clear.

In the quiet that follows, Nessie reaches over and eases shut the lid of the laptop. Devender leans back as if he's glad to let someone else touch the machine. Barely concealed disdain wrinkles the skin around his eyes.

"David," says Nessie, "you can consider this my resignation."

This last word releases a dark force within Warwick. He spits verbal railroad spikes, says she's unstable, crazy, psycho. She ignores his rant. Gathers her laptop into her bag, pulls her jacket on. No hurry. Smiles at Devender and the Goldman men at the table. "Nice not knowing you all," she says. "Last in, first out."

Once she's gone, Warwick regains some of his old self-control. "Give us another month," he says, dabbing at sweat with a handkerchief. "Let us come back and try this again. You saw how well it worked till she interrupted the thing. Right, Devender? You see it?"

But the trance is broken. The magic trick is ruined. We all know. We're not getting a deal today. We're not gonna make that debt payment. We're at the end of something, we just haven't admitted it yet.

CHAPTER 24

I call Nessie, but she doesn't pick up. Warwick phones me, I don't pick up. We're a vicious circle of not answering each other's calls.

I need a beat to figure out what's happened. Nessie told me once not long ago that she was thinking about taking a sabbatical. Something longer than a beach vacay. More like a trial of another phase of her life.

"What would you do?" I asked.

"Something creative," she said.

"Your job is creative."

"Something real," she said. "Something tangible. Something you can hold in your hand."

The news spreads quickly through the little society of Warlock & Co. The office space in the Garment District remains ghostly all day. A few people come in: a network admin, junior product leads, but the engineers make no showing, not one. Warwick never comes in, either. He fires off texts from downtown all afternoon. DOC IS DOING DAMAGE CONTROL WITH DEVENDER, he writes. WE CAN TURN THIS AROUND. I don't bother to ask what he hopes to accomplish. I tell him that it looks like all of Nessie's engineers have called out for the day. Passive resistance.

CUT OFF THE ACCESS OF ANYONE WHO DOESN'T SHOW UP.

I stare at the words, uncomprehending. I know that he knows we can't do anything without an engineering team. He must be tossing off texts in a fury, a rhino thrusting his horn at anything within range. Then he sends me a picture of a business card with a message in blue ink written on the back: DEVENDER SAYS YOU GAVE THIS TO ONE OF HIS PEOPLE. I start to sweat even before I read my handwriting: TELL NESSIE HOW YOU REALLY FEEL.

I DON'T KNOW WHAT THAT IS, I write.

I am wiping sweat from my forehead, rubbing my neck while I wait for him to respond. The truth is, as I look at these handwritten messages, I *do* have a faint inkling that I wrote them. Sitting at a table somewhere, late at night. I just can't remember why, what drove me to it. Tell Nessie how I feel? No way. I shake my head, shake off this weird feeling, this sadness I get when I remember writing these notes. I try to come up with an explanation for what the message means—not for myself, but for Warwick, if he asks, when he asks.

YOU WERE RIGHT, he writes at last. WE SHOULD HAVE TOLD HER SHE WAS FULL OF SHIT RIGHT THEN AND THERE.

I stare at his words, weighing a response. Nessie's gone, I think. It's suddenly so real. We're never going to trade knowing smiles across a conference table while Warwick drones on. He texts again, moments later:

DID YOU LOCK HER ACCOUNT? CHANGE HER PASSWORD. SHE WANTS OUT, SHE'S OUT.

I'm grateful that he doesn't dig in further. Doesn't ask what my feelings for Nessie are. GIVE ME A SEC, I write. I log in to the network control panel and reset Nessie's password. Remove all her admin rights. Then I return to the text conversation. OK, IT'S DONE.

I feel as if I've betrayed Nessie, but what other option do I have? Warwick owns the company. It's his life, truly. He has no girlfriend, no wife, no kids, no hobbies, no real friends that I know of. Everything that he does is the company. *I'll do the other stuff after we make it big,* he told me once. *The big house in Scarsdale, the toothy kids, the classy marriage to a woman from a blue-blooded family. I'll get there in time.*

Warwick keeps texting, keeps asking who's shown up, who hasn't. I don't know how to tell him the truth. NOT LOOKING GREAT, I offer. Then, shockingly, one of Nessie's engineers shows up—a crack in group solidarity in the form of Priti, one of the newest members of the team.

Priti wears fancy new sneakers, has a high-class Boston accent. Nessie says Priti has real potential, might be a real asset one day, assuming she quits worrying about what her dad, a big-deal civil engineer, thinks about her chosen career. Right now, she seems distracted, sorting through her bag as she walks to her desk.

"Hey," I say, smiling hard. "Glad you decided to come in."

Seeing me, Priti blinks like someone caught out past curfew. "No, no," I say, "it's all good. You're doing the right thing. Don't worry about what people think."

Priti takes her laptop out of her bag. Slides it gently onto her desk. Taps the top of the laptop with her fingernails and says in a quiet voice: "I just wanted to return this. I didn't want anyone to think I was stealing it."

That's when I realized I got this wrong, got everything wrong. "Come on," I say, "you can't all just blindly follow her."

Priti pauses, turns back. The abashed look is gone. How quickly she pivots, drops the mask, reveals her real self. "Blindly follow? Holy shit, Graham, you're one to talk. But I'm not going to try to convince you," she says. "I'm out of here. They've already been at Killian's for an hour, so I'm late to the party."

She heads back to the elevator, and I follow, forlorn, knowing it's pointless. After she hits the "Down" button, she says, "Did you hear the latest? Warwick's threatening to sue her. She doesn't even have another gig yet. He wants to make sure nobody ever hires her. It's sick."

"That doesn't sound like Warwick," I say.

Priti doesn't say anything else, won't even look at me.

Back at my desk, the office space is quiet, still. Usually, I like this feeling. As if I'm guarding the wall alone. Today, it feels wrong. I still can't quite believe Nessie has quit. She won't come off the elevator anytime soon. She won't be here when I work late. I still don't understand what happened. Despite seeing and hearing what happened in real time. She'd been frustrated, sure, but she had agreed to our plans for the meeting. I didn't see this coming.

Killian's, the Irish pub where the engineers have gathered, is only a few blocks from the workspace. No one has invited me. But Priti mentioned it so casually that I'm sure no one will mind. Besides, I'm sure Nessie will want to see me. I've got plenty of questions to ask her. Like: *Have you lost your mind?*

The walk there feels familiar, like I'm meeting folks for a regular happy-hour drink. Briefly, I have this image of walking along this sidewalk with Nessie, just the two of us. A good night. Can't remember when or why. I need to talk to her, convince her to take back everything. There's still a chance I can fix whatever went wrong, I think. I push open the door to the pub and see Nessie and a dozen others. I don't have my coat off, but already I can feel that I'm not entirely welcome. To Nessie's tribe, I represent one of Warwick's people.

"Thanks for coming," Nessie says without a smile.

"We've certainly got plenty to talk about," I say with a chuckle. She nods, turns to talk to someone else. Obviously, she can't just talk to me. She's the person everyone is here for. Her time is the only currency. I'm perfectly willing to bide my time, wait my turn.

One of the interface designers corners me near the jukebox for what feels like an hour. He tells me how happy he is for Nessie. He says this has been a long time coming. Apparently, he connected her with the creative director at Bergdorf's, and she's going to design the display for one of their holiday windows on Fifth Avenue this year. A real coup. "It's been, like, a dream of hers forever," he tells me, and he goes on, but I keep thinking, *Wow, how come Nessie hasn't told me about this?* Then, I remember her password. Briefly, this makes me happy, decoding the meaning of *B3rgd0rf-w1nd0ws-1117*, but then I remember that I wiped out this password, locked up her account a few hours earlier.

Someone pays to play Great White's cover of "Once Bitten, Twice Shy" five times in a row (and counting). The designer tells me that he's sure the reason Nessie was never granted full partner status is simple: she's a woman. He insists that I convince him he's wrong. I shrug. "Nobody is a full partner," I tell him. "Just Warwick. The name of the company is an aspiration, not a fact. There is no *& Co.* It's all aspirational. It's just Warwick. He's the company. He calls the shots." The designer doesn't believe me. He pokes me in the chest and spills his drink. I'm in my own private hell. Finally, I say, "Hold on a second," and I unplug the jukebox. Everyone glares. But someone had to do something.

Sometime after six o'clock, the group dwindles to three people: Nessie, Priti, and me. Priti has her peacock-green coat on, and she holds her purse, but she never leaves. She's tearfully telling Nessie that she's never had someone who inspired her more. Nessie keeps reassuring her that she'll be fine. Nessie promises to text her tomorrow. That she should stay positive. "We'll find something for you," she says.

I interject with some of my own advice, trying to help extricate Nessie. "You could always just, you know, stick with your job at Warlock." They both look at me coldly. "Hey, whoa," I say, "don't get me wrong, I want Nessie to stay, too. We can still be one big happy family, can't we?"

Priti gives Nessie one last hug, says goodbye. Not so much as a wave to me.

Nessie puts her hand around a drink that I have not seen her touch. I've been just sipping beers myself. I want to be clearheaded.

"You're teetotaling, too," I say.

"Yeah," she says, "I have things to do. A whole life to sort out. Thanks for sticking up for me today."

"I could've done more."

"No shit, Graham. I'm being sarcastic."

"Right."

Nessie waves at the bartender, who strolls up and leans over the bar. "You ready to close the tab, doll?" Nessie nods, and the bartender wanders back to sort Nessie's credit card from the cache on the counter.

"I'm still reeling," I say. "I just—I didn't see this coming. I thought the algo was working so well."

"It was," she says.

"But the demo? Those answers? You should have stuck to the script."

"The algo works perfectly," she says. "It gives truthful answers. Warwick doesn't like the truth. Despite whatever he claims."

"Can't we fix this? Whatever it is that's wrong between the two of you? Did Warwick do something? I know he gets sort of out of hand sometimes. Together, we can keep him in check. Isn't that the deal?"

She shifts in her seat, rips a cocktail napkin to bits with gathering agitation. As if I'm reciting something she has committed to memory.

I say, weakly, "I'm just trying to patch things up."

The bartender returns with her card, a paper receipt, and a pen. She signs the receipt and reaches for the card and then stops, turns to me.

"Do you remember," she says, "when I met your mom?"

Of all the words she could have said, of all the questions to surprise me, few could have disarmed me more. I stare at the credit card on the table. A quick montage of memories, Geraldine visiting the office after we signed the lease, Geraldine lying in bed in a dark room, Geraldine the last time I saw her. At last I lift my chin. "I'm sorry, Nessie. I don't know what you're talking about."

Nessie leans a little closer, watching me. "She was sick," she said. "She was in the hospital. You asked me to bring her soup. Do you remember? She wasn't herself anymore. You were in the middle of this big blowup with Warwick. Yet another fight over the algo. So you asked me to go instead. To make sure she was cared for. It was the sweetest gesture I'd ever seen."

I want to lie to her, to claim that I remember, too. But she looks so intently at me that I know she'll see right through me if I do. "I don't think—" And then I stutter, start again. "I think you're mistaken. My mom died more than a year ago. I don't think you ever met her. Maybe I'm wrong. When was this? Was it at the end? That was such a bad time. I've tried to forget so much of it."

Nessie's mouth tightens, a fake smile, a quick nod. I've let her down, but she's not surprised. "You're right," she says. "My mistake. I'm thinking of someone else."

I feel the urge to stop talking. But I can't just watch her leave in silence. "Hey, listen, Nessie, are we okay? I mean, you and me? I have a hundred questions about what went wrong with Warwick, but I don't think any of them really matter if there's something that I did. Did I do something? Did I not do something? I feel like maybe there's a misunderstanding that I could sort out if you'd let me. We're friends, right? We help each other out?"

She looks at me with such sadness that I am alarmed. Her eyes shine in the reflected light from the TV over the bar. I have never seen her shed a tear. Not in the ten years I have known her. "You think you know someone," she says, voice crackling, deeper than usual, swollen by regret.

"Right," I said.

"But you don't," she said. "You don't and you can't. I could sit you down and tell you everything I know about your life, and it wouldn't be the whole story. There would be so much that would get left out. Stuff I don't know. Things you feel, thoughts I couldn't know. And even if you recorded every conversation or captured on video everything we ever did or saw together, that still wouldn't tell you everything about us, about life. The part of the story that no one sees, the part that matters. The part inside, the human part. The things that can't be explained."

She wipes at her eyes, as if she's furious at herself for the tears. I stare at the tattoos on her arms because I can't bear to look at her eyes. "Nessie," I say. "Nessie, please. Tell me how to help."

She shakes her head. "You can't see. You can't be different because this is you. The real you. It's all in there. It must be. You still remember, somewhere. You just can't get to the memories. It was you, we were both there, and I know there's a better version of you inside, walled off but not lost. Maybe you'll never see. Maybe that's for the best. Go back to being who you were. Go back to believing it's a good idea to disrupt the world. Keep following Warwick's lead. You need that. Someone who keeps messing up the world so you can keep fixing it."

She pulls on her denim jacket. She's got a cabbie hat, too, now. Something I didn't notice earlier, at the client meeting. She's changing, I'm losing track of her. I understand then that this is it. I know that I can go on without her. I went on after my mother died. I went on after college when all my friends went in other directions. You learn to deal with loss and endings; loss is just part of the equation. But I do not want to go on without Nessie. *Tell Nessie how you really feel.* Like a shipwrecked sailor hopelessly striking wet rocks for fire, I tell her that I'll miss her, that I have no idea how to cope without her; but those are words that friends say to each other, and I want something deeper. I have no good choices. I have no idea what to do. I push forward, leaning toward her, my lips for her lips, and I hope she feels the same.

She leans aside, ducks my kiss. Somehow, she saw it coming. Confused, sad, at a loss, I apologize. She takes her bag and she's gone, the door of the pub swinging in her wake. I'm standing alone and looking after her when the bartender saunters over, looking sheepish, trying to catch my eye.

"Hey," he says, "your friend forgot her credit card. Could you call her, ask her to come back?"

"No. No, I don't think so."

My phone vibrates in my pocket. I don't need to look at the screen to know who sent a message. Not Nessie. I didn't realize it, but I've been getting messages from Warwick for an hour. He's still raging over everything that has happened. All the slights, real and imagined. I ask where he is, where to meet him. She's right. In the end, it's easier to do as I'm told than to forge my own way.

Warwick is on his third or fourth old-fashioned by the time I arrive at Grand Central. We always meet for drinks at the bar overlooking the concourse. We sit on stools at the railing, the perfect perch for commenting on the world. He likes to point at the suburban commuters hotfooting it for trains and say, *There but for the grace of God go I.*

The bartender shakes my drink in an aluminum shaker while Warwick raves about the wealth he could have had if he hadn't sold his dot-com holdings after the crash. His old blues standard. He acted rashly. He had no eye for the future. He let himself get caught up in the panic of all the other everyday rubes. He didn't trust his gut. I've heard this hangdog coulda shoulda woulda speech before. Soon, he'll start to list all the people who failed him. I interrupt.

"What are we gonna do about Nessie?"

"Nessie? Screw her."

"What happened between the two of you?"

He puts down his drink with a hard clack. "Me?" He laughs. "What happened between the two of *you*?"

I look away, toward the Main Concourse, up at the green ceiling with its false constellations. "Nothing," I said.

"Exactly," he says, leaning back. "I'll tell you what happened. She stopped believing. What have I always said? We're going to make the world a better place. One little change at a time. Eventually, all the changes will add up. Until then, we've got to prop things up, juice the status quo, tell the story people need to hear. Fake it till you make it. Nessie didn't want to play that game. That demo today was the last straw. Devender needed to think our chatbot was completely perfect. Nessie had to play it her way. *Let the algo be the algo,* she said. Look where it got us. Nowhere. No dice. And do you know the worst part? She's got her team stirred up, ready to *vamos*. We're at a dead end. No way forward, not really. It's game over."

He picks up his glass, but it's empty. He palms the empty vessel, studies it.

"Then you start over," I say. I take a deep breath, puff up my chest a little. "You've done it before."

He regards me with a wistful expression. As if there is, in my suggestion, something that reminds him of better days. He puts an elbow on the bar, cups his chin in his palm. *Tell me,* his posture says.

"I'll find some new engineers," I say. "I'll put together a job req tonight. I'll reach out to a staffing agency. Maybe we hire some consultants to fill the gap. Maybe this is a good thing," I say, thinking about Priti's last hug with Nessie, about the designer who raged at me while Great White played endlessly. "Not everyone was really a believer," I say. "Not everyone was all in."

"You're a rare breed, Graham. Loyal till the end."

"That's my story," I say, "and I'm sticking with it."

CHAPTER 25

I still look for her. There is no reason for her to return to the coffee cart near the office where she bought her morning joe back when we saw each other each day, but I'm all eyes whenever I wait in line, just in case.

About a week after she quit—a week of no response to my apologetic texts and emails—I looked her up in the payroll system and took the train to the postal address where we mail her W-2s each year. I walked the length of her block, a Washington Heights hood with row houses, a road that slopes to the river, maidenhair trees with branches tented over the street.

I knew her building even before I found the number on the doorframe. Felt like I'd been there before. All these row houses were pretty much alike. Been in one, been in them all, right? But there was something more there. I couldn't see it, but I knew there was a courtyard behind it. Maybe a door that led into her apartment. I could imagine slipping through; oddly, in my imagination, I was going *out* with her rather than *in*, as if I lived in there once, sat inside with her in a sitting room, answered the phone when it rang, debated interior decor with her. A vertigo of lost possibilities made me unsteady on my feet. I sat on a bench in nearby Riverside Park and waited till my head cleared. Then I went home.

Weeks pass. Maybe months. I lose track. The nights are longer than the days, the temps drop, the globe tilts. I'm home from work, and it's dark already, but it's not time to sleep. I sit with my laptop, clicking around on social media. I scroll through tweets and posts and photos from people I know or once knew, people I haven't seen in person in years—decades, sometimes—and it's hard to tell who's putting up a front, who's talking tough, who's hurting, who's hurt, who's virtue signaling, who's spoiling for a fight. Is that what all this technology gets us? Just one more place to parade all our self-deceptions, all our make-believe lives?

I stand at the window, where I can watch traffic patterns on the street, the line of cars at the Lincoln Tunnel. The relentless traffic, the gridlock that I dislike but that I also count on because it reminds me that there are millions, billions, of strangers out there still fighting their way through. A silvery streak passes in the air, another, two more; before long, a silent, thick snowfall begins.

Flakes disintegrate before they reach the ground: beautiful, picturesque. The city looks like a diorama. A perfectly planned and executed window display. This metaphor stirs up a recollection, a stray memory. Specifically, the interface designer who bawled me out while we stood next to the jukebox. He told me Nessie was doing a display window for Bergdorf on Fifth Avenue.

I put on a coat, and downstairs I hail a cab. The ride crosstown is short, but it takes an eternity. I close my eyes, and before long I'm lost in a pretend reality where I run into Nessie right in front of a window she designed, and I tell her what she's designed is amazing, and she asks what I'm up to, and I say, *God, where to begin,* and we walk through windy streets, talking, laughing.

The cabbie drops me at the main entrance for Bergdorf Goodman. Already, I can tell what I'd hoped for isn't about to happen. All the windows along Fifth Avenue are papered over with the same message: BERGDORF WINDOWS 11/17: I'm a day too early. Today is only November 16. I loosen my scarf, feeling prickly, agitated. Did I really believe I would run into her? The very idea is preposterous.

Lost in thought, I walk along the building, hands in pockets. Each window is papered over till the last one. Here I find an opening, a keyhole into the interior, where bright lights burn, where people wheel carts, heft large boxes, roll fresh paint on walls. A whorl of creators at work. I see her at once. She's swinging a hammer. She's stringing a wire. What are the odds? *It doesn't matter what the odds are,* I think, *when it's happening right in front of you.*

She works at her task, not alone but not interacting with the others until another worker comes over, says something, and she looks up, smiles, wipes her hands on her work pants, stands. The other worker unrolls a large piece of paper, a schematic, a plan, perhaps. Together they look at a paper, at something I can't see, then back again. Nessie's hair is up in a knot spun around a pencil. She's wearing an untucked button-down shirt with sleeves rolled up, a white tank top, white chinos, white Converse sneakers. She looks radiant, happier than I've ever seen her. Someone moves a cart behind her, and then I can see the full display, the window view that soon shoppers from the tristate area will come to see. Nessie has created a vast replica of the Manhattan skyline. Not just a small parcel. The whole western edge of the island, from the Battery to the last bridge to the Bronx. A soaring line of tall buildings made of glass, clear as volcanic crystal, radiant in spotlights.

She walks to a box at the edge of the island, opens a lid, and turns a crank. All at once the entire panorama of this miniature New York City comes to life. Tiny cars on the West Side Highway, lights turning on and off in windows, the soaring towers of Midtown. In the foreground, like a framing device for the view, I see a dingy building that looks like the rooftop of an old motel. Standing at the roof's edge are two small animatronic silhouettes, a man and woman who take turns drinking from a bottle and pointing. Everything about it is familiar but strange, a view that I know without looking but that I've never seen before. It's beautiful and hopeful, this grand reproduction of the city at night; watching it, I can remember standing somewhere similar and feeling hopeful for what tomorrow would bring, for what was unknown, unwritten. I belonged in that dream world.

Nessie and the other worker watch the display for a few moments and then nod, say a few words, and turn it off. There's still so much to do. Nessie takes a ladder and walks away, someplace I can't see. I wait for her to return. She doesn't come back. I take a few steps closer to the window glass. If I cupped my hands to the glass and peered hard, I could see farther inside. But something holds me back. Not far away, the front door of the department store is still lit, open. I could go inside, find this window, call her name, see her again. But I don't.

There's so much I want to tell her. Warwick has turned disaster on its head. He's already saying that Nessie's resignation, the desertion of all the engineers, is the best thing that could have happened. He keeps saying that he has a new view on trust. He says he wants to quantify loyalty. We can gamify it. He wants to hire some pure-math postdocs, wants me to poach a quant from the crew at Goldman. I could tell her everything. But she doesn't need to know. I get that, now. I see that, finally. She's moved on, started something new. Now it's my turn.

This is the last time I'll see her. I stand in the cold night staring at my reflection in the window, lost in thought. KNOW WHEN TO LET GO. Yes. I wrote down a message like that as a reminder to myself once. I remember how hard-won the idea felt at the time. I'm not sure where I wrote it, or why. But it feels like a credo for me at this point. You let go of something, it frees you up to grab whatever comes next—whatever chance, whatever idea, whatever person.

Around me the snowfall intensifies, the flakes tracing elaborate spirals in the light of streetlamps. I think of my mom, who loved first snowfalls; in one of my very earliest memories, she bundled me in a coat, hat, and mittens, and we rushed outside to catch flakes and look for patterns in the shapes, the colors, the sizes. Snow fell so fast and hard that night that there was a film on everything perpendicular to the sky: the lawn, the trees, our car, the driveway, the roof, our shoulders, our shoes, the top of her head. And it kept coming down, everywhere we looked. *If this keeps up,* she said with a laugh, *we'll have a new world by morning.*

ACKNOWLEDGMENTS

I wrote and rewrote this story many times, and along the way I benefited from thoughtful readers like my wife, Raina, and my friends Matt Neuroth, Felise Cooper, Joelle Renstrom, Michael Holtman, Greg Trefry, and Yu Wong. Your ideas made my idea far stronger, and your support has been invaluable.

I would have given up on this book if not for Elias Altman, whose suggestions as agent and adviser made it remarkably better; and I am grateful for the deft guidance of Laura van der Veer and her team at Little A, who elevated the book with precision and thoughtfulness. I'm also grateful for the fellow writers, family, and friends who encouraged me over the years it took to get here. There are too many of you to list; you know who you are because we've laughed and sighed about life together, often till late at night, maybe recently, maybe decades ago. I've never forgotten. Thank you.

I sold this book a few weeks after my mom died. She read it in an early form and said, "This is your best work yet. Now you just have to get it published." She was always certain I'd get the job done. I, on the other hand, had serious doubts. You were right, Mom! I wish I could write you back into this world.

The last thank-you—the most important one—goes out to Raina, Yasmine, and Maddox. I am so grateful for our life together. I can only write because of you.

ABOUT THE AUTHOR

Photo © 2024 Sharona Jacobs

Bryan VanDyke thinks about the internet for a living. A former staff writer for *The Millions,* he is a graduate of the writing programs at Columbia University and Northwestern. He lives in New York City with his wife and two children.